A SAM JAMESON
NOVEL OF SUSPENSE

CORPSE POSE

LESA KNOLLENBERG

LITTLE CREEK PRESS®
AND BOOK DESIGN
MINERAL POINT, WISCONSIN

Little Creek Press.
5341 Sunny Ridge Road
Mineral Point, WI 53565

ORDERING INFORMATION
Quantity sales. Special discounts are available on quantity purchases by corporations, associations, and others. For details, contact info@littlecreekpress.com

Orders by US trade bookstores and wholesalers.
Please contact Little Creek Press or Ingram for details.

Printed in the United States of America

Cataloging-in-Publication Data
Names: Knollenberg, Lesa, author.
Title: Corpse Pose / Lesa Knollenberg
Description: Mineral Point, WI: Little Creek Press, 2023.
Identifiers: LCCN: 2023918912 | ISBN: 978-1-955656-64-1
Subjects:
FIC030000 FICTION / Thrillers / Suspense
FIC031080 FICTION / Thrillers / Psychological
FIC031000 FICTION / Thrillers / General

Book design by Little Creek Press

AUTHOR'S NOTE: The true heroes of any story are the survivors left behind to make sense of the unfathomable. If you're in pain or experiencing difficult thoughts, please call 988 to reach the Suicide and Crisis Lifeline. You're not alone.

To those courageous
enough to trust.

MOUNTAIN POSE is the foundation for all standing poses.
Use it whenever you need to feel centered and grounded,
prepared for any instability that lies ahead.

CHAPTER 1

"IF YOU'RE TOO CLOSE TO SOMEBODY'S GOODNESS, then stagger yourselves."

The yogi, hands clasped behind his back, stepped carefully between jewel-toned mats. He sported a carpet of black curly hair that trickled from his bare chest to the waistband of his running shorts to mysterious places beyond. It was another lesson in resisting distraction during hot yoga.

"Breathe in through your nose and out through your mouth," he said, but somebody to my south was still enjoying last night's garlic, and the lanky college student in front of me smelled like a keg. Class had barely begun, and little beads of perspiration were already popping along my hairline as the temperature in the room climbed to a balmy 105 degrees.

"Reset yourself here in mountain pose. Stand at the top of your mats, facing the mirror." I scanned my classmates—beautiful bodies facing forward, palms outward. Nobody else seemed self-conscious about their creeping underwear or the ramifications of having yogurt for lunch. The only thing circling their heads seemed to be headbands and man buns. They all appeared regally rooted while I felt completely unmoored.

"Turn sideways on your mat. Bend at the waist, spreading your legs to create an upside-down V." My neighbor's goodness was, indeed, right there looking at me. I shifted to the right of my mat and bent over, looking right back.

Judging by her solid abs, she was disciplined. Although she had long coltish legs, mine were more muscular and defined from years of running. She had a sinewy grace, but I knew I could out-squat her. I'd put my neighbor at around twenty-five, ten years younger than me. Those ten years had taken a toll. But I was here, in hot yoga, pushing myself past comfort, hoping to replace my grief with something new, like peace.

"Let's move to tree pose." The instructor's voice had a Doppler effect as he moved around the room. "It's deceptively simple: plant one foot firmly on the earth. Focus softly and surrender."

My foot slipped and I lost my balance. "It's hard to wobble," he said, and I felt like he was calling me out. "We all hate it—especially in front of other people. But that wobble is growth. It's you, challenging yourself. Wobbling is good."

Bull. Wobbling meant you were weak. It meant that no amount of control or vigilance would protect you from losing your stability and what you loved most. If I had learned anything from the world of running, it was that being tough yielded results. There was always a better way: more protein, heavier weights, less sugar, more grit. It was all about taking control.

I put my foot down like a petulant child and reset. The class moved to warrior II. Finally, something I could do; warrior II was definitely in my wheelhouse. I did it perfectly in my head, but one look in the mirror and I saw that I was crooked and squat and, as far as I could tell, the only woman in the class without toenail polish. *It's not about perfection*, I reminded myself. *It's about the pursuit.* As I tried to enjoy the pursuit, the heat and the wafting aroma of patchouli made me woozy. I stayed in the subpar pose until the final reward—savasana.

"Savasana—or corpse pose—gives you a chance to reset. We're trained to think that all the good stuff happens when we're pushing ourselves. Savasana contradicts that. Sometimes it takes a few minutes for your body to assimilate what just happened; honor that. Namaste," the yogi said. We responded in kind. As he opened the door and left, I felt the magic and safety sealed up with us breeze out the door. After only a few minutes of stillness, restlessness took over. I opened one eye to peek at my fellow yogis and made sure I wasn't the first to break the spell. Then I rolled up my mat and followed the fresh air, feeling better about myself, my neighbor, and humankind.

Dim lights and scented candles created a mystical feel in the lobby as I moved around sweaty bodies toward the door. The energy was subdued, demonstrating one of the unwritten customs of yoga—the *After*. *Before* class, there is polite chatter and small talk. *After* draws respectful whispers, as if nobody wants to sully the air. The body and the soul are quietly realigned, and they both need to fit in the car. Moving among the little cliques of hushed groups, I found my shoes and was the first to escape from the studio into the cool night air.

Dusk made a showy appearance as I walked to my car. The parking lot was full of bumper stickers on Subarus promoting the farm-to-table movement, the Clean Lakes Alliance, and puppy yoga. It was a good time to be crunchy in Madison. Wisps of wind dried the sheen of sweat on my arms, and my hunger was talking. *Hummus with red peppers. Red seems more wholesome than green. A protein smoothie? Something salty after all that sweat. Sweet sounded bett—*

Thoughts of food dissolved as I looked at my car. As I edged closer, it looked like there was a long, vertical scratch on the driver's side door. I squinted and sped up to get past the dumpster that blocked my view.

As I got closer to the car, my stomach dropped. It wasn't only one scratch. Violent slashes covered the metallic blue, and all that I'd done to be open and zen in the previous hour evaporated as my chest tightened and my heart rate soared. I glanced toward the studio, hoping nobody else could see what I saw; carved into my poor little hatchback were five letters, each a foot tall:

Bitch.

DOWNWARD-FACING DOG is an inversion pose that simultaneously calms the brain and energizes the body. It offers a new perspective when the world feels upside down.

CHAPTER 2

I FLINCHED AS IF THE WORD *BITCH* WAS CARVED INTO MY OWN EXTERIOR and clutched my yoga bag closer to my body. My knees felt pliable, like they were carved from butter. The block letters were scratched violently into the paint, a hand fisted with dark menace straight down to the primer.

Behind me, voices erupted from the studio's open door, and I started to sweat again. I didn't want to be seen like this. I couldn't be the pariah who brought violence to an otherwise serene evening. Even as a newcomer to the yoga world, I knew there were rules: One didn't use plastic water bottles or talk during class. Phones were turned off. And certainly, one didn't ruin a good, peaceful vibe with vehicular profanity as the sun set in the west.

I dug in the bottom of my yoga bag, desperate to find my keys. If I turned the car around, I could buy myself a few minutes until I figured out what to do. Slowly pulling into a spot far from the building with *bitch* facing away from my gentle yogis, I sat in the car with my chin to my chest while I tried to slow my heart. I decided to call Finn, my youngest brother and a Madison cop.

"This better be good," Finn said before I even said a word.

"It is."

"Because I'm in Milwaukee."

"I'm sorry. I wouldn't call if it wasn't important."

"I know, TP." *TP. He couldn't be too mad. Hearkening back to his nickname for me—The Pain—felt like a loosening.* I hesitated, wishing I didn't need him, wishing I had called simply to check in. We used to talk almost daily, but things had changed since our parents' accident. There were newly exposed fissures between all of us, deep and raw. Besides, Finn worked so much overtime that he sucked the marrow out of any day off. I didn't want to get in the way. I closed my eyes and tried to imagine a way out of this conversation.

"Sam. Focus. What's up?"

In the tiny crack of decency that his voice conveyed, I decided to jump in. "My car got keyed."

"Bummer. Happens a lot. How high is your deductible?" He lowered his voice and said accusingly, "You do have insurance, don't you?"

"Of course I have insurance. I'm not an idiot."

"Debatable. Deductible is probably $500. Do you need money?"

"I got it, Finn. But it's not that simple. It isn't your typical—"

"Seriously, Sam. The Brewers are down by one, and the winning run is on second. Spit it out."

"It wasn't just keyed. Somebody scratched the word *bitch* into my car."

"No shit?" He chuckled; a low, raspy big-brother sound that made me roll my little-sister eyes. "Who did you piss off now?" He barely waited a second before barreling ahead. "Wait. It could be that wench that ran the 800. Where was she from? Villanova? She always hated you."

"Stop. That was years ago. And she wasn't a wench."

"You're right. More like a shrew. Who else hates you?" He chuckled again. "This could take all night, TP." His teasing felt so familiar. I realized with a pang how much I'd missed it in these last few months.

The sound of his chuckle was heartening, too.

"Funny," I deadpanned. "Look, this happened while I was in a yoga class, and I want to know if I should call your department and file an official report. I mean, I know I should, but—"

"Hell, yes, you should. Why wouldn't you?" I could hear the crowd roar in the background. The runner must have made it to third.

"Never mind," I said. "I'll handle it. Maybe I'll just pay out of pocket."

Finn made a noise between a growl and a groan. "This isn't something else you need to handle on your own. Ask for help like a normal person." Ouch. That jab landed hard. He knew I hated asking for help, but it felt cruel, considering what we were going through.

"I'm trying," I said reluctantly.

We were both quiet, giving the silence some heft in our conversation. He blinked first. "Okay, look, I'm out in the concourse now. What's really going on?"

The noise behind him stilled, and I realized I had been yelling. "It's embarrassing."

"So what?" He took a breath, as if to remind himself that I wasn't nine years old. He started over. "Okay. I'm sure it's embarrassing, but make the call, and don't overthink this one." He seemed to reconsider. "Unless you're worried that it's true—that you really are a bitch?" I couldn't tell if he was being serious or sarcastic, but I could hear in his voice that he was smiling.

"Sam," he said gently, "you might be a pain in the ass, but you aren't a bitch. Go ahead and call the station and have somebody come out."

"Okay. Thanks, Finn. I appreciate—"

"I know you do. Promise me you'll call if you need anything," he said.

"I will," I said. I wouldn't.

As Finn disconnected, I heard the crescendo of a roaring crowd, but it was hard to tell if the mayhem was good or bad. Whatever happened, I made Finn miss it.

I called the nonemergency number for the police and described my situation. Dispatch said they'd send somebody out and that it would be a short wait. They didn't define short. When I finished the call, I kept the phone to my ear, hoping to look inconspicuous to anybody walking by. I wanted to cry but squeezed my phone even tighter, trying to keep Finn's voice in my ear, trying to hold myself together.

"Hello?" I called out as I opened the studio's interior door. The other students had cleared out, leaving the lobby empty. I jangled my keys, a trick learned while working the late shift at a movie theater. You'd be surprised how easy it is to accidentally scare people after a midnight showing of *The Rocky Horror Picture Show.* Now I make it a practice; a little jingle of the keys, and people know you're coming.

A young woman was bent over the reception desk, hair so dark it was almost purple, and it angled toward her face. When she looked up at me, the sleek bob righted itself like a well-choreographed cascade. She looked spritely and organic, with a name like Moonglow or Yarrow.

"Forget something?" In one fluid movement, she righted herself and closed her laptop while assessing me at the same time.

"No, my—my car got keyed," I said quickly, gesturing toward the parking lot.

"Just now?"

I nodded. "During this last class. I called the police, and they're on their way. Mind if I wait inside? It's kind of creepy out there."

She looked at the wall clock and back down at her laptop. Her eyes were deep orbs of brown, both welcoming and wary. I recognized an employee who wanted to go home.

"I can wait outside," I said, backtracking toward the door.

"It's—it's no problem. It's all good. I can stay for another half-hour. I have some work to finish up, anyway." She nodded toward me, a reassurance of sorts, and I started to feel a little better.

"Thanks. I hope it won't be long." I lowered myself onto the couch by the door and propped my bag at my feet. "Let me know if you need to leave."

She went to the back room, and I leaned into the cushions and sighed. My body ached, my skin felt dry and deflated, and as I looked around, the empty lobby didn't seem as dreamlike as before. In contrast with the stark yoga room, the lobby was usually a sanctuary of plum-colored furniture, twinkle lights, and tranquil music. Now with the twinkles turned off and fluorescent lights on, the carpet looked dirty. Mismatched flip-flops collected in a small heap in the corner. The harsh lights made me feel conspicuous, and I desperately wanted to go home. Forget the peppers; I closed my eyes and fantasized about cheese puffs and a shower, in that order.

I thought about my poor car—and Finn's question. Who *had* I pissed off now? Nobody recently. I had been mostly keeping to myself, filling my days with my new job at the bank, trying hot yoga, and tackling administrative minutiae for my parents and me. I had made a practice of keeping my life small. Singular. Contained.

As if summoned, the receptionist came back into the lobby, carrying a glass of water in a paper cup. She handed it to me. "I know some of the other studios serve coffee and tea, but we're basic. Just water."

"Basic is good. I've been to almost every yoga studio in town. There are so many great ones, but this one felt—I don't know—safe. Tucked in." Something about her prompted oversharing and being the only people in the studio felt conspiratorial. "Thanks for the water." I toasted her with my cup.

"I've only been here a few months," she continued. "When I moved here this was the first studio I tried, and right away, I knew this was where I needed to be. It's addicting, isn't it? Yoga? I had to get a job here because I couldn't afford all the classes I wanted to take. This is home now."

Her all-black yoga ensemble matched her olive skin and highlighted a trail of bracelets on each wrist. The bracelets traveled up her forearm and made me doubt she had trouble affording anything. I self-consciously smoothed my hair and was trying to think of something to say when headlights from the parking lot flashed through the studio windows and arced around the room. A police cruiser had pulled into the lot, so I grabbed my stuff, thanked Moonglow/Yarrow, and headed back to my car.

Officer Sutton was friendly and efficient. His eyebrows were large and dark but well-defined. Even his pores were large. None of this was unattractive. In fact, it gave him a rugged quality that was quite appealing. It was a different kind of attractive—

"Ms. Jameson?"

"Yes. Sorry. What were you saying?"

"I'm gonna go file this report. I'll be back in a few minutes."

He headed toward his patrol car and I climbed into mine, wishing to be anywhere but here. The sun had set quickly, spreading its heft over the horizon before tucking in for the night, and the apartment building across the street began to come alive, lamps popping on like fireflies. Lights came on, and lives continued, all while I sat alone in the dark. I wanted my mom. My dad. I was thirty-five years old, alone, and tired of feeling sad and off-kilter.

It had been almost four months since my parents died. They had been out for dinner with friends and were run off the road by a drunk driver on their way home. For the first few weeks after the accident, I moved through the world in a numb trance. My brothers and I made the requisite decisions, and friends and family kept us afloat. But after the lasagna pans were washed and returned, I found I couldn't readjust. The accident had landed me in a vortex of grief; I couldn't imagine a life without my parents and floated, directionless. As a former marathoner, I knew how to run from things. But after my parents died, I couldn't elude the pain. My brothers had pulled away, and I collapsed inward, but mostly I cried in my car. My little hatchback had been an insulated chamber that kept my pain private, and I held grief hostage in the passenger seat.

And now that was damaged, too.

I checked my phone, which had been left on silent mode, seeing that a call had come in while I had been scrutinizing Officer Sutton's face. The call came from a number I didn't recognize but an area code I did.

My hometown. Another thing to run from.

Rather than listen to the message, I scrolled down to read the transcript. Seeing her name stopped my heart.

Hi Sam. It's Pen. I've just been trying to—I wanted to—oh, I'm sorry. It's been so long, and I have been thinking about you since I heard the news about your parents and I sent you a note, but maybe you never got it. Well, this isn't turning out like I wanted at all, but can you call me?

My heart started again, escalating. Pen's message was a jolt of nostalgia, hope, and embarrassment, the full house of conflicting emotions. I read the transcript again but couldn't bear to hear her voice. I wasn't ready.

Memories of Pen rolled into memories of Ashley, of course, and I put my chin to my chest. Pen and Ashley represented the best and worst of me, and the openness I had just created in yoga was now sandbagged by shame.

How did I fall for that? How did I—

"Excuse me?" A male voice and a rap on my window made me jump. I instinctively moved away, twisting my neck in the process. Officer Sutton peered into my window, clearly trying not to frighten me but aware that he had failed. He stepped back as I got out of my car.

"Sorry to startle you. We're all done here, Ms. Jameson. And I wouldn't worry. Most times, things like this are random. We've been getting more calls about vandalism in this area." He turned toward me and lowered his voice. "But do me a favor; be careful. Walk outside with somebody. The minute you get in your car, lock the door. Be aware of your environment at all times."

I thanked him and watched him walk away in the night. It was darker now, and the receptionist had turned out all the studio lights and was approaching my car.

"How'd it go?" Her bracelets rattled as she tucked a weighty key ring into her yoga bag.

"Fine. It's more a paper trail than anything." I nodded toward the police car idling nearby. "He said it's most likely random."

"He took long enough to get here. Probably couldn't tear himself away from the donut shop." She rolled her eyes. "Cops. They're all jerks."

I laughed. I hadn't heard a cops-and-donut stereotype in a long time. But a glance at her told me she wasn't joking at all. "Not all of them," I said. "My brother's a cop."

"Oh. Well, brothers are a different story." She waved me off. "Although they can be jerks sometimes, right?" she added, seemingly to save face.

I thought of Finn's protective nature and didn't respond. It had been a long night, full of things unsaid and emotions unexpressed. I was losing a grip on the composure I had been faking, and it was time to go home and unleash. "Thanks so much for staying longer than you wanted," I said.

"No problem. That really sucks," she said, motioning toward my car door. "Are you okay to drive home? Sometimes things like this don't affect you until later."

"I'm fine, slightly embarrassed. It'll be interesting driving around like that. It's like those cars wrapped in ads for cheese or insurance. Maybe I can make some money somehow."

She laughed. "At least you have a sense of humor about it. I'm BJ, by the way."

"And I'm Sam. Or 'Bitch.' I'll let you decide." I smiled weakly.

"You sure you'll be okay?" she asked. She tipped her head, and in the light, I saw a smattering of freckles that danced across her nose.

"I'm fine. It's just one of those things," I assured her. But as I crawled back into my desecrated little car and locked the doors, I had a feeling that it was much more than that.

CRESCENT LUNGE relies on the strength and flexibility of your legs.
If you can, look up and stretch toward your fingertips.
Reach for what you want.

Carefully.

CHAPTER 3

I SLEPT WITH MY BEDROOM WINDOW OPEN TO TAKE ADVANTAGE of the sweetness of early July, before the summer heat gets oppressive, the petunias get leggy, and the neighbors mow their lawns at daybreak. After a fitful night I woke early, glad for the fresh start and ravenously hungry.

And then I remembered. *Red peppers. Yoga. My car.* The faces of the police officer and the studio receptionist wove themselves into my consciousness like blurred, judgy avatars. None of it felt real. *Wait. Maybe it wasn't.* With the naivete of a Disney princess, I jumped out of bed and raced downstairs, rushing to the garage and my car, knocking over an open bag of potting soil along the way. I moved to the front panel to find the word *bitch* staring at me like it was iridescent, highlighting the obvious while exposing the watermark of shame underneath.

It was undeniably real. And although Officer Sutton assumed vandals were to blame, I wasn't convinced. Regardless, I'd need to rally. As I cleaned up the potting soil, I tried to set an intention for the day, newly adopted from yoga. Unlike marathon goals that felt fierce and strong, pushing past a threshold, yoga intentions felt softer and compassionate, something to cultivate. Most of my yoga intentions circled around self-acceptance—something that consistently eluded me—but I decided that my intention for the rest of the day would be to *choose courage.*

I'd start in the car. I crawled into the beast and appointed it the "Bitchmobile." I opened the garage door and whispered *I can do this,* repeating the mantra from my running days. I could almost hear Coach Fulsom's gravelly voice, the backdrop of most of my challenges, self-imposed or not: "Settle in. Don't let anybody derail you. Run your own race." Although I'd had many coaches over the years who helped me win at State in high school, train over the summers, and even a pacing guru my family hired one year, my collegiate coach made the most impact. Coach Fulsom was a mirror. He helped me discover things about myself in ways that had nothing to do with speed or distance. He saw my potential as a runner and a human and even encouraged me to consider running semi-professionally. "You got grit, girl," he'd bark.

And now? It was taking grit merely to leave my garage. As I pulled my car halfway out and paused under the heavy garage door, my next-door neighbors headed toward me on the sidewalk. They were a lovely older couple who walked daily, barely knew me, and were always so cheerful that it made me nervous, like I could disappoint them easily. I hit the brakes and pretended to be on my phone until they got closer. I gave them a quick wave, waited until they had passed behind the car, and then backed out of the drive.

First hurdle cleared. I drove on. People at stoplights did double takes at the keying, but I forced myself to look straight ahead as if I was a contemplative driver or listening to NPR. My heart was pounding, and my neck was stiff from not looking left or right. Trying to ignore people's reactions felt badass, like dipping my toe into the "so what" pond.

After I got my groceries (where plump red peppers were on sale), I pushed myself even further and took the long way home. Lake Mendota sported patches of deep indigo with little black and gray birds riding the crests of the waves. Runners along the lakefront took advantage of the cool morning and unoccupied trails. I envied them.

I pulled into the parking lot of a local bike shop and watched the runners while I let my intention carry me into the next hurdle: returning Pen's call. I had her number from the day before and started to dial, but as I chewed on the possibility of what to say, a wave of nerves rose in my stomach and I quickly hung up. *Why am I so nervous? What's the worst that could happen? She'll reject me? It would hurt, of course, but I'd get through it. I've been through worse.*

The possibility of rejection aside, I knew my hesitation to call was rooted in fear. Reconnecting with Pen meant opening a door into the past, something I had avoided for years. If I opened that door, there was no screen to sieve only the good things, and I knew with certainty that pain would be on the other side. Ashley would be on the other side. Her face waved in front of my memory like a hand in the dark. Pretty, manipulative Ashley. Pen always called her a firecracker. "Grandpa says there are people who like to set the world on edge," Pen had said. She and Grandpa had been right.

If Ashley was explosive, then Pen was restorative. She always put me back together. Pen had taught me about French braids and jump rope tricks and the joys of eating brown sugar right out of the bag. We traded clothes and deodorant and fears of tampons. When we got older, she was part of my foundation; simply standing next to her made me feel whole. She had seen me from the ground up and knew me in an unadulterated, authentic way. Not being near her anymore only compounded my loneliness.

I put my phone face down on the passenger seat, not ready to open that door. Then I remembered that pesky intention, *choose courage.* I forced myself to dial again.

She answered after two rings.

"I love I love I love Marcus Stein," I sang softly, a ditty Pen and I had made up about our crush, a football player less interested in us than watching his own flexed biceps in study hall.

"I can't believe it. Sam Jameson." Her tone was flat; it felt like a bad sign. This was exactly what I worried about—our connection meant more to me than it did to her.

"It's me," I mustered, not trusting my own voice anymore.

"It's so good to hear from you," she finally said, her tone now lyrical and familiar. Hearing the genuine response made me squeeze my eyes shut with relief. "I can't believe you would call back right this minute," she said. "I just drove past the local car wash, and they had a 'help wanted' sign out front. Remember that summer?"

I remembered that summer. I could instantly recall the smell of the briny detergent and the hours we spent folding small square towels. We were the only females working at the car wash, and I could still picture the tan lines around the velvet choker she wore. The visual was cemented in my memory, a path right back to her.

"I do," I whispered back, eyes closed to fight the tears. "How are you?"

In true Pen fashion, she ignored the trivial and plunged instead into the deep. "I was devastated to hear about your parents, Sam. I loved them so much."

"They loved you, too." My throat was starting to close up, and I couldn't speak.

"I tried to reach out when I heard the news," she said. "Did you—did you get my note?"

I sighed, disappointment in myself adding to my shame. Her note was among others that I read quickly after my parents died, put in a basket with intentions for handwritten responses, and hadn't touched since. Except, of course, to be dusted with guilt. "I did. I'm sorry I didn't respond. I've gone dark in so many ways. I even had to get a new job. It's all been too much."

For five years, I had been happily employed as a middle school guidance counselor, spending my energy helping kids figure things out. Because I had experienced a solid, loving family, and some of my students had no idea what that was like, I felt the need to make up for the disparity. It felt good to give back. But in the aftermath of losing my parents, my heart gave out. Although I loved the kids, being around that much vulnerability and loss every day took too much out of me. I wrestled with the decision like a welterweight, but ultimately I had to protect myself. Ignoring the advice to avoid big decisions while grieving, and taking advantage of my empathetic principal, I quit my job. Once free from my contract, I found a simple job as a bank teller, assisting people with their withdrawals instead of their worries. I still think about the kids daily, but I'm hoping the next counselor on the mat has more tricks up their sleeve to fight the good fight.

"I get it," she said. "I just needed you to know how devastated Mom and I were. Are."

"Thanks, Pen. And how is your mom? Does she still make those hella big monster cookies?"

Pen laughed. "She does. She'll be so excited you and I talked. She adored your whole family. Speaking of, how are your brothers?"

I sighed. "We're all struggling. You know Eli and Levi. They're so much older than us that they're fairly removed from it all. They're back east, back to their lives. That leaves Finn, Buck, and I here to deal with everything." I didn't have the reserves to go any further than that. "Do you keep in touch with—with anybody from Omaha?" I wasn't quite up for finding out about Ashley yet, either. "I haven't talked to anyone," I added.

"No kidding," Pen said wryly. I laughed. "People ask about you," she said. "My job takes me to Omaha every other month, so I see people from high school. They always ask." She almost interrupted herself. "Wait. You didn't suddenly get back on social media, did you? I followed you for a while."

"I had to quit because of the trolls," I admitted. "They felt free to comment on every race or uniform slip. I couldn't stop reading the comments—there are some true assholes out there—so I finally shut down my accounts for good."

"That answers one of my questions," Pen said. "I thought maybe you were back. Remember my old horse, Boots? I posted a picture of him on Instagram a few years ago with the tagline 'My first love.'

Somebody commented on it this week. Thought I'd take a stab that it was you," Pen said.

"Wasn't me. Is that weird? To comment on past stuff?"

"Kinda. It means that somebody went back through my whole account. It's a little stalkerish," Pen admitted. "I can't figure out who it is, either. The account is just called justus82."

"Greatest year ever. So one of our classmates?"

"That's what I'm guessing," Pen said. "They left a blue heart and commented, "You haven't changed.""

"What does that even mean?" My mind stumbled over the possibilities. "Could be anything. It's pretty innocuous."

"Good word. You sound like Mrs. Thein," Pen laughed, referring to an English teacher that taught us to love "just the right word." Just the thought of the wool-wearing, literature-loving instructor warmed me.

"Do you keep in touch with Ashley?" I finally asked, although my voice sounded regrettably timid.

"Nope. But my mom is part of the grapevine from the old neighborhood. Somebody told her that Ashley ended up in Chicago. Single, one kid, parties a lot."

"I guess I'm surprised you don't keep in touch," I said. "I figured the two of you would still be tight. She always felt more like your friend than mine."

"That's funny. That's how I felt about you two."

I remembered my intention and made myself wade in deeper. "Well. This brings back some bad memories."

"It does," she said softly.

"That's part of the reason I called. I feel lost most of the time and don't really know why. Mom and Dad's accident shook us to our core. My brothers are handling it in their own way, but we can't seem to help each other."

"I'm so sorry, Sam. It's got to be hard on you all—for different reasons."

"It's making me realize how small I've let my life become, and I'm trying to figure myself out. This new grief, of course, but the old stuff,

18

too. Guilt over the stuff we did. I did."

Pen inhaled a breath so deeply that I could hear its layers. "I know. It weighs heavy."

"Memories pop back into my head, and I cringe," I said. "I know we were young, but still. I'm trying to process everything, I guess. It all hurts so much. I'm trying different things to feel better." I pulled back from a full-on cry. "You'll love this—I even took up hot yoga."

"Yikes," she said, but not unkindly.

"I know. I was skeptical at first. But it's something brand new, so it isn't tied up with any memories, good or bad."

"I get it," Pen said.

"The sweat is awesome—"

Pen interrupted me, which was familiar, too. "I guess my Instagram stalker is right. It's nice to know some things haven't changed."

I laughed. "Still love to sweat, which is why I take *hot* yoga. But I'm also trying to learn who I am without running. Or running from things. Being still and mindful is really hard. I was surprised."

"Are you *super flexible* now?" She said it with a tone reminiscent of days when we had no idea about sex but could mimic innuendos.

I laughed. "I'm trying. I just want to learn to be flexible out in the world like I am on my mat."

"How bohemian of you. I suppose you're vegan now too?"

"I dabble."

She groaned. And then got serious. "Listen, I have to run. I'm already late to pick up my twins, but it's been so good to hear your voice. Can I call you later?"

"Of course. And I can't wait to hear about the twins."

In a familiar flurry of last-minute incomplete thoughts, she started three sentences that she left hanging, and we promised to catch up soon. After we hung up I took a deep breath, muscles finally softening, and cringed when I thought about what I had said: *I want to learn how to be flexible out in the world like I am on my mat.* Dear Lord. But it was true. It's what I set out to do—learn to be more spontaneous and open. Reaching out to Pen was a tentative but courageous step. I added her contact information to my phone, and simply seeing her name in my hand made it tangible. She was back.

EXTENDED SIDE ANGLE POSE promotes grounding and body awareness. Its expanse promotes free thinking and imagination. It might even inspire you to try something new.

CHAPTER 4

ONCE UPON A TIME, SUMMER MEANT SPRINT INTERVALS and new training shoes. Now summer meant trying things like meditation, quinoa, and getting my friend Celia to work out with me. I called and she answered, sounding like she was inside a vacuum cleaner.

"C? I can barely hear you. What are you doing?"

"We're touching up our pedicures. I swear they don't last anymore. Bitsy's lasted longer than mine did this time."

"You painted your dog's nails?" Bitsy is some sort of specialized diva breed, pampered beyond reason.

Celia laughed. "No, I had them painted."

She took me off speaker, and her voice became clear. I could even hear the faint southern drawl that snuck into conversations when she forgot to rein it in. "The manicurist here owes me for all the free highlights I give her. I could trade her a haircut for a pedicure if you want one. Your feet look like Old Man Hickory's."

"That guy from the wellness convention? Gross. I haven't thought about him in forever." Celia and I met at a temp agency one summer in college, selling a myriad of products at trade shows. It was an enchanting summer with retail during the day and dive bars at night, which put a damper on my training mileage and made my fall season painful, but worth it. Sometimes the agency would put us up in a cheap hotel, which was basically tuition for our crash course in friendship. I returned to school my junior year knowing entirely too much about sausage casing, macramé underwear, and Celia's propensity for cowboys.

"Speaking of feet," I said, "find your cross-trainers. Today's a perfect day to work out."

"Nah. Busy."

"Doing what? Your nails? C'mon, Celia, you need this." I turned down my street, where the sidewalk was mercifully free of pleasant neighbors. Pulling into the garage, I closed the door immediately, turned off the car, and sunk back into the seat. Challenge completed. Now it was Celia's turn.

"Why? Why do I need this?" Celia whined.

I hesitated. I had been worried about her lately but needed to tread carefully. Although charmingly impervious to criticism, she was also incredibly vain. "Little things, like I've noticed you breathe harder when we go up any stairs. And you have a little sweat mustache sometimes. That's new."

"I have a mustache? Dammit. I'm newly waxed. Seriously, nothing lasts anymore."

"It's a sweat mustache, Celia. I think you need to get a little exercise, that's all, to get healthy. I've noticed you don't have as much bounce in your step. You have a little less chocolate in your shake."

"Stop," she said. "Healthy can suck it. And you're one to talk."

"I have a reason," I shot back. The car interior was getting hot, but I held my ground.

"Sorry. I know you've been through so much lately. But I just can't go today," she tried.

"Why?"

"Besides Bitsy's runny nose, Tommy is back. I gotta be available."

Tommy is Celia's enigmatic boyfriend, who travels extensively and wears a diamond pinky ring. He's shorter than Celia but makes up for it with confidence, and although he's the opposite of her usual type—he's bald and a good fifteen years her senior—he pampers her, too. As close as Celia and I are, I've only been around Tommy a handful of times. The first time I met him his phone never left his ear, and the second time he commandeered the conversation at dinner but picked up the tab. He had just been in Chicago and brought elaborately wrapped chocolates from a well-known confectionary "for you girls," and he wasn't satisfied until we each unwrapped one and took a bite. It was a kind gesture, so I feigned enjoyment in the dark chocolate and still had the remainder in my kitchen drawer. According to Celia, Tommy is high maintenance but worth it. She dropped everything when he was back in town, a handy excuse to avoid spending time on anything uncomfortable. Sweating would be uncomfortable.

"Tom can lend you out for an hour. I'll pick you up at noon. Go find some shoes that don't have heels or end in the words Choo or Blahnik. It'll be good discipline."

"Fine," she said, with a clipped tone. "Discipline is annoying as hell," she added before she hung up.

That meant I had about an hour to kill. I left the dark garage and put away my wholesome groceries in my bright, orderly kitchen. It was a brief moment of composure and I stopped, took a deep breath, and soaked it up. I sat down at my laptop to research what Pen had been up to all these years, but I couldn't go through with it. Whatever I found would bring up feelings; I wasn't ready to move away from this fleeting equilibrium.

Avoidance was the one old friend I had managed to hold on to.

Instead of doing something useful, I spent my extra time googling the "wench" that Finn had mentioned earlier. We were rivals throughout my running career, hating each other from a distance but needing each other for success. I found out she was now running semi-pro and holed up in a training camp in Arizona. Between hearing about the wench's success and my second conspicuous drive in the Bitchmobile,

I had replaced my composure with irritability by the time I arrived at Celia's at noon.

Ten minutes later, Celia finally emerged, a luggage-sized gym bag over one arm and diet soda in her hand. She was wearing short shorts and a skin-tight V-neck. She lobbed her body into my car and let out a deep martyred sigh. I chose to ignore it.

"I just hung up on my sister," she said. "She's so judgmental. She tried to hide it, but I could hear it in her voice. You know."

But I don't know. I'm the only girl in my family, so I don't understand the intricate layers of having a sister. Growing up in a sea of testosterone, I've never been a girl's girl. Boys are simple—every man for himself. Sports rule. The word *butt* used at the most inappropriate time results in the biggest laugh. Boy language is easy to decipher, and boy confrontations are direct. A well-placed "What the hell?" in our household meant, "Why did you do that?" The "because you're a douche" retort meant, "I was kidding. Relax," and it was over. Boys are simple.

Girls are not. From what I can tell, the language of girls is a labyrinth of implied communication, and most girls are privy to a nonverbal Spidey sense that they all seem to understand but consistently eludes me. I learned this the hard way, being one leg in a triad of friends. I always felt the least connected, like I wasn't quite getting it. Sister language seems to be especially indecipherable if you grew up with brothers. I've seen Celia reduce her sister to tears with no less than a raised eyebrow. So I find I'm most comfortable in the company of men, and especially lately, even more content to be alone.

After the jarring incident with my car, however, I needed reassurance. One of the things I missed most lately was calling home. Things never seemed real until I told my parents, something I could no longer do. While I still talked to them in my head and my car, this time I needed a real conversation with somebody else who cared. Celia was the next best thing.

"Did you notice the side of my car?" I asked.

"No. Why?"

"Somebody keyed it at yoga last night."

"Bummer." She was zipping up the various pockets of her bag, unimpressed with my news.

"They scratched the word *bitch*."

She stopped her rummaging and looked up. "No shit?"

"That's exactly what Finn said. You're riding shotgun in a Bitchmobile."

She laughed, then self-corrected. "Are you okay?"

"I am today. Last night I was a little freaked out, but today I'm badass."

"Why didn't you call me?"

"Because Officer Sutton was at my service," I sang.

"Was he cute?"

"Sort of."

"Still. It must have scared you."

I busied myself with some careful parking as we pulled into the gym lot. "I'm fine. It's probably some punk. It's purely a hassle at this point, but I'll get it fixed this week."

She turned her body toward me and cocked her head.

"I swear," I reiterated.

"Okay. I'll let it go. But I still don't get why you're even taking yoga. You work out enough."

"It's something to try," I said, not wanting to admit to Celia how being orphaned had left me completely adrift. She'd been supportive and compassionate whenever I needed her over the past four months, but I wasn't sure she'd understand my attempts to create a new, examined life rooted on my yoga mat.

Once inside the health club, I flashed my ID and guest pass at the front desk. The foyer was thick with parents waiting for family swim and more than one dad held the hand of a floatie-wearing toddler while watching Celia cross the lobby.

Celia is buxom. The first thing you notice about her is her large, bossy breasts. They enter a room before she does and demand attention. If the two of us walked by, you would notice Celia's breasts, then her long, saffron-colored hair, then maybe you would notice her tight sweater, wondering all the while why she was alone.

When I'm with Celia, I'm invisible.

But this fitness world was mine, and I was in charge. Celia's energy palpably changed as she took in the surroundings: suspended running track, weight machines, treadmills, cross-trainers, and stationary bikes, all facing a bank of televisions like cars at a drive-in. It was the ultimate exercise buffet, and I liked almost all the offerings. Moving my body was the only thing that had given me a small break from my grief, so I had been coming to the gym and alternating machines on a whim. The only thing I couldn't do was run. It was too close to my pain and too close to my parents. They had been at every track meet, every finish line, every awards ceremony, and running was in our genetic makeup. I couldn't do it without them.

After being back at the gym for a few weeks, I realized that pushing my body wasn't enough; the grief was getting heavier. I needed to try something else. I couldn't commit to a lunch date or a phone carrier, but the one decision I made wholeheartedly was to try yoga. I was tired of feeling off-balance, so I promised myself that before I tried therapy, I'd attempt to regain my stability on the mat. I found the hot yoga studio, where I felt both anonymous and safe, hoping to sweat out my sorrow.

In the locker room, Celia took her makeup bag to the mirror, and I took the opportunity to sit on the bench and breathe. For some reason, my heart was racing. When Celia came back, she looked exactly the same to me, except she suddenly smelled like baby powder.

"You know that stuff is bad for you, right?" I asked. "The powder?" I started to explain, but the bright room began to get gray. My legs felt like mile twenty-two of a marathon. I sat down and put my head between my knees.

"Sam, honey?" Celia sat next to me.

"I feel dizzy all of a sudden."

"It's all this freaking oxygen. People weren't meant to sweat like pigs. And it smells." She put her hand on my back, and despite the overpowering smell of Celia's talc, I was starting to feel normal again. The room was back to its original hue. I put my palms on my knees and pushed myself back up.

"I feel better. Probably too much coffee. Let's start with the treadmills." We left the locker room and headed straight to the open pit of the health club. Bodies glistened, weights clanked against weights, and thrums of bass from the nearby turbo-kick class syncopated the room. We found two treadmills next to each other, and I tried to talk Celia through the digital start-up.

"This is so stupid," she mumbled.

"Sometimes getting here is the hardest part," I said. "You've already done that."

"Still stupid."

We started with a slow walk while Celia found her pace, then lost herself in a reality show on the bank of televisions. The runner on my right was a woman with a foot flop so loud it would've given Coach F. facial tics.

I plugged in my headphones and walked. I increased my speed and the volume on some classic U2, but even Bono couldn't drown out the flop queen's uneven gait. *Tap-BAM tap-BAM tap-BAM!* Her right foot slapping on the rubber echoed off the gym walls. Even worse, she was on her phone. I increased my pace a little more and tried to focus. Her side of the phone conversation was vapid, her voice loud, and my irritation was wound around this notion like a thick and bulky rope: *She should be paying attention.*

She was taking running for granted; she wasn't following the rules. Runners have an inherent responsibility to strive for more. My arms pumped, power starting from my shoulder and surging to my closed fists. *You never take anything for granted, running or otherwise. You make your bed, pick up litter, and change the filters in your furnace to protect yourself from the unexpected. You don't let anybody damage your car, and you protect what is yours. You pay attention. You stay in control. And you certainly don't let drunk drivers take away what you love.*

There it was.

A tiny sob escaped from its pent-up hold in my chest. After reassuring myself that Celia and the flop queen hadn't noticed my downward spiral, I increased my pace again. My shins and calves woke up as I eased into a slow jog. I took deep, cavernous breaths and blew the bad air out and away. My feet landed softly on the treadmill like they should, and my brain backed away from abject panic.

Another deep breath, and I had regained my composure. For a brief second, I felt like myself again. I snuck a look at the flop queen. She was off her phone but still flopping. According to the dashboard on her treadmill, she was running a nine-minute mile.

I set my machine at eight.

My quads felt strong in a way they hadn't in a very long time. I went a little faster, and my arms returned to their familiar position. My breathing steadied, and my brain settled in. *This.* This is where the power lived. I hadn't had this feeling in a very long time. I was home.

Home started getting a little hot, however. My skin started to feel prickly as the heat became uncomfortable. Sweat began to cover my face while a chill covered the rest of my skin. Celia said something to me, and I turned to her. Although I could hear her voice and see her lips move, I couldn't decipher what she said. Time slowed and the world went gray. I felt like I was going through a tunnel and slammed the power button on the treadmill to stop.

The round red power button was the last thing I remember before the gym went quiet, and darkness blanketed the tunnel from all sides.

LOCUST POSE can have a profound effect on your nervous system while reducing anxiety.

Try it next time you're faced with terrible news.

CHAPTER 5

"FEELING BETTER?"

The industrial lights above me looked like overlapping suns. I blinked slowly to make sense of things and focused on the face floating above mine. The face held luminous features, too—a sexy mouth, a salt and pepper mustache, and straight, white teeth, like piano keys, only whiter. Crystalline blue eyes bore into mine. They were extraordinary.

"Hello?"

The perfect mouth formed a perfect word.

"Are you okay?" the marvelous mustache tried again. I nodded, although I wasn't sure I was okay at all. I nodded anyway.

"Sam!" Celia's shrill voice pierced the celestial ether. "What the hell happened? You scared the shit out of me! I was starting to get into my groove, and then you wiped out. I thought you tripped, but then you wouldn't answer!" Celia's voice became louder as she wound up the instant replay. "I couldn't figure out how to get off this stupid machine, and your eyes were rolling back in your head, and you were freaking me out!"

Mustache put his sweet hand on her arm to stop her tirade. "Let's see how she's doing," he said. He put two fingers gently on my neck. I didn't hate it.

"Don't worry," he told me while pressing into my carotid. "I'm not some freak; I'm an EMT. We can call for an ambulance, but let's make sure you're stable first." He kept his fingers on my neck and consulted his watch. In the periphery, I heard somebody announce that they would call 911.

"Call who—the ambulance?" Celia got involved again, much too loudly. Worry creased her forehead.

"We don't want to take any chances." Behind him, the fluorescent gym lights that once looked like suns were nothing more than bright circular bulbs. "They'll check your friend here and make sure she's okay."

"My friend's name is Sam. She's single." Celia announcing my single status? That, I hated.

Mustache smiled and turned to me. "I'm Ryan. I was behind you on the gauntlet, watching you when I saw you go down. Have you had anything to eat today?"

Wait. Was I concussed? Or just hungry? Wait...maybe he was asking me out? Was that a thing? I hoped Celia heard it. Then maybe she would take the hint and back out of this scene. God. How am I this desperate? Must be the concussion.

I stopped the spiraling in my head and tried to get my mouth to move. "Um, yeah, I ate. And I'm better now. I don't want an ambulance." I tried to move up on my elbows and immediately felt woozy, so I gently leaned back down. "I'm fine—no ambulance, please," I repeated to Mustache. Ryan. I looked to Celia for support.

She got it. "We'll stay here a minute, and then I'll take her home," Celia said, bending down to swipe the hair off my forehead. Her boobs threatened to tumble out of her tank as she leaned over. "I'm Celia, by the way." Out of habit, she demurely tipped her head.

Ryan readjusted his stance so he was on his knees; apparently, even heroes get leg cramps. In the process, he turned slightly away from

Celia. I couldn't shake the feeling that the world had somehow turned upside down. This guy was ignoring Celia and was interested in *me*. Nobody bypassed Celia for me. His hand was still on my arm, and I closed my eyes for no other reason than to slow time.

"You can cancel that wagon," Ryan said to somebody nearby. I noticed that the clanging of weights had resumed, but there was still an uncomfortable quiet in the gym. Ryan checked my pulse again while I tried to think of something to say.

"Sorry. I'm ruining your workout," I said.

"Are you kidding?" he said kindly. "This was much more exciting than climbing stairs." He looked toward the treadmill I had flown off and then back up at me. "Are you hurt anywhere? You fell gracefully, but you must have hit somewhere."

"I think I'm okay." Embarrassment eclipsed any potential pain. "Thanks for your help." I suddenly felt air on the exposed skin right above my shorts and couldn't think of anything else. *What if I landed in an unflattering angle? Do I move his arm to readjust? What bra did I wear? What if—*

"I've actually noticed you here before," he said. "I should have introduced myself earlier." He leaned in so that only I could hear. "But this will be our 'meet cute' story."

I smiled and carefully reached for the bottom of my tank. Mercifully, it seemed to have covered what it should. The gym manager came over to check on me, and other people moved away. My pulse settled, and I slowly sat up. I felt much better, so we assured Ryan that I was fine, thanked him, and Celia led me back to the locker room. She held my elbow like I was the Queen Mum, nodding to gym patrons along the way. She packed up our belongings, and we walked to the Bitchmobile, where she tucked me in the passenger seat and drove straight from the club to a nearby urgent care. Although I protested, it was a good idea. There was no wait, and an amiable nurse with an unfortunate Texas-shaped bald spot took my vitals. He was gentle and attractive, making me glad Celia stayed in the waiting room.

When the affable doctor came in, she asked me to repeat my story while she examined me.

"What is your diet like? Do you find your symptoms worse after you eat? How often have you been lightheaded in the last week?"

"Good, no, and this is the second time. I'm actually very healthy. Honestly. Maybe I have a virus, or I'm anemic or something. I'm sure it's nothing."

"Has there been stress in your life lately?"

I hesitated. *Let's see. My parents died, I switched jobs, I don't see my brothers anymore, my car got "bitched," and I ran for the first time in a while today.* I decided to stick with the basics. "Yes, but this seems to be related to exercise."

"Interesting. Okay. We'll need to order some blood and urine tests. We can have the lab do that today, but we won't have any results for at least twenty-four hours. We'll send the results to your primary doctor." She moved to the nearby computer screen and logged in. "Dr. Aponte is your primary?" I nodded. Dr. Aponte had been my doctor for years. Even hearing his name felt like a dose of comfort.

The urgent care doctor continued: "Watch for concussion symptoms, too. Do you have somebody to drive you home?" Although I assured her I did, it was a commentary on the state of my life that Celia was my most responsible adult.

Celia drove the Bitchmobile to my house with a quick stop at her condo to pick up her dog. Once in the car, Bitsy settled in my lap, and I leaned back into my seat. A small headache promised to reveal itself soon.

When we got to my house, she appointed herself Nurse Crotch-it and walked me up the steps slowly. She settled me safely on my couch, and I faced the open window, overheated and owly.

"I'm pretty sure it's Nurse Ratched," I corrected her.

"Whatever. How are you feeling, Peanut?" She sounded genuinely concerned as she sat next to me and used her feet to push my ottoman away, sideways. I moved forward to straighten it, but Bitsy jumped on my lap again.

"I'm fine," I said. "But I'm mortified. And I'm never going back to the club again." My skin itched, and I felt like I was wearing wool.

"You will. You need it. Plus, you'll want to see Cutie Ryan." She sang it in a playground voice, and I rolled my eyes.

"Stop," I told her.

"I gave him your digits," she sang.

"What?" I said it so loudly that Bitsy jumped. "When did you have time to give him my phone number?"

"Listen. You looked like hell and had old mascara puddling under one eye. If he's still interested after that, then God love him. I didn't actually give him your number, but I did casually mention your last name as we left the gym. Now we'll see if he's smart enough to find you."

I shook my head as she left the room, and Bitsy followed. I straightened the ottoman and then closed my eyes. Although I appreciated Celia's caretaking, it was exhausting to feel so vulnerable. For someone who liked to be self-reliant, this was a new level of distressing, this unvarnished lack of control.

Celia returned, carrying two glasses. "The level of organization in your fridge is hilarious, you freak. One of these days I'm going to find your cupboards alphabetized." She handed me a tall glass of cranberry juice. "No vodka for you," she said, taking a big swallow of her own glass, clearly more vodka than juice. She settled next to me and tucked a throw blanket around my feet. It was too hot, but the gesture was sweet so I let it go. Bitsy sidled in between us.

She turned to me. "Seems like you're having a crappy week," she said softly. "And you don't seem very freaked out by any of it."

"I don't think I can right now, you know? I feel like I'm on one of those rackety bridges—up high, over some river or canyon—and I can only handle watching my feet move. It's all I can do to inch forward. If I look down or think about the other stuff that's going on, I'll fall. The enormity of everything is too much to handle."

"I get it," she said. "But I don't think it's healthy to avoid stuff."

"Healthy can suck it," I said. She smiled, and we were done.

We had barely started watching a replay of the most dramatic rose ceremony in *Bachelor* history when Celia decided she was famished. "All that working out," she claimed. "Do you have jalapenos?"

"They're in the 'J' cupboard. If not there, try the 'H,'" I joked as my phone buzzed with a text. It was a number that wasn't in my contacts, and I didn't recognize it, but the message was simple: *I know who you are*

I didn't know how to respond. Normally I'd assume it was a wrong number and let something like that go, but I was damn tired of being passive.

I texted back: *?*

It garnered the same response: *I know who you are*

I tried again: *Who is this?*

No reply. I immediately did a reverse phone lookup, and regardless of which site I tried, was told there was "no contact information available." I was getting itchy again and threw off the blanket. I ambled to the bathroom after getting up too quickly.

When I had settled myself down and back onto the couch, my phone rang. I grabbed it quickly, ready for war. Once again, an unknown number. I picked up anyway.

"Hello?" I answered gruffly.

"Sam? It's Ryan."

"Ryan?" I flashed to earlier. I couldn't exactly remember his face—it was a montage of mustache and straight teeth with a little Rob Lowe thrown in—but I remembered his voice. My brain swirled. *Could the weird text be from him?*

"From the health club," he added as if I'd forgotten. Things were happening so fast. I turned toward the kitchen, waving at Celia to get her attention, but her back was toward me.

"Did you just send me a text?" I blurted.

He hesitated. "No. Should I have? Is this a bad time?"

I shook my head, trying to rattle myself back to coherence. "No, I'm sorry. I got a weird text a minute ago. This is a great time," I said lamely.

"Wanted to see how you're doing." His voice was sympathetic and smooth—a baritone with a touch of tenderness, like a gym teacher when the jocks aren't around. It was calming. "That was one mean tumble," he said.

"You're telling me. I bruised more than my ego."

"I hope it won't keep you away from the club. Will this make you afraid to get back on the 'mill?"

Gym rat vernacular aside, he was charming. I relaxed and something in me remembered how to flirt. "No way. I grew up in a household of boys. I'm not allowed to be afraid of anything, well, except for snakes. Snakes are gross."

He laughed. "Noted. No snakes. I'm sorry we had to meet that way, but I'm still glad we met. Would you be up for getting a drink sometime?"

"Considering how you helped today, I definitely owe you one."

"How about tomorrow night? We could go watch the ski show on Lake Monona. They're doing a tribute to *The Wizard of Oz*," he added.

"That sounds perfect." My dad's face popped into my head, and I knew he'd want me to put on cautious brakes. "Can I meet you downtown?"

"That's probably a good idea. You can't be too careful. What if I'm some sort of creep?"

"Then maybe I should introduce you to my brother, the cop."

Celia came into the room. She shook her head with such vehemence when I mentioned Finn that I heard her earrings jangle. I waved her off.

"I never step away from a challenge," Ryan said.

"Noted," I replied.

We made our plans, and later, Celia took matchmaking credit. Although the night was shaded by the unnerving text, I put it aside. I was surprisingly thrilled that Ryan had called, I was starting to feel better, and Celia made the most dramatic nachos in my kitchen's history. The night was a win.

The next morning, I opened my eyes slowly, trying to adjust to the shapes in the room, trying to remember why my brain hurt. It felt like somebody was standing on my head. Memories of falling off the treadmill and meeting Ryan swam to the surface while the wisps of a nightmare slowly disappeared. Their intersection made me dizzy. I got up slowly and made coffee. It was a start.

Morning routines have become my panacea: coffee, a load of laundry, the news à la Gayle King. I know how to stutter-step my way into a day. Daily habits propel me but are strictly limited to *what comes next*, a strategy I developed in the last few months. I can't leave grief in charge of the agenda.

My new routine included a Sunday morning flow class that was gradually replacing my Sunday morning grief. I substituted movement and focus for memories of church services flanked by my brothers but tucked safely between my parents, leaning on their arms and smelling coffee on their breath, and where my dad would write math problems on the church bulletin and pass it to my brothers during sermons. I hadn't been in a church since the funeral, but I found yoga provided that same safe grounding.

Although sore from my fall in the gym, I dressed slowly and headed to the studio for my fix. I parked as far away as possible, with the word *bitch* facing some bushes. The receptionist from the night of the keying was behind the desk.

"Hi. It's Sam, right?" She turned toward the computer, checking me in for class.

"Right. Sam. How you doing?" I cringed. I sounded like a stereotyped mobster. I was gripped by embarrassment for causing Friday night's scene while simultaneously trying to remember her name. I took a quick glance out the window to make sure the scratches on my car couldn't be seen while I gathered myself. The receptionist—BJ, I suddenly remembered—looked at me quizzically. Another yogi approached the desk to check in, so I waved a thanks to BJ and slinked away.

I settled onto my mat in the large, heated room for our flow class. It was to be taught by Nena Wilhelm. I had heard students cast her name about like she was a deity but hadn't ever taken her class. She was a little intimidating; she owned the studio, and the success of her minority-owned business, especially in an industry woefully short on diversity, was celebrated in Madison.

The door opened, and Nena Wilhelm floated in. She was a beautiful woman with flawless skin, long willowy legs, and muscular arms. She wore understated gray and black yoga clothes, but her headband was wide and wild, with tropical royal blue and orange framing her face.

"Welcome," she said. "I'm glad you're here."

Sunlight melted from the window onto my mat, and the background music was lighthearted. My body followed Nena's cues, and my mind stayed numb until she paraphrased a quote from Maslow: "In any moment you have two options: to step forward into growth or step back into safety."

We were in a side-angle pose when she casually dropped that bomb. I was instantly disappointed in myself for not paying attention. That was the kind of dogma I was there for. I watched Nena from my sidelong view as she weaved her bare feet (note: turquoise toenail polish) around mats like puzzle pieces on the floor, smiling at newbies and gently assisting the shoulders of regulars. She was graceful and polished, like a dancer. Something about her felt familiar. And then it struck me—she had the same mannerisms as Pen. I smiled as Pen's face waved in front of my memory, then flitted away as we moved to warrior II. Once I realized their somatic similarities, the parallels between my new yoga teacher and my old friend were obvious. Nena, of course, was older than Pen had been the last time I'd seen her, but the gestures and demeanor were the same. Or maybe I wanted them to be alike: nurturing, all-knowing, giving me insight into what Pen might be like as an adult. Nena seemed to circle the room and, surreptitiously, my history.

Nena instructed us to move to our stomachs for chaturanga pose, and I immediately remembered laying on Pen's bed on our stomachs, listening to Hootie and the Blowfish, and memorizing the liner notes. I recalled the smell of Pen's basement, the delicacy of the Swiss lace curtains on her bedroom dormer window, and the way I had once coveted her Barbie Dream House. Pen was the closest thing I had to a sister, and no matter how much time we spent together, I never got tired of her. One of our teachers once asked if we had magnets at our sides: "Doesn't matter if you're in different classes or in a crowd; you two always seem to find each other."

Class flew by without a morsel of mindfulness; instead, it created a preoccupation with Pen. An hour later, I was back home and showered. The sun seemed to be following me, so I grabbed my laptop, perched on the patio, and let it catch up. I searched online and quickly found Pen Edmonton, project manager for an insurance company in Bar Harbor. It wasn't a surprise that she ended up in Maine; her parents had grown up there, and the family vacationed there every fall. Her father's obituary—he was never without a Pall Mall between two ashy fingers—told me that Pen and her mother lived near each other, her mother in the family's original house.

I closed my eyes, enjoying the sun's warmth on my face, glad for the reassuring details about Pen. The next logical step would be to look for Ashley.

As best friends, Pen and I were paired like salt and pepper until Ashley moved to town. At first, we ignored her. She had a strange accent and wore a belt buckle as big as a salad plate. The accent turned out to be fake, but by then, we were captivated. When we discovered she had a sense of humor and a Sport & Shave Ken doll with drawn-in genitals, we welcomed her as our third—our cumin, or garlic, or something that seemed the same but was different. Spicy. Ashley made life exciting and was also the catalyst for some terrible decisions I made down the line. I had long ago entombed our relationship; it was best to leave it that way.

But when I stood up to go inside, Nena Wilhelm's Maslow reference popped into my head. Was I going to step forward into growth? Or remain stranded in safety?

Although my relationship with Ashley had turned sour before it ended completely, maybe reconnecting with her would be a healthy, courageous step forward. I typed her name into my laptop's search engine, and results popped up immediately. I read the first result.

In an obituary.

I read it three times.

> Ashley Leigh Limbaugh, 35, died on February 2. The world has lost a light. She will be sorely missed by her mother, Evelyn, her son, Dakota Munn, and everybody who knew her. Ashley was beginning to be recognized as a bright star when she was tragically taken from us. She was a role model for so many people. She was preceded in death by her father, Theodore Limbaugh, and her grandparents. The family is being served by Godwin Funeral Services and will receive condolences on Saturday, February 23, at Crestlawn Mortuary, Chicago, from 10-12 pm. Interment to follow at a later date. Instead of flowers, please consider a donation to the family.

It didn't feel real, although my body still reacted. My lungs felt like they were being squeezed, restricting any breath. I read it again. Ashley was dead. She had been a difficult person to love, but still—I did. And she had a son. Since there was no mention of the boy's father, that meant he was now orphaned. My lungs felt strangled again. Would Ashley's mom raise him? The sun that had been trailing me all day wasn't enough to stop the cold coursing through me when I thought of that poor kid. Her mother was difficult—acorn, meet tree—so Ashley and her mother had a complicated relationship. Anybody close to Ashley had a complicated relationship.

It had been years since I'd seen her, but I could instantly conjure her up. She was tall, with eyebrows painted dark, and mahogany hair from a bottle that left her bathroom counters stained and her mom constantly pissed. Her wit should have come with a warning; she could cut you down faster than Emeril with shears. Her apologies were epic, and I've never laughed as hard as I had with Ashley. She was challenging and unpredictable, and now she was gone.

I needed to move. I jumped down the few patio steps and paced in my backyard. My feelings for Ashley were knotty and messy, and the more I thought about it, the faster I walked. There were so many things to unpack and I dug in, parsing each memory that revealed itself. When I noticed the sun had lowered itself closer to the tree line, I realized how long I'd been outside.

I called on a skill I'd perfected in the last few months—detachment. I had done a little research after my parents died, hoping to understand how I could consistently be so numb. Turns out it's a survival technique, and it has a name. Classic dissociation. The part of my brain that protects the rest of me like a conscientious eldest sibling, sets aside traumatic news until little bits of it can be integrated. It's a handy device that keeps me on autopilot; it gets me through my day.

For all the work I've done with muscles, tendons, and fascia over the years, that protective part of my brain is my strongest body part. When I heard the news about Ashley, it took over until I could process it in safe little pieces. Although I had ridden a high after finding Pen and hit a low when finding out about Ashley, I was able to mute it all for an immediate concern: I had a date.

Back inside, I checked my phone and saw that Celia had texted three times and called twice.

Celia: *Hi Peanut! How are you feeling?*

Celia: *Hello?*

Celia: *WTF! R U OK?*

Nurse Crotch-it deserved some answers. After all she'd done to take care of me, she was entitled to an update. But now I was really late, and a text would have to suffice.

Me: *I'm good! Really sorry, was catching up on stuff and now I'm running late for my date. Can I call you later? Love you!*

Celia: *k*

Despite my "love you," I got the lowercase "k." She was definitely mad.

A half-hour later, my phone rang while I was fine-tuning my makeup. I expected it to be Celia, but Pen's name popped up. I immediately picked up like I always had without thinking about my date or Ashley or that I was running late.

"Penelope," I twilled, something that used to drive her up a wall. She hated her full name, a nod to an ancestor she never knew. "Are we going to talk fourteen times a night, like we used to?"

"Sam," she said quickly. "It's Ashley. It's terrible."

"I just found out, too. I can't believe it," I said, quickly switching gears.

"How did you find out?" she asked.

"I looked up her name after we talked. I found the obituary. I didn't want to call back right away in case you were with your kids. But I still can't believe it."

"I know. Did the obituary mention how she died?"

"No," I said.

"I talked to my mom. The grapevine got to the bottom of it." Based on the sound of Pen's voice, I sat on the closed toilet lid to prepare myself for the news.

"Was she sick?" I asked. My mouth was dry.

"No," Pen said, taking a jagged breath. "It's worse. Ashley was murdered."

A favorite with athletes, **HALF PIGEON POSE** creates a deep stretch in the leg muscles. It opens up the hips and strengthens the legs while creating that realignment we all crave.

CHAPTER 6

ASHLEY. MURDERED. PEN'S WORDS WOULDN'T FIT INTO MY BRAIN, like one of those wooden toys that helps toddlers learn to sort shapes. I couldn't fit the word *killed*—a hard-sounding, vicious word—within the space designated for flighty, manipulative Ashley.

"Are you sure?" I asked, stalling, hoping.

"I'm sure. Mom heard it from a couple different sources. Ashley was stabbed, Sam. Frickin' stabbed."

"Where was she? Was it random?" I asked.

"Not random. She was in her own apartment. According to Mom, there still aren't any suspects, and it happened in February."

Right before Mom and Dad, I thought, and was instantly ashamed of my own centrism.

"What about her son?" I asked, afraid for details. "Was he there?"

"No, he wasn't there, thank God. And now I guess he's living with Ashley's mom," Pen said, silencing us both. That would be another tragedy in the making.

"I can't believe this," I said. "She was—"

"I'll be right there!" Pen yelled to someone else, returning to me with a whisper. "I have to go. Sorry to drop this news and bail, but I knew you'd want to know. I'll check in later."

She disconnected and her voice was gone, replaced with dead air. *How am I supposed to process this? To go on with my day as if this horrible news about Ashley never happened?* I stood in front of the mirror, looking at the grown-ass woman staring back at me, knowing she was still a scared teenager at heart. I watched her summon her resolve, tucking her hair behind her ears and tucking the distress away. For later.

<hr>

Ten minutes early, I waited for Ryan at our prearranged spot outside the downtown post office. I was worried that I wouldn't recognize him; I wasn't exactly lucid when we first met. I doubted he was flawless as I remembered. I was also unsure of what to do with my limbs. *Folded arms? Leaning against the mailbox?* I tried a few things out to see what felt natural. Nothing did. It had been so long since somebody made me this nervous. My one long-term relationship had been doomed from the start when my brothers didn't trust him. It took me two wasted years and the discovery of a hidden Tinder account until I came to the same conclusion. Since then, it has been hard to have confidence in anybody.

Ryan walked up the sidewalk carrying a wicker picnic basket, wearing khaki shorts, and sporting a plaid shirt that stretched at his biceps. Better than flawless. He gave a quick wave from a distance, and when he got close, he leaned in for a half-hug while a hint of citrus and something outdoorsy wafted around his collar. The scruff from his beard grazed my cheek. It was a gift basket for the senses in a long season of drought.

We walked the two blocks toward the lake while I tried to remember how small talk worked. I shouldn't have worried; Ryan's conversation skills carried us both, and it felt effortless. He was, in a word, charming. He was also observant. As we walked by a terrace in front of the county courthouse, brimming with dollops of golden flowers and dark centers, I felt a rush of warmth as I realized they were black-eyed Susans, one of my mom's favorites. I instantly pictured her kneeling in her garden, rubber gloves caked with mud, weeding away anything that would stifle the flower's dramatic display.

"They're beautiful," Ryan said, nodding to the terrace. "Daisies?"

"Black-eyed Susans," I mumbled, the lump in my throat making me incapable of saying anything else. As we approached the lake, the musty smell of lake water and music from the ski team's home base attacked our senses before we could even see the boats. More people joined our trek, collective anticipation at its best. Lake Monona's bank was grassy and warm, and Ryan put down a homespun quilt for us to sit on. He poured wine and toasted to summer, and for one tiny moment, life felt good.

And yet I hadn't been myself. The water ski team, fresh off winning a national championship, gave us something to focus on while we were breaking the ice, but I was still affected by the news of Ashley. Focusing on a date when a childhood friend was dead—murdered—seemed worse than irreverent. While I tried to keep it compartmentalized in a corner of my buzzing brain, Ryan had been a beautiful distraction, a distraction that held my hand when the show was over and gave me a comfortable kiss after walking me to my car. It was easier to focus on that.

The wind was so strong the next day that the quiet creek across from the bank had miniature whitecaps. The sun was shining, but the water churned as if the combination of good news and bad had no choice but to combust. I could relate. I stared out the front window of the drive-through bay, grateful for the rhythm of work as I toggled between processing Ashley's murder and my date with Ryan. Each customer exchange was a gratifying diversion, where credits equaled debits and the whole transaction balanced out.

When the morning rush eased up, I sat, chin in my palm like a schoolgirl, reliving the night before. There were so many good moments: how I flushed when he touched the small of my back as we stepped around blankets and quilts spread on the grass, the way he listened intently even though he couldn't always hear me, and the way he helped the people next to us open their wine. Shallowly, it was fun to be with someone so attractive, consistently drawing women's attention. That was a new one for me. In fact, a day later and it was still hard to believe the whole scenario. I could still taste the heady merlot he opened before unwrapping a platter of cheese and crackers dotted with clusters of grapes. It had been a culinary production. *Who does that much work for a picnic?* There were cocktail napkins. *Who remembers cocktail napkins?*

Somebody near me in the break room slammed a locker, and I jumped. Aside from slamming lockers, the daily activities in the bank were like a metronome, calming my anxiety with rhythmic purpose. Deposits in, withdrawals out. Four quarters to a dollar. Loans paid on time. During my break, I called the auto shop my parents had always used and made arrangements to drop my car off after work. Another task accomplished.

Things picked up at noon and cars waited in line, three deep in each lane. A white van with dark windows pulled into the farthest lane, and the engine idled so loudly I could hear it even without the bay speaker. I kept an eye on the stereotypical janky white van while I finished up the cars in order, then turned on the far lane's intercom.

"May I help you?"

There was no immediate response.

I lowered my head, spoke closer to the microphone, and tried again. "Can I help you?"

The driver's side window began to come down as my heart rate began to rise. Light slowly creased the driver's face.

It was Ryan.

"Just a deposit, ma'am," he said as he packed the tube, and it flew toward the bank. When the tube reached me, I opened it to find a small bag of chocolate coins wrapped in gold foil. They had begun to melt, and the smell of chocolate filled the bay. Relief filled me, too.

"Thank you," I started to say on the mic, but Ryan was pulling away. He smiled and waved and turned into the day's traffic. And then he was gone. After the flurry of customers was over, I ate one of the sweet chocolates and spent a lengthy amount of brainpower trying to create a witty text to Ryan but ended up with the classic "Thank you." He didn't respond.

After work, I changed into my workout clothes and left my banking attire in the break room. I had already packed my triathlon bike in my car, so I parked the Bitchmobile at the repair shop, left my keys in the drop box, and rode to my aunt Dorothea's. My legs felt shaky for the first few blocks, but it wasn't long until I caught a rhythm. The wind had downgraded to a strong breeze, barely moving the trees lining craftsman houses and their cleanly edged yards. The smell of chlorine from the nearby community pool brought back memories of late afternoon swim practices with caustic coaches and swim lanes that felt as long as highways. The bike ride was cathartic with movement and fresh air, helping me round out the edges of the chaos in my life. Seeing my aunt would help, too.

Aunt Dorothea, my mother's oldest sister, had always taken her familial role seriously. When we were children, she was warm towels and homemade blueberry muffins. After my parents died, she promoted herself to a new position that included sending newspaper clippings about gynecological care and hardy perennials. She made insinuations about my nonexistent love life and subtle reminders about how often I should launder my sheets. Her sovereignty was made worse in the last few months after the Elizabeth Circle chose her chicken salad to be their Lenten standard, putting it in the St. Paul's Lutheran Church national cookbook and calling it "out of this world." It catapulted her to celebrity status, which was going straight to her head.

"Hello?" I said through Aunt Dorothea's front screen door.

"Hello, Sam? Come in, honey," she yelled back.

I walked through the unlocked door of her bungalow and found her in the kitchen. NPR played in the background, and my aunt looked to be caught up in eight different projects at once. Flour littered the kitchen counter, and the smell of chicken stock permeated the room. She came to me for a quick hug and returned to her chores.

"Sit, sit," she said as she waved her hand toward the kitchen table. "I'm finishing up here," she said, wiping her hands with the bottom of her apron. "Do you want something to eat?" She stopped her buzzing to look me over. "Is something wrong?"

"No," I said, taking a seat at the table. "I dropped off my car at that place on Burmeister and thought I'd stop by." I sat at the head of the dining room table and played with the edges of the placemats. Since it was mid-summer, they were, of course, red, white, and blue. She had always traded out her decorative mats with the holidays, the same rotation embellishing her table my whole life. "Everything is fine. Although it has been a weird couple of days," I admitted.

Despite promising myself I wouldn't tell, details came spilling out while she listened, her bony hips leaning against the kitchen counter. Naturally, I didn't want to tell my aunt about my date; it would generate an onslaught of questions and advice. Just for a while, for a few selfish moments, I wanted to keep the memories of the night contained, secreted away, in a tiny little box I could open and view at my choosing. I wanted to quietly preserve the memory of our lakeside date and the chocolate coins in my backpack. The memories were draped in newness, and just for a while, I wanted to keep them covered.

Instead, I told her about my car being vandalized, carefully avoiding the "bitch" part. Dorothea is a fierce mama lion when somebody she loves is wronged, and somebody tagging her niece the B-word would have certainly rankled her. Despite promising myself I wouldn't tell her about my fall and trip to urgent care, I couldn't stop myself from sharing a watered-down version that I'd been feeling a bit woozy. She pulled herself tall, abruptly, ready to pounce.

I held my hand up. "It's nothing. It's only after I exercise," I said.

"That doesn't sound right. When will you see a doctor?"

"This week," I assured her. "I promise."

She nodded, appeased. "And other than that, how was the play, Mrs. Lincoln?" She tipped her head, pleased at her own wit, and pulled a wad of white tissue from the sleeve of her faded denim shirt. Her hairstyle, the same for thirty-two years, was shellacked from the rows of Aqua Net cans that I knew were lined up under the bathroom counter.

"There's more. And it's worse. Do you remember my friend Ashley from Omaha?"

Something crossed her face when she heard Ashley's name, and she pursed her lips. "I never—"

"I know you didn't like her. But I just found out she died."

The look disappeared from her face. "Oh, dear. That's terrible. So young. How did you find out?"

"I called Pen." Now I got the eyebrow lift of approval. She had always loved Pen. She sympathetically *tsked* and shook her head.

"According to Pen, Ashley was murdered, Aunt Dorothea. I can't believe it." My voice shook. "They still don't know who did it."

My aunt stared at me. Although she didn't say anything, eight different emotions crossed her face at once. She came toward me, put her hand on my shoulder, and leaned toward my face. "Are you okay?"

I nodded. "I think so. I'm still trying to process it."

"This is too much. Life has certainly taken some terrible turns for you girls." She patted my shoulder and returned to the kitchen. When in doubt, make tea. She grabbed the avocado-colored kettle from the stove, filled it with water at the sink, and then absentmindedly let the water run untended down the drain. We were both quiet. She watched the water, and I watched her, confused by her sudden silence and ragged movements. Usually poised and fluid, she looked on the edge of something.

Dorothea has always been a commanding presence in my world. Being with her makes me feel twelve years old and safe. I've watched Aunt Dorothea with fascination my whole life, and although she is full of surprises, this diffidence was new to me. After starting the kettle on the stove, she sat down at the table next to me, and I could see something troubling behind her trifocals. I waited it out, mostly out of my own exhaustion, and we watched finches chase away the blue jays, bullies of the bird world, from her backyard feeders. The sun slanted in through the back door, creating an apron of light into the kitchen.

"I've been thinking," she started. "I think it's time for you to dig in." She flattened her palm on the table and brushed nonexistent crumbs onto the floor. She finally looked up at me, and I noticed the beginnings of a rheumy film in her eyes. It made me uncomfortable and prickly. "Especially on the heels of all this bad news. I feel strongly about this, Samantha. I'm worried about you."

"I know—" I started to agree, but she shut me down with a shake of her head.

"It isn't about being busy. I know there has been plenty to keep you occupied with your teller job and all that probate business. You're all too busy; your brothers barely return my calls, and I have a feeling you aren't seeing them much, either."

I continued to play with the placemat edges. Dorothea watched my hands. "And it isn't about needing money, either. I assume you'll have plenty from your parents' estate, and I can tell you haven't been spending it on new clothes or your home." I wanted to roll my eyes, but her seriousness kept me respectful. She steeled herself, straightening in her chair. "It's about getting back out there. Back out in the world."

She leaned in as I leaned back. "You probably don't think you're ready, but sometimes that's when we need a thing the most." She eyed me carefully. "I know how hard it is to move past the pain. When your uncle Rich died, there were days I couldn't even imagine life without him. And after your mom—your parents—died, well." She let the sentence fall, unfinished. "But for every day that I was miserable, I learned that the next day might have some peace and grace. Maybe I could see the smallest inkling of hope or understand that I could still miss them *and* enjoy the rest of my life. It's hard to pull yourself out of the grief, and sometimes the only way to start living again is to help somebody else."

I knew she was right. In the "before" days, before my parents died, my role as the careworn middle school guidance counselor was to help kids navigate the awkward years. It felt good to help. At first, the connections I made with students seemed one-sided, but a few years in, I started getting thank-you notes for making a difference. Always from the ones I wouldn't expect. And truthfully, I hoped to help them avoid the mistakes I had made. For years I had watched adolescents start sixth grade with innocence in their backpacks and leave in eighth grade with cynicism showing like a whale tail. It had all changed so much since I was a teen. I had worried about missing my favorite television show if I had too much homework; my middle school students had Netflix on their phones but missed their mom between her two jobs. I used to worry about what my mom served for supper; the kids I worked with worried about the cops with warrants. We avoided being called on in class, not called out on social media.

So much had changed.

"You need to be teaching again. Helping young people." Aunt Dorothea continued. "You need to—"

"You're right," I interrupted, louder than necessary. I cleared my throat, unsure what would come out of it. "It is time. And I have an interview scheduled for next week. A private school, for the fall semester." That stopped her cold. It was also, unfortunately, a lie. I couldn't handle this conversation, knowing I was the cause of my aunt's earnest worry. I felt self-conscious and needed an out. I took it.

"You what?" She looked shocked and relieved but also a little lost without being able to finish her spiel, obviously practiced. "An interview? A private school? Well, that sounds perfect."

I nodded, so technically, I wasn't adding to the lie. Plus, I had no fake details to offer and am not that great on my feet. I put my hand on top of hers. "But thank you for the pep talk."

Dorothea nodded and seemed to acclimate. She blew a little puff of relief. "I knew you could do it. No hill for a climber." Then she remembered something, and her dull eyes brightened. "How are the benefits? You'll need insurance." My trip to urgent care flashed in my mind. *You have no idea.*

"I'll ask," I assured her, squeezing her veiny hands again. We smiled at each other and turned back to the finches, who had bravely scared the blue jays away. "Speaking of jobs, I better go. I still need groceries. I've got nothing for lunch tomorrow."

Dorothea brightened. "Let me make you something. I have this chicken—"

"It's okay," I said, once again, too loudly. "I need to get enough for the week. But thank you."

"Why don't you borrow my car, then," she said, moving toward her purse on the desk. "Let me get my keys. I'm not going anywhere."

"I couldn't, Aunt D. It might be a couple of days until I get my car back, and you'll need wheels before then. Besides, I have my bike."

"Nonsense. I can walk most places. And if I need a ride, I'll call you." She handed me the keys and looked at me over her glasses. "It'll give me a chance to see you again soon," she said, almost wistfully. I stood up and leaned in for a hug, wrapping myself in the combined smells of fabric softener and flour, feeling her scrawny shoulder blades, hoping to reassure us both.

Dorothea's car was fun to drive, and it was a relief to feel normal after being conspicuous, like a clear face after chicken pox. Her car was some model of Chevy that my brothers would know—they knew thousands of chassis, models, and makes, but it was the interiors of things that threw them. All I knew was that the car was sporty and red and a refreshing change without remnants of grief patterned in the upholstery.

Pulling into my driveway, I noticed a small box on my front porch. Strange. I hadn't ordered anything. My postal carrier usually wedged packages inside the storm door, but this sat square on my welcome mat. I took the box from the porch and went inside, sitting on the couch with the box on my lap as if it were a dirty cafeteria tray. Possibly a prank by my niece Ella, who, like her dad, Buck, thought she was funny. But something about it didn't feel right. It was sealed with packing tape, but there were no labels, bar codes, or official post office stamps. The box was smaller than a breadbox and bigger than a bagel. Maybe it was food. Once in a while, I ordered protein bars from a health food store in upstate New York; maybe this was a free sample, and the label fell off.

Even though my palms were sweating, I pulled off the tape and lifted one flap of the box. Newspaper covered the opening, making it impossible to peek in. I pried open both box flaps, carefully pulled out the newspaper that rode on top, and threw it to the floor. Once I could spread the box open, I looked inside and let out a high-pitched yelp.

Coiled at the bottom of the box was a snake.

COBRA POSE represents our capacity to overcome fear.
A cobra uses its strong spine to lift its head. Mimic that same strength
when you're in cobra pose to engage your core and lift your good heart.
See if you can push yourself past fear into love.

CHAPTER 7

I SHOVED THE BOX OFF MY LAP, AND IT FELL TO THE FLOOR, right side up. I expected the horrid creature to come slithering out toward me, but there was no movement. Instinctively I pulled my legs up on the couch, watching for any twitch near the box while I swallowed the bile that crept up my throat.

I waited, completely still, talking myself down from the nausea while I focused on the box.

My blood propelled adrenaline through my veins so loudly I couldn't hear anything else. *Was that a rattle? Definitely a rattle. Wait—no, it's my heartbeat.* I continued to watch the box until my vision got blurry.

Time for action. I grabbed a broom from the nearby kitchen closet and tentatively poked the box with the handle. Still no movement. I prodded harder until I turned the box on its side and could see the snake sitting askew. I screeched, even though it was still coiled and didn't appear to have changed positions. It looked undeniably real. It didn't look alive, but I wasn't going to fall for that. I reached the broom handle toward the snake, and for a moment, I could imagine one of my brothers jumping out to scare me. But they weren't there. It was me, alone, poking at a snake with a broom.

The snake still hadn't moved. This gave me a little respite, so I sat back down on the couch to assess. Using the broom handle, I inched the box toward me in tiny increments to inspect it. I moved it closer until I was convinced the snake was dead and then leaned back against the couch to breathe. My living room was completely still except for the drone of the refrigerator.

I wanted to call my dad. I wanted him to get rid of the snake, fix my car, and smooth my hair while I fit my head into that little crook between his clavicle and chin. He'd tell me I could handle it and convince me it would all be fine. But my dad wasn't there. Nobody was. I needed to get used to this feeling of being alone, and I knew I was sturdier than this. Four stalwart brothers had trained me; I could deal with a stupid dead snake.

For a brief moment, I considered calling the police, but I let that idea slink away without acting on it. It was only a snake. This thing that was making my heart race wasn't life or death. I thought of Ashley and how afraid she must have felt. How, at some point, she must have realized it was the end of her life. She must have been so frightened. Bloody. Alone. The bile crawled up my throat again, and I closed my eyes. I said a quick prayer for Ashley and took some deep breaths.

The phone rang and I jumped. I rebounded when I considered that it could be somebody who could help. It wouldn't count as desperate if *they* called *me*. It was Celia, and she started in right away.

"Seriously? You're not going to tell me about your date? I've texted you three times!"

"I know. But there's been a lot going on."

"Did you sleep with him? You slept with him. That's why you aren't talking."

"No, I didn't sleep with him." *But I would have, given the chance.*

"What is going on with you?" Celia asked, so I told her about the

54

snake. She squealed and freaked, as expected, and her squeamish response increased my resolve to be brave. She wanted me to call the police. I declined.

"At least call that officer who took your statement about the car."

"Officer Sutton? I'm sure he has better things to worry about. Seriously, Celia, I want to figure this out on my own."

"Are you freakin' kidding me? Somebody destroyed your car and sent you a python. There's no figuring it out on your own."

"Somebody keyed my car, and I'm guessing this is a garden snake that was delivered to the wrong address." The words fell flat without any conviction to fill them up.

"Whatever. Do you want me to come over?" Celia's voice dropped an octave and she whispered, illustrating how much she didn't want to come over.

I finally acquiesced, purely to get her off the phone. "No, I'll take care of it. I'll call Officer Sutton. Or maybe Finn. Let me figure this out, and then I'll call you later and give you every detail of the date."

"You better," she pouted. "I put a lot into this guy. I deserve details." Amazing. She could make anything about her.

I carried the box—at arm's length—out to the garage and set it on my potting table, then slapped on my gardening gloves while steeling myself at the same time. *I can do this*, I told myself, repeating my running mantra. *I can.*

I used my garden clippers to pull out the rest of the newspaper that was layered inside the box. It was the local paper from a week earlier. I flipped over the box with an embarrassing little scream and backward hop, and the snake landed upside down on the table, exposing a dull beige underbelly. Using the same clippers/scream technique, I flipped the snake over to see stripes of yellow and brown intricately patterned across the top. The scales were like little pieces of mica lined up perfectly on a Goodyear tire. There was a sheen to it that would have been interesting if I wasn't nauseated. But this was revolting. And disturbing.

I grabbed the box and examined it closely. Laying in the bottom of the box were little white pellets, which I assumed were snake scat. I channeled my inner forensic biologist and surmised that although once alive and producing scat, the snake had died in this box.

A snake on my doorstep. *Who would do this? Most of the people who were close to me knew my fear of snakes. This wasn't a prank—it was mean. And combined with the car vandalism and that creepy text I got, unnerving things were piling up.*

I immediately thought of Tyler, an ex-student of mine. What had started as a school-sponsored mentor relationship ended quickly when he blamed me for getting expelled. He had only started trusting me when a staff member turned him in for aggressive behavior, but I couldn't convince him it wasn't me. I hadn't thought about Tyler in a while, but the acne-tipped teenager had an inordinate amount of hate and a yen for showboating. He was capable of something like this. Maybe he was the little miscreant that keyed my car, too. *But why now?*

I left the snake in the garage and went inside. First, I called Catherine, a coworker from the middle school and left a message asking her for any information about Tyler. As a current school district employee, she had access to his school records and her distaste for the boy as motivation. Then I poured myself a glass of wine and researched snakes. Two glasses later, I confirmed I had been sent a common garter snake, probably a female. Knowing it was a garter didn't help, except to note that it hadn't been venomous. That was reassuring. Somebody hated me but didn't necessarily want me dead.

I finally gave up and crawled into bed. After laying awake with the television prattle for company, I convinced myself the boxed snake was a pubescent prank. I promised myself to deal with it in the morning, and after creating a false and tentative sense of safety, I fell into a fitful sleep. Dreams of snakes, ashes, and alarms flashed like a strobe until I finally awoke to a ringing sound, with no idea where I was, what day it was, or what was creating that incessant noise. I finally swam my way to consciousness and realized it was morning, and the sound was my phone. By the time I found it the ringing had ceased, but there was no message, and I didn't recognize the number.

I looked at the time. Damn. I had forgotten to set my alarm and was already half an hour late. I jumped out of bed; you don't do "late" at a bank.

As I rushed through my routine, my phone rang again from the same number. This time I answered.

"Hello?" I said brusquely. "Hello?"

There was silence on the other end and then an abrupt disconnect. I hung up, uneasiness creeping up the back of my neck.

The phone rang again. I barely let it ring once.

"What?" I snapped. Fear and anger reached up together and pushed me to overload. My wet hair dripped on the carpet, I was late to work with nothing clean to wear, and a snake lay in a box where my car should be.

"Sam Jameson?" a man asked, obviously taken aback at my tone.

"Yes—this is Sam. Can I help you?" I backed off a little but still sounded terse.

"This is Justin from Dr. Aponte's office. We have results from the tests you took at urgent care this weekend. Can we schedule a time for you to come in this morning?"

"Can't you tell me now?"

"No," Justin said. "Dr. Aponte would like to see you."

I closed my eyes and slowed. This guy didn't cause my problems and didn't deserve my ire. "Okay. Would noon work?" I asked nicely this time.

Justin was unfazed. "That won't work," he said. "Be here at eleven."

<hr/>

I traded an early lunch with my coworker Stephanie, who knew her way around a rumor, remaining cryptic when she got chatty. At 10:55, I was settled in an exam room and once again didn't know what to do with my arms. I sat on one of the clinic chairs, then climbed on the exam table, wrinkling the paper. That felt too eager. The second chair was too far from the computer. The second I returned to the first chair, Dr. Aponte opened the door with a quick knock, saving me from myself. He greeted me then logged on to the computer for the test results. He typed unnervingly slowly.

"Looks like you had some excitement this weekend." Dr. Aponte said. "According to the blood work taken at Urgent Care on Saturday, you have a slight hormonal imbalance," he said after scanning the screen.

I took a swollen breath, and my shoulders relaxed from their stronghold around my neck.

"The test results indicate that the level of sodium in your blood is low. Your electrolytes were dangerously low, too."

He swiveled in his chair toward me. "Do you drink a lot of water?"

"I try to." This was little and white, but it was technically my second lie in twenty-four hours. Amid all the changes in my life, I had been slacking on my routines, notably water intake, which wasn't like me. Over the years, I've learned to be very disciplined about my nutrition. After an over-zealous coach taught us how to ration carbs until pre-race meals, I experimented with macronutrients and had it down to a science. I'd have to start paying attention again. But sodium? Child's play. I could do this.

"We'll need to do one more test to monitor for something more serious called Addison's disease. But I suspect that adjusting your sodium will eliminate your hyponatremia—feeling lightheaded and nauseous."

He looked at me resolutely from under bushy eyebrows. "Have you been under more stress than usual?"

I didn't know how to begin to answer that, so I went with straightforward. "Yes."

"Anything you want to talk about?"

"Not really."

"Okay. But know that if you aren't feeling safe—for any reason—we have solutions. For the physical symptoms, we'll start with good old-fashioned sports drinks or electrolyte powders. Make sure they aren't full of chemicals, sugar, or especially potassium. Potassium could make your sodium concentration fall quickly, with dangerous results.

Add one or two drinks a day, especially after exercise. I think you'll notice a difference right away."

I nodded somberly as if my brain was patiently listening and not a spider monkey after eating Fruit Loops. This didn't seem like *my* body we were discussing. I'd spent years pushing myself to peak performance and knew every tight tendon or imbalance that could affect my running. I knew when I needed more fiber and when I was low on iron. I could even tell when I ovulated. But this was strange new territory, a sneaky nuisance with implications that could be large or small. And all I could focus on was that although Dr. Aponte was a phenomenal doctor, he was not so good with a razor and had missed a swatch of stubble along his jawline.

"Sam?" he said, a little more gently. "Even if this is Addison's, you'll be fine. And in good company. JFK had Addison's, too."

After my appointment I sat in the parking lot, facing a row of pines that bordered the clinic. Behind the pines were apartments, and I could see a woman reading in her high-backed floral chair through the trees. She looked quiet and self-contained, adjusting her reading glasses and playing with one strand of streaked, gray hair. I could imagine that she was nurturing. Wise. It made me miss my mom even more. I had been going to this clinic long enough to call her from this spot after other appointments. I'd called her with good results after a questionable pap smear, another time with fears from a fuzzy mammogram. When I was younger and got sick at school, she'd pick me up and even if I was miserable, I couldn't stop my face from smiling as I walked toward the car. She always made things better.

I thought again of Ashley and the son she left behind. The familiar sensation of grief started low in my gut, taking the path it had learned in my body. As I headed back to work I set it aside, but promised myself that it was time to air myself out when my shift was done.

Ever since I was little, nature has been my restorative well. Moving my body and being outside centers me in a way that works every time. Mom often reminded me that when I started kindergarten, the routine and stimulation of a busy classroom overwhelmed my little five-year-old body. My parents tried earlier bedtimes and cutting out sugar, but I got crankier as the week wore on.

One fall day, we went for a trail ride on a converted railroad track. After speeding ahead of my family on my bike and returning to them again, I yelled, "*Now* I remember me!" My need for renewal has been the same ever since.

After a claustrophobic afternoon at the bank, I headed to one of my favorite trails in the arboretum. It starts in a wide-open prairie and narrows into dense, fragrant trees. When I started my hike, thoughts of Ryan, Tyler the delinquent, and JFK bumped into each other like runners lined up for the mile.

After a quick scan for snakes, I stopped in the middle of the trail and lifted my head toward the sky. The sun was making a slow trajectory toward a row of border pines. Closing my eyes, I could hear my dad's voice: "Soak it all up. Do you feel the wind on your face? Hear those birds? Take a deep breath. Can you smell the evergreen?" His voice, his timeless repose, both calmed me and grounded me.

My dad knew everything. Once, lying on our backs watching the sky, he had convinced me that he could move the clouds with his mind. And then he did. I saw it. Things felt possible when I was with him, and this dose of nature was doing the same. It also reminded me of yoga, this stillness and rekindling, although instead of sweat, the trail had a peaty, damp smell—a combination of decay and bloom. This grounding allowed me to hold one thought at a time and try to rationalize all that had happened to me. The car damage? Random vandalism. The dizzy spells? Understandable and conquerable. The snake—although creepy—was an accidental misdelivery.

When I opened my eyes, three nuthatches with clean gray and black stripes triangulated around a tall pine in front of me. Spastic and agitated, they picked at the bark protecting the sparse tree. Their chaos picked at my optimism, too: *But Ashley is still dead.*

Screw you, nuthatches. My goal, learning to live *within* chaos, meant I needed to challenge myself with things that were outside my comfort zone. Since losing my parents, I'd tried a new job, hot yoga, and reaching out to Pen. And now, especially after the news of Ashley's death, I needed to keep pushing myself past the familiar and be open to new things. New things like playing the Dobro guitar. Or eating Indonesian food. Or, I finally decided, pursuing Ryan.

⚜

The last time I asked somebody out, I hid in the bathroom so my brothers wouldn't hear. It was freshman year, and I awkwardly asked Brandon Hernandez to the winter dance, knowing that if he turned me down my life would end, and I would move to the swamp—the swamp of Nebraska. My brothers hated Brandon Hernandez and if they knew I was calling him, I would be banished to the same swamp. I almost got away with it until my oldest brother, Eli, heard me through the bathroom door and started singing "Gettin' Jiggy Wit It" as loudly as possible. Brandon Hernandez assumed I was messing with him and hung up. I didn't talk to Eli for a week.

This time I was just as nervous. I planned on using the few seconds of the ringing phone to calm myself down, but he answered right away.

I jumped in. "Hi, Ryan. It's Sam."

"Hey! Ready to admit you were wrong about the Chiefs?"

"Never. But I do have stats to prove that your Packers are overrated. I was wondering if you'd like to hear them. Do you happen to have plans for tonight?"

He took a quick inhale. "Sorry, I do."

I shouldn't have called. I look desperate.

"No problem. Just thought I'd check," I said quickly. *He probably already has a date. With a model. She's probably a Rhodes scholar with an English accent and has never even heard of the Nebraska swamp. I should have—*

"Sam? You there? How about Friday?"

I did a tiny fist pump. "Yes. That works."

"Good. Bring your lame stats."

"I will. Do you like Indonesian food? There's a new place on the east

61

side that I want to try," I said.

"Never had it. What are your views on Italian food? I'm a big fan of Bellatonia. Ever been?"

Bellatonia was a venerable downtown favorite, dark and romantic. I hadn't ever been there, so technically, it was venturing out. We made our plans, and I hung up feeling daring and adventurous. Take that, Brandon Hernandez.

I went home and parked in my garage, where the snake still coiled in its box. I shivered. But armed with my new confidence, I decided to figure out where it came from. I hadn't heard back from my coworker from the school about Tyler's whereabouts, but I could at least rule out a prank by my niece. I texted her.

Me: *Can you stop over tomorrow?*

Ella: *?*

Me: *Date this weekend, need fashion advice.*

Ella: *SHUT UP! Be there after practice.*

Taking control was satisfying. That night I slept hard. The next morning, I dropped Aunt Dorothea's car off at her house and hid the keys under the metal milk box on her porch. I walked the few blocks to the east, wishing I had sunglasses. As I rounded the corner, I could see my car parked adjacent to the auto repair shop, the driver's side panel clean and sleek. Closer to the garage, a couple of the mechanics stopped to assess me before bending back to their work. A radio blared. Inside, the shop smelled of gritty oil and stale cigarettes.

"My Toyota looks great," I told the attendant at the front desk, pointing to my car. He consulted a large desk calendar with folded edges and dirt-smudged estimates, found the notes on my car, and tipped his head at me.

"I know who you are," he said.

"What?" I stopped digging in my bag for my credit card.

"I know who you are," he repeated. I looked up, taking in the tangled eyebrows that were like a shelf too heavy for his face. According to the stitched nametag on his coveralls, he was "Ed," but an old boyfriend once told me that those nametags were fake. Shops ordered uniforms with random names, letting employees choose whatever name they wanted.

"Still runnin'?" He asked as he looked me up and down.

It wasn't unusual for locals to remember me. Anybody who read the sports section might be familiar with my name. But still. I looked at "Ed," with his shelf brows and fingernails ringed with oil. He didn't seem like a track and field devotee. I nodded and handed him my credit card, and he took forever to print a receipt. A quick signature, and I was almost out the door when I realized Ed still had my card.

I made it back to the foyer as he was walking toward me, hand outstretched with my card. "Hey—I didn't mean to scare you," Ed said. "My daughter ran track about the same time you did. You were kinda famous in our conference."

My face flushed with embarrassment. *Nice. Way to assume and overreact in one exchange.*

I tried to regroup. "What did she run?"

"The 400. And she was glad she never ran against you."

"Oh—thanks. And thanks." I pointed to my credit card.

"But do you? Still run?"

"No. I don't. I ran professionally for a few years after college, but it got hard. Collegiate perks really spoil you and without endorsements, it's hard to make a living. You end up working, running, and avoiding injury all on your own."

"I figured. It's a lonely sport."

I nodded, still awkwardly holding the foyer door.

He continued. "I figured you made it pretty far. But yeah, it's a tough sport, most of the time, hoping you don't get hurt. I figure you gotta be careful," he said.

I nodded and turned away, almost running to the safety of my car while his parting words echoed in my ears. "I figure you gotta be careful."

I figured faux Ed was right.

It's hard to breathe with the compression of any forward bend. It requires awareness. **WIDE-LEGGED FORWARD BEND** has all the benefits of that compression but with a stronger base. You might need that extra support if you don't like what your awareness reveals.

CHAPTER 8

ELLA BREEZED THROUGH MY FRONT DOOR AT 5:30. "I only have like ten minutes. We were supposed to have tournament practice at three, but Paige suddenly remembered she had to work at four. Like she didn't know tournaments were next weekend?" She slipped off her shoes and put her snarl of keys on the foyer table. "Who's the dude? Is he hot?"

I took a breath for her. "Very hot. We've already been out on one date, but this time I want to wear a dress."

"You do know people don't use the word 'date' anymore?" Air quotes helped illustrate her point.

"I know. But I'm old. Help me find something that makes me look young."

We started up the stairs to my bedroom, Ella first. She had one long braid that reached past the number of her practice jersey. She wore shorts that barely covered her ass, something my father would have never let me wear, although since the moment she started walking, her butt cheeks had always fallen out of her shorts. Except for the fact that now she was taller than me, she really hadn't changed.

In my bedroom, she stopped and looked around. "Aunt Dorothea would say this is 'neat as a pin,'" Air quotes again. She walked over to the closet and pawed quickly through my limited choices. "When's the last time you shopped? We could do something with this. This skirt is cute—wait, you've already been on a date? And you didn't tell me? Where did you go?"

Her whorl of thoughts made me dizzy. "The ski show on Sunday night."

"That's either lame or cool—TBD. Where'd you meet him?"

"At the health club. I was on the treadmill—" I stopped myself. Although she seemed superficial to the untrained eye, Ella was sensitive. She didn't need to worry about my health. "I was sweaty when we met, so I'd like to up my game. How is volleyball?"

"It's good. Right-side hitter this season. Coach said if I work on my serves, I can maybe start. Paige and Miranda, too. Although they're pissing me off lately. They're so mean to our manager. He's just a freshman—a volunteer—and they treat him like crap."

I stopped digging through a drawer to look at her. "You don't join them, do you?" I sounded accusatory. She bristled.

"No, Aunt Sam, I would never," she said, folding her arms across her chest.

"Sorry. Really. I'm a little sensitive about that issue."

"Why. Were you bullied?" She smiled. "I wouldn't be surprised. I've seen pictures. No offense, but you've grown into your looks." She went back to raiding my clothes and moved her search to the back of the closet where small sizes lived.

"Very funny. No, I wasn't bullied." I hesitated, calculating the small chance that there was some sort of pedestal I could tumble from. I decided it was negligible.

"*I* was mean," I said quietly.

She spun around. "What?"

"I was a mean girl. I was mean to people. Especially a freshman boy."

She cocked her hip and stared at me, hand clinging to a hanger. "No way. I can't see it."

"It's true. It was bad." I moved to sit on the bed. "I think you've heard me talk about my friend, Pen. Old school BFFs. We did everything together for a long time. And then we added a new girl, Ashley, to the mix. Somehow that turned us a bit." I sighed as memories and guilt intertwined. *And now she's dead.* The thought roared in my head so loudly I was sure Ella could hear. I looked down at my hands, trying to decide how much to tell her. She had moved to sit next to me, quiet and wide-eyed.

"We had this weird dynamic. We started picking on people—joking at first." I searched her face, hoping for understanding. There was none. "And then, I don't know. It started getting mean, and we would try to antagonize people. Especially this kid, Larry Jacobsen. We could get him so riled up about anything: his clothes, his freckles, his lunch." The memory of Larry, his greasy hair and big brown eyes, made me close my own eyes with shame. "He was obsessed with knives and was always getting suspended for bringing some weird knife to school. His mom was also known for her mood swings and freaky behavior. We used all of that against him. His mom had some severe mental challenges, obviously, but we were too clueless to understand stuff like that. To us, it was freaky."

"Freaky how?" Ella was listening intently, something I didn't see often. I wished it wasn't for this particular story.

"She would berate us for walking too close to her house one day, and then stop us and start a conversation the next. She drank a lot. She was also notorious for picking up guys at the convenience store, which was more fuel for gossip. A couple of times she showed up at school in her bathrobe, looking for Larry."

"Oh my God. I would die."

"I know. One year for Halloween Ashley wore a bathrobe and held an empty bottle of booze, and wore a nametag that said 'Larry's Mom.'"

She gaped at me, and I didn't like the feeling. Recalling this was awful.

I made myself continue. "Poor guy. He was very protective of her, which is why we pounced on him."

"I really can't see you doing this," she said softly.

"I know. Making fun of him made me uncomfortable at the time, but not enough to do something about it. On some level, I thought he deserved it because he made fun of me during my chunky days." I glanced at Ella. We hadn't really talked about my chunky days, my own middle school struggle with my confidence and weight. Athletics— and learning the joy of feeling strong instead of skinny—eventually helped me sort things out. I had always intended to be a role model rather than a storyteller when it came to my struggle with my body, but I questioned that decision now. Ella was probably the closest thing I'd come to having a daughter, and I hadn't ever shared the most significant things about me.

"Aunt Sam," Ella said, shaking her head.

"I know. I feel terrible every time I think about it. I'm going to find him and apologize. I'm embarrassed about it and even more embarrassed to tell you about it."

Ella got up from the bed and thumbed through my jewelry box. A pall in the room curled the edges of the air. I pushed myself off the bed, too. "So be careful. Don't do stuff you'll regret later. Don't follow Paige and what's-her-name down that path."

"Miranda," she said absentmindedly. I stood next to her, and we perused my jewelry in silence. I had it separated into little white boxes and their lids. One of the necklaces looped in a perfect circle, reminding me of the disgusting snake.

"Is this Grandma's?" She pointed to a silver bracelet, teal beads and silver charms threaded in a row.

"It is."

"She always wore it with that black and white jacket," she said, running her fingers over the beads. While we stood, her left foot turned inward. It was a tiny movement, but I knew her well enough to know it meant she was feeling nervous. Uncomfortable. I also knew that when both feet turned inward, she was on overload and ready to shut down.

"Would you like it?" I asked her quietly.

She picked it up and put it in her palm. I started to say something and then watched her, holding a piece of my mother, sorting through her own memories for words that would hold.

"Sure." She put the bracelet on her wrist. "I don't want to forget anything about her. About them."

It was brave, her wish to remember. "Do you want anything else that was hers?" I opened another flat box with my mom's costume jewelry laid out on dark green velvet. I hadn't looked at it for months. Ella went straight for another bracelet, one my mom wore almost daily, and the second I saw it, I could remember my mom's skin and hands, the way they held a book. My heart clenched.

"Okay to take this?"

"Of course. She'd love knowing that you have it," I told her.

She ran her finger over the top of the velvet, put her head on my shoulder for a couple of seconds, then looked back down at my jewelry. I wanted to say something wise and comforting, but the moment was gone. Besides, my throat had been sore from grief since the first bracelet.

"Don't you have any bigger earrings?" Ella asked, her voice forced and animated.

"Not really." I waited a beat. "I might have been a mean girl, but I'm not a slut."

"Gawd." With an eye roll.

Not much later, Ella and I were both satisfied with my outfit, a simple white skirt, lacy top, and strappy sandals. "Don't forget to over-accessorize," she reminded me as we headed back downstairs. "Just when you think you're done, think of me and add one more thing. And do we need to talk about protection?"

"Funny. Not." Then I remembered the snake, the real reason I invited her over. "Hey, did you drop something off for me? On my front porch?"

"What?" She had already started looking at her phone. "No. Why?" Although preoccupied, she sounded genuinely clueless. She's not a good liar—perhaps a family trait—and has an obvious mouth-rubbing tell when she tries.

"Never mind. Have fun at volleyball."

She gave me one last eye roll and was out the door. I closed the door behind her and returned to my bedroom. Discarded clothes were scattered on the bed and my jewelry drawer was still open, a reminder that even the smallest decisions are worth taking seriously.

Time in the bathroom was a novelty for me. With four brothers barking at the closed door, I never had the luxury to spend time on myself; minimalist grooming became a habit. So I blasted some Queen Bey and primped. I even broke out the new mascara without finishing the old one. That's how hopeful I was. I found my mom's silver hoop earrings from the stash Ella and I had unearthed. My fingers wrapped them tightly, and I held them in my closed palm for a second before I put them on. Fully accessorized. Ella would be proud.

Bellatonia perched on the corner of two busy streets, the faded brick hidden behind gnarled bushes. I found a parking spot one block over, which was rare. Clearly, a sign that this date would be phenomenal. I lucked out again with a prized window seat in the bar, where I promptly ordered a chardonnay from an irritated waitress. I was taking my first long gulp when I saw Ryan amble toward the restaurant. He wore a crisp white button-down shirt, dark jeans, and mirrored sunglasses.

I downed the chardonnay.

Why was I so nervous? I'd dated good-looking men before, but Ryan was different. He seemed on the cusp of reckless. It was like the woo-woo yoga folks sometimes said: if you ask the universe for something, it answers. I had been wanting to learn how to be spontaneous. The universe had offered me spontaneous—in mirrored sunglasses.

Ryan entered the bar folding the glasses into his shirt pocket. As he looked around, I gave a genteel wave, as if I didn't care if he joined me or not. My heart thumped as he came close.

"Hey," he said as he kissed my cheek. This time he smelled nautical, a nod to crisp colors and bright skies.

"Hey," I said, "You look—" but the waitress had materialized before he even sat down.

"What can I get you?" she asked, facing Ryan.

"A Manhattan. With rye. And she'll have another pinot grigio," he told her, nodding toward my empty glass. She hovered momentarily, but Ryan turned his attention to me, unleashing a crooked little grin that kept me from amending the wine order. His smile was one of the few things that I liked off-center.

"You look amazing," he said, leaning toward me. "You look good in lace."

"Thank you. And thanks again for your deposit at the bank the other day," I said.

He puffed up a bit. "Buddy of mine lent me the van. I thought it'd add to the mystique." Our drinks were delivered to the table, and I took a greedy gulp. The grigio was average but it settled my nerves, and I felt a slight shift inside me somewhere. I relaxed just a little. When our table was ready, we were led to an intimate corner with a candlelit table and good acoustics. I went from relaxed to relishing. My date was attractive and attentive, the conversation was light and lively, and our waiter had a sense of humor. I ordered a dish without garlic.

"So tell me more about the great Sam Jameson," Ryan said. "I know you have poor taste in football teams, and I already know some about your running career. But who is the woman behind the myth?"

I laughed. It was easy, this conversation with Ryan, and it fostered a new sense of hope. The wine helped, of course, and candlelight on the table made those baby blues shine, and every once in a while, a thought popped into my head that dulled some of the luster: my parents would never meet him. I wasn't picturing us on a wedding cake, but my parents—especially my dad—had always been my litmus test for guys. If I left for a date and returned to the porch light on, I knew my dad didn't like him. If the light was off, Dad thought the guy was acceptable. Dad still didn't trust him, but the guy was acceptable. If it's true that a girl's self-esteem can be tied to the strength of her connection to her father, I should be golden. My connection to my father was on such sturdy footing that I felt more than worthy; I felt treasured. It's something I wish for every little girl everywhere.

"Sam?"

"Sorry. I was trying to justify the myth. But I can't."

He laughed and raised his glass. "No doubt."

"Seriously, I had a good run. Literally. But I can't take the credit; it's good genes. Both of my parents were athletes, and my dad was a sprinter."

"I noticed you used the past tense. Are your parents gone?"

A sense of loyalty to my parents nudged me into telling him about the accident. It wasn't something I usually shared with people this early in the getting-to-know-you phase, and I was clumsy about it.

"I'm so sorry." He leaned in and took my hand. "That's tough." His thumb rubbed the top of my hand, and I remembered what comfort felt like. Those days after my parents died, I took such stock in people's generosity with touch. After a while, people stopped feeling the freedom to touch me. I missed it.

"I never thought I'd be here, you know? Without parents, I mean. I really miss them."

He continued to rub my hand. "'How lucky I am to have something that makes saying goodbye so hard.' Didn't Shakespeare say that? I'm sure that isn't comforting, but it's true. Not many people have the type of parents you do. Did."

I nodded and took a sip of wine to avoid the "big ugly cry," as Oprah calls it. "Luckily, I have four brothers, so there's always somebody bossing me around."

"Four? Let me guess. You're the baby? Finally a girl, but they'd already named you Sam, just in case?"

I nodded. The waiter stopped at our table for a quick check-in, but I had barely touched my food.

"What's that like? Growing up with four brothers?"

"It wasn't bad, really. Two of them are much older, so they weren't around as much. I'm closer to the youngest two, Finn and Buck. Finn is the cop I mentioned, and Buck and his family live outside of Madison."

"He's the one with a daughter you talked about—Bella?" he guessed.

"Ella. We're the only girls in the crew, so we pool our evil and hang out regularly. Her mom is around, too, but Ella and I are close."

"Right. Ella. And you told me about Finn the other night. Buck is the oldest, then Finn, then you. But what about your other brothers? You haven't said much about the other two."

The truth of that sentence pained me. "Eli and Levi? They're older, so they weren't around as much. I always idolized them, but we haven't spent a lot of time together. Our relationship is weird right now; I hope it's that we're all giving each other some space. After my parents' funeral, Buck and Eli got into a fight, and we've kind of divided along age lines."

"What kind of fight?"

I hesitated. It seemed a betrayal to my brothers to share a complicated family argument. "It might help to talk about it," Ryan said gently.

I considered that. The memory of those days after the accident had been sealed up in my head for months without any fresh air. I had discussed it with Celia, but it was probably time to unpack it and look at the debris again.

"Eli and Levi, as the oldest, always think they're in charge. But Finn, Buck, and I had lived with Mom and Dad most recently, so we thought we knew what they would've wanted. We had big decisions to make about cremation or burial and smaller ones, like choosing the music for the funeral." I smiled. "Buck was pretty sure Dad would have wanted Patsy Cline.

"Nobody can push buttons like a sibling, and my brothers and I are professionals. I guess losing my parents exposed the cracks in our family. It was like each decision turned those cracks into open wounds, and that's where all the pain and anger—" The back of my throat began to ache again as I recalled the raw anguish that had erupted from those arguments.

I cleared my throat. "How's that for mixed metaphors? I think I got three in there." I busied myself with my napkin and took a self-conscious swipe at my mouth.

"What about your family?" I nodded at him. "You haven't mentioned yours much, either."

"Only child. Dad was a cop; Mom stayed home." He looked toward the bar. "They were older when they had me, and I think they had given up on having kids. Dad died in 2007, and Mom is in a nursing home in Baton Rouge. We have a complicated relationship. I'd like to move her up here, but it's more expensive, and I'm paying for everything. That's when you wish you had brothers or sisters." He looked over at me. "Nobody to push my buttons."

"Sometimes that sounds appealing," I smiled. "Sounds uncomplicated. But I can't imagine life without my family. My niece, especially."

"Still," Ryan said. "I'd have given anything for siblings."

"In theory. In reality, they're a pain in the ass." But even as I said it, I couldn't help but smile.

"Like how?"

"Here's a perfect example. We lived on the edge of a subdivision, and I had a pet chicken named Romeo," I said. Ryan smiled, earning him more points for literary appreciation. "The other chickens were mean, but he'd let me hold him and even ate from my hand. We spent whole days together, and he would follow me everywhere.

"One day, I couldn't find him, and I was devastated. I looked everywhere. My brothers helped a little, but one by one they lost interest. When it was time for supper, my mom called us inside. I was too distraught to eat, but she made me sit at the table anyway. My parents were old-school: we all had to wash our hands and comb our hair before we could come to the table. My brothers even wet their hair down. I can still picture the comb lines in their hair when we bowed to pray."

I had told this story before—it represented our family well—but this time, while telling Ryan, my mind was recalibrating the story against loss. It was *before. Before Mom and Dad died. Before Ashley was killed.* I looked up at Ryan, afraid that I had said too much. I had let the wine and a good audience buoy me and hadn't been this uncensored in a long time. But Ryan was leaning back, his arm crooked around the chair next to him, looking at me like I was a candy bar and he was a diabetic.

"Once we prayed, all hell broke loose. With four hungry boys, the food started disappearing. Quickly. Plates got passed, but if you didn't pounce, you didn't get any. As the main dish came my way, I asked what it was.

"'Chicken,' Mom said without looking up. The room got quiet, and the plates got still, and I screamed as I pushed my chair over and ran from the room.

"As I ran upstairs, I could hear my brothers laughing, which made it worse. I ran into my bedroom, slammed the door, and threw myself on the bed. Once I stopped crying, I heard scratching from my closet. I opened the door and out flew a very pissed-off Romeo. My brothers had put him up there once they found out we were having chicken for supper."

Ryan tipped his head back and laughed. It felt good.

"More wine?" The waiter was back. "Or dessert?"

"Just the check," Ryan said, looking at me but holding up his finger to claim the bill.

"Nope. It's on me," I argued. "I'm the one who invited you."

He turned to the waiter, nodding. "I'll take it." He still had his finger in the air.

"But—" I tried to stand my ground.

"Forget it," Ryan said. "Let's consider it my atonement for ordering chicken." He raised his glass, and I followed. "To Romeo," he said.

Once outside, we stood on the sidewalk. The state capitol building stood like a citadel, lit from the inside, proudly guarding the brilliant night sky. Ryan reached for my hand, and we watched the foot traffic around the Capitol Square until he turned to pull me in for a kiss. Our arms intertwined between our chests, a soft touch and a barrier all at once. When the kiss ended, we faced the capitol again.

After a few moments, he lifted our still-clasped hands and kissed my fingers. "How about another drink? I know a place that has a great hazelnut port."

"Sounds good. Walkable?"

"Not really. The port's at my place."

BRIDGE POSE strengthens the pelvic floor, opens up our hips, and helps firm up the buttocks.

Isn't that enough?

CHAPTER 9

WE TURNED AWAY FROM THE CAPITOL, hands still clasped, walking slowly back toward the restaurant. "Where are you parked?" Ryan asked.

As I lifted my arm to point toward my car, I tripped on the uneven sidewalk.

"I'll drive," Ryan said, putting his arm around my waist.

"It was the sidewalk," I protested as we walked toward his car. He smiled.

And although it was truly the sidewalk and not the wine, I didn't protest anymore. There was something delicious about being supported. Our hips were close together as we walked, bumping against each other inconsistently, each accidental bump a small thrill. In the parking lot, he kissed me again before opening the passenger door. The car was a sweet little two-seater with a plush interior, and I sank deep into the cushion as we drove to his house on the west side of town. The night was cool and damp, and we listened to jazz as we drove with the windows down. I felt a lightness—a freedom that the wine, music, and a bright sky had braided together. It was a permission slip to forget the angst that had been breathing down my neck.

His house was a small Tudor in a suburban neighborhood. We pulled into his garage, and he immediately lowered the door behind us. Apparently, we wouldn't be leaving for a while. The garage was spectacularly clean, with crisp, white drywall meeting a sleek and spotless concrete floor. Tubs with laminated labels lined shelves against the front wall. It was foreplay for the fastidious.

I waited a few beats for Ryan to come around and open my door, but when he stopped behind the car to check his phone, I hopped out on my own. A shoe rack next to the door held four pairs of shoes with mates so close and perfectly aligned that they looked like one unit.

I followed him up unfinished pine stairs into the house. It seemed large for one person, especially on an EMT's salary, but was decorated tastefully, as I had expected, with black leather furniture, Frank Lloyd Wright-inspired tables and lamps, and minimalist art. We drank hazelnut port, which was terrible, but I still sipped as he gave me a tour of the lower level, starting in the living room.

"Now this," he said, pointing to a framed picture on the bookshelf, "is priceless." I picked up the custom frame that held a stock certificate for the Green Bay Packers. I moaned.

He grabbed it back. "You can't touch it if you aren't going to revere it." I immediately thought of Celia's quick, raunchy humor. I could have used her.

"I've been a stockholder since 1972, and they've had their ups and downs. But some things are worth waiting for." He looked at me long enough to make me uncomfortable, and then he kissed me. This time I wrapped my arms around his neck and kissed him back.

"So I feel like I spent the whole dinner talking about me," I admitted when we took a breath and sat on the couch. "Tell me about you."

"Not much to tell, really. Grew up around here, played ball in college, love my job. Boring."

"What kind of ball?"

"Baseball. Chicks dig pitchers." He smiled. "Now I play softball—a coed league that I've been on for years. You should come play with us sometime. Or do you throw like a girl?"

"Yes, I do. Thank you. But I'm sticking to noncompetitive sports for a while. Actually, I've been trying hot yoga at the studio down the street."

He gave a short nod of approval. "That sounds relaxing."

"It's not relaxing at all; it's surprisingly intense. It's harder than you'd think."

"I bet," he teased.

"It is. B.J. Raji swore by it."

"Right. A defensive tackle from the Packers doing yoga." He swirled his glass before taking a drink. "No way. He was over 300 pounds."

"More like 350. He can even do the splits. I read an article about how yoga completely changed his body. He was so muscular and tight that he turned to yoga for help. Once he started a yoga practice, his muscles got more elastic. He played some good football after that."

"Wow," Ryan said, putting his wine glass on a coaster. "A girl who does yoga and knows her defensive line. Where have you been hiding?"

We kissed. And kissed some more. I wondered if kissing had changed since I'd done it last. *What if there was a new way to do it? What if I was doing it wrong?*

There was tongue; there was fire. It seemed to be going well. It was weird when you thought about it. How do people even learn how to kiss? What if, instead of learning from movies and books and watching others, we were the first people ever to kiss? "*I like you. I know I want to mash something of yours against something of mine, but what? Elbows? Nah, too hard. I know; I want your face pressed against mine. How about lips? It feels good, but is it—*"

"Sam?"

"Sorry," I said, but still worried that this seemed like a lot of kissing. *Was this normal?*

We kissed again, and his tongue found places my dentist had missed. When he pulled away, he touched my forehead with his.

"Upstairs?"

It had been so long since I had felt seductive or attractive. The base instincts that had been dormant in me for so long resurfaced, and for once I didn't overthink it. He grabbed my hand, and we climbed the stairs.

His bedroom was tasteful and classy. Earth tones and neutrals, with a small reading lamp next to the bed coating the room in a soft golden glow. *When had he turned on the light?* A new worry about disrobing in front of somebody new started to germinate, but he stepped back and traced his hand down my side. "You have a great body," he whispered in my ear.

"Do you have—"

"Got it," he said and leaned over to the nightstand to open a drawer, exposing a box of condoms. He grabbed one and we moved toward the bed, a king-sized behemoth with a tasteful black duvet and untold tales inside. But I felt safe and adventurous, and although it had been a long while, I seemed to remember what to do.

⧫⧫⧫⧫⧫⧫

I woke up alone. The room was light with the muted morning sun, and it felt late. My clothes were draped neatly at the end of the bed, and I rushed to put them on in case Ryan walked in. What happens in the throes of a romantic adventure is different than seeing each other naked, bent over, in the light of day.

I found my way downstairs, taking in more details of Ryan's house that I didn't care about the night before. A plate of fresh pineapple, a mug, coffee in a carafe, and a tented note sat on the island in the middle of the kitchen.

"*Hi. Got called in for an early shift and didn't want to wake you. Make yourself at home, and I'll pick you up at 11. Until then, su casa es mi casa.*"

Which told me two things: I had an hour to snoop, and his Spanish needed some work.

I looked around me, taking stock. White cupboards framed the gray and white granite island, and the countertops were bare except for an intricate wrought iron wine rack. No canisters, plants, or dirty dishes muddying the austerity. It was clean and sparse. I loved it.

The window was open, and I could hear the thrum of construction vehicles in the nearby subdivision. The smell of fresh earth combined with freshly ground coffee made me feel domestic. I ate some of the pineapple and it was divine, which is usually the case when prepared by someone else. Looking for a storage container was the perfect excuse for a kitchen cupboard raid. You can learn a lot about a person from their pantry. Cereal? No carb issues. Using handwritten recipe cards? Sentimental. It seemed Ryan was a foodie, based on the expensive-looking knife block on his counter. But upon further investigation, I could tell the knives had been rarely used. His cupboards revealed whey protein powder, sugar-free gelatin, and gluten-free crackers in front, but a half-empty box of Twinkies hidden in back.

My search of the pantry had barely ended when I heard a noise in the living room. My heart stopped. The kitchen cupboards were all wide open, and it felt like my pants were down. I started closing doors quietly while listening intently for another noise.

Nothing.

"Ryan?" I called out, but everything was still. Even the backhoe was quiet. I tiptoed into the living room and found our wine glasses from the night before. As I took them to the kitchen, I noticed I had one more cupboard to explore. It was next to the refrigerator and held office supplies and mail. As I eased it shut, I noticed a business card sitting on top of a manila folder: Eugene Gauthier. Criminal Defense Attorney.

Why would Ryan need a defense attorney?

I picked up the card and looked at it, turning it over. On the back, hand-written, Eugene Gauthier had written these words: Call me if she decides to file that restraining order.

I was instantly cold. Putting the card back quickly—exactly where I found it—I started to open the folder. Then I recoiled. Once I looked at the file, I was done. This relationship wouldn't unfold naturally, and besides, this was wrong. It was all wrong.

But. A restraining order?

I quickly closed the cupboard and backed away. The reality of this situation dawned on me slowly, gravely, and cemented my feet to the floor: I had literally opened myself up to someone I barely knew—someone with a restraining order. Of course, this was a huge leap, but it was becoming increasingly clear to me that I had a stalker.

And the guy I just slept with had a potential restraining order.

According to the microwave clock it was almost eleven, and Ryan would be home soon. A wave of dread ran through me. Should I leave? Face him? I wasn't sure I could pretend I didn't know about this; I'm a terrible actress. But if I asked him about it, I'd need to confess to snooping. That didn't seem like a good option with somebody who has a restraining order. If I left—got a cab or an Uber—would he hunt me down?

This new information didn't match the man I had disrobed the night before. I needed more time to process this and decided I couldn't ask him about it. I had been intruding on his life, and it was none of my business. Maybe there was a good reason for the business card in his cupboard. Maybe we'd laugh about it later. I would let him drive me to my car, and then I'd consider my options.

Retracing my steps, I raked the carpet with my fingers in rooms where my snooping was obvious. I looked in the bathroom mirror, practicing a false sense of lightheartedness. I would be calm. I would be noncommittal. I would, as quickly as possible, get the hell out of there.

As I came out of the bathroom, I heard the grind of the garage door. Ryan was home. I raced downstairs.

WARRIOR I symbolizes a spiritual warrior—strong and brave in the face of adversity. This pose requires constant realignment while facing what's ahead.

CHAPTER 10

I SCRAMBLED TO SIT ON A STOOL NEAR THE ISLAND and pretended I was composed and serene, casually scrolling through my phone as if my heart wasn't pounding. Ryan entered the kitchen through the garage door, twirling his key ring around his finger.

"There she is," he said, closing the door behind him with his foot. He wore navy pants and a navy shirt with the EMT emblem marking the right sleeve. He moved next to me, cupped my chin with his free palm, and leaned over for a kiss.

"A sight for sore eyes," he said. A blend of wintergreen gum and woodsy shampoo clouded him. Combined with the tight-fitting monochrome uniform, he was a study in masculinity. But even a whiff of mint and virility couldn't assuage my fears. I let his small kiss land on my lips and then moved away.

Ryan kept his hand on my chin. He tilted his head to search my face. His eyes were still blue and beguiling, but the peppered hair that was once so charming now looked old. He suddenly reminded me of a schnauzer. Funny how the light of day and a restraining order can change things.

"Morning breath," I explained, covering my mouth with my hand. He stepped back and smiled.

"Even your morning breath is cute," he said. He set his keys on the counter, a tiny framed picture of Brett Favre chained to the fob. "I have some mouthwash in my bathroom. For next time." He grinned.

"Oh? Really? Is this a common problem for you? Women with bad breath who spend the night?" My attempt was lighthearted, but it came off shrill.

He laughed. "No. Not at all. I like to be prepared."

"Good to know, Boy Scout. Should we get going?" I slid off the stool and headed toward the door. "I know you're on your lunch break."

"Sure." But he didn't move. He looked around the kitchen, and I followed his gaze. Did I leave a cupboard open? Could he tell I had just scoured his kitchen and his secrets? I felt heat rising from my neck. A dense silence knocked around the kitchen while he scanned it.

"I see you liked the pineapple," he finally said.

The pineapple. Yes. He made me breakfast and left a note.

"Yup. Very good. I love pineapple. Thanks. We really better go. You need to get back to work, and I need to shower." At the mere mention of anything pertaining to nudity, I blanched. I grabbed my purse from the kitchen counter and headed toward the door, hoping he would follow. He did.

The ride to my car was awkward, with spaces where conversation should have been and where mouthwash would have been nice, after all. I accused myself of being unjustifiably nervous. I could, after all, be jumping to conclusions; a restraining order isn't a murder conviction. There might have been a million explanations for the file in his cupboard. A simple misunderstanding, perhaps. He could be an undercover cop or have a jealous ex-girlfriend with plans to vilify him. He could be helping somebody out. As a matter of fact, it was all pretty vague. All of this could be easily explained.

Or he could be a creepy stalker. A serial killer who beds desperate yoga students and poisons them with freshly sliced pineapple.

His car, which had felt leathery and cozy twelve hours earlier, now felt stifling. There was no airflow, and our bodies were much too close. I remembered the night before when we had kissed over the gear stick. Now I plastered myself against the passenger door and feigned interest in the sidewalk.

"Is something wrong, Sam?" Ryan finally asked after silence filled the car like fog.

"No. I'm just—" I steeled myself and cleared my throat. "I'm just embarrassed. This isn't like me. I don't typically spend the night so soon after meeting somebody, and I'm just embarrassed."

He started to speak. "We—"

I started at the same time. "I—"

"Look," he said, forcing his words over mine. "I was going to say that I don't do this, either. This soon, I mean. I thought we had something different."

"I know." I stopped there because I didn't know. I didn't know what to say or what to think. When we got to my car, I tried for a rapid exit, unbuckling my seatbelt and reaching for the door. I wasn't fast enough, and Ryan had quickly made it to the passenger side. He opened the car door and held out his hand. I ignored it as I swung my legs out of the car and tried to stand gracefully. My purse strap caught on the seat belt, and I stumbled onto Ryan's boot.

"I got it," I said awkwardly as Ryan tried to help, and I yanked my purse free. I moved away from him and the confines of the open door.

"Thanks for everything, Ryan. And thanks for dropping me off. I'll talk to you later, okay?" I let the words topple out of my mouth as I walked backward on the sidewalk, trying not to trip again. A quick little wave and I was almost there, disentangling myself from Ryan, his car, and uncertainty. Ryan lifted his hand in a return wave and got back in his car, looking bewildered. A bewildered schnauzer. I opened my car door and threw myself behind the wheel, then pulled out my phone and pretended to read something until he pulled away.

I sat in my car, trying to settle myself down with deep breaths. Damn. It had been exactly a week since I sat in the yoga studio parking lot, trying to settle down after my car got keyed.

My weekends sucked.

Since hearing Finn's voice made me feel better last week, I decided to try it again. I should tell him about Ashley. Or I could ask him about restraining orders, and he could mansplain. That would be familiar and cheer me up. Growing up, he was a blowhard but also my benchmark and main source of entertainment. Maybe we weren't that far away from that now.

He picked up quickly. "Yo."

"Hey, loser. You busy?"

"Yes, but you probably need something."

Suddenly this didn't seem like a good idea. "I don't need anything."

"Okay," he said, drawing out the last syllable for annoying emphasis.

"I wanted to call my brother. Is that a crime? You're the expert."

"No, but you usually want something."

"This time, I don't." A beat. "I just miss you."

He made fake scratching noises on the phone. "Hello? Hello? I could have sworn you said something nice."

"Shut up. Can't you be normal for once?"

"No. Seriously, what's up?"

"Seriously, nothing. I miss you. We haven't hung out in a while. We used to spend more time together."

"We used to have more time to spend."

"I know. Wouldn't you kill for one of those summer days when we did nothing all day?" The way I threw out the word *kill* so casually made me cringe. *How did that one-syllable word get so watered down? How can I use it so carelessly, especially now?*

Finn laughed, bringing me back. "That's when we usually got in trouble," he said. "Remember the time we got busted for cussing at the Widows Waverly across the street? They were leaving for church, and we hid in the bushes in front of our house. We yelled every dirty word we knew at them." He laughed, a deep chortle that sounded like my dad's. "Like they would have no idea it was us. I still remember the younger one shaking a finger at the bushes. What was her name again? We got in so much trouble for that one."

"Shirleen. It was totally your fault, Finn. You were a terrible influence on me."

"You haven't turned out so bad."

Silence. Another beat. "Wish we could go back," I said, my voice sounding more like a little girl than it should.

"Me too. I miss them," he said quietly.

"Me too."

More silence, but this was more companionable.

"Listen, I hate to do this, but I have a game in like twenty minutes," Finn said.

"No worries. I'll let you go. You playing Carpenter Field?"

"Yup. You should come down. You haven't been there for a long time, TP."

"Maybe I'll surprise you. I'll hide in the bushes and heckle." We hung up, and I felt better until I remembered why I had called.

There was a power yoga class starting in an hour, and I decided to go. After so much time bouncing around in my own head, I needed a break from myself. I stopped at home to change my clothes, then drove to the studio, parking in my usual spot. I had claimed it from the first day I joined the studio; I liked that it faced a linden tree, leafy, full, and secure. Regardless of what happened the last time I was here, sticking to my routine was my version of a "screw you" to the disturbing things that had been happening to me.

Inside, I stopped to take off my shoes in the lobby. A beige jacket hung on the coat rack, a relic from cooler days. It looked left behind and lonely. BJ called out to me from the reception desk, startling me from my cloud of reverie.

"Hey, Sam," she called, familiarity in her voice. "Going to Nena's class?"

"I am. Do you need my card?" I asked, hoping to circumvent any small talk and hide how wretched I was feeling about life.

"Nope. You're all checked in. We're in the back room."

The back room. My favorite. It feels removed from traffic and any judgment, imagined or real. Walking down the hallway to the back room is more than a metaphor for the single-mindedness to come. It narrows things down until it's me, my mat, and my new blend of sodium water.

I found a coveted spot in the middle of the room—not in the front (God forbid), not in the back (can't see the mirrors for alignment), and not too close to the heat source (I made that mistake once and almost keeled over). When you're early to class, you get to be Goldilocks. I spread out my mat and moved to my back to relax and get my mind yoga ready.

I heard rustling to my right and opened my eyes to find BJ unrolling her mat next to mine. She was definitely yoga ready, with her designer mat and stainless-steel water bottle. In the time I'd been laying there trying to detach, she had changed into black yoga pants and a purple tankini. The purple tankini perfectly matched her purple headband. Next to her, my black tank and capris looked goth. She spread a pink sweat towel toward the edges of her coordinating mat. I was using a Shrek towel, a gift from my niece.

The door opened quickly, and Nena stepped into the room. "Welcome," she stated simply. "I'm glad you're here."

She looked at me and smiled and I felt called out, ala teacher's pet. It reminded me of the first cringeworthy class I'd taken. My stomach had growled intermittently and despite what the cautious instructor advised, I pushed myself too hard. I was sore for days. In those early days, I felt most comfortable in rabbit pose, head down and body rolled into a tiny ball, like a hiding bunny. After a couple of classes, rabbit pose began to feel tight and closed-off, and I found myself looking forward to chair pose, perching on an imaginary chair with arms in the air. Chair pose sounded innocent, but like its Sanskrit name, Utkatasana, it was powerful and fierce.

It was time for fierce.

"Let's begin today's practice in child's pose," Nena said. "While you're moving there, I'm going to walk around and deliver foam blocks. I've noticed a reticence to use the props, and I want to remind you that they're simply here to help. They aren't a sign of weakness; they're gentle support. We can all use that, no?" She placed two rectangular blocks next to each mat. I eyed them but never touched them. I wasn't a wimp.

"I also recommend that you take a minute to think of an intention for today's practice. What brought you here? Dedicate the next hour to something or someone that you want to focus on." I decided my intention was to get centered again. And not be a wimp.

The poses and the music continued to crescendo, and I was beginning to feel strong again. By the end of the vigorous class, I had created small puddles of sweat on my mat. During one particularly difficult sequence, we took a downward dog to rest, and the sweat that rolled down my body dripped from my head and splattered on my mat. It sounded exactly like rain. I looked over at BJ. She didn't seem to be raining sweat, and I silently cursed those women with their revved-up metabolism and appropriate sweating. Women without any unwanted body hair. Women who were probably camp counselors going from swim lessons to beach volleyball without changing their two-piece swimsuits. They could jog without wearing an underwire bra. They were sweat-free, carefree, pony-tailed, and, worst of all, unaware of how lucky they were. She probably never slept with anybody that had a restraining order.

BJ noticed me looking at her and smiled. It wasn't an easy glance, under the armpits during a downward dog, and when Nena quietly walked up behind us, we quickly looked away as if caught cheating in algebra.

After some long, peaceful moments and a heartfelt "Namaste," I stayed supine on my mat and hoped my sweat had simply evaporated on its own. It hadn't. BJ was rolling up her fancy mat, and Nena walked over to the small space between us. "Nice to see you two," she whispered. BJ and I each responded with a smile, much too eagerly. BJ followed Nena out of the room. The rest of the class was still reverential, so I tried to delicately mop up sweat puddles with Shrek, then quietly rolled up my mat and left.

Outside, I walked tentatively to my car. I almost expected a repeat of the last time. But it was unscathed, and I climbed in with relief. I checked my phone and saw a text from Ryan: *Hey. Thinking of you. Movie tomorrow night?*

I deleted it quickly as if it could stain my screen. The last hour had restored my faith in myself, and I wanted more time to figure things out. Aunt Dorothea was famous for her "Come to Jesus" meetings with people to shake some sense into them; it was time for one of those myself. Although sweaty, I turned left where I usually turned right and took myself to a coffee shop. I'd never held a "Come to Jesus" meeting before, but it seemed a good day to start. Throughout my years of counseling, I taught students coping mechanisms ranging from self-awareness to delayed gratification. It was time to use those strategies myself. So much had happened that I wasn't taking seriously. It was time to research Ryan's potential restraining order and see if I could find more information on Ashley's murder. The coffee shop, rich with antiques and quilts, seemed a wholesome place to regroup, and I had settled into my second cup of chamomile tea when my phone rang.

"Sam?" It was Celia, her voice high and screechy.

"What's wrong?" I whispered, knowing it must be bad. She never calls me Sam.

"I need you to take Bitsy. Can you come and get her? I'm leaving this minute. I have her leash and bed by the door. Can you come?"

"Hold on, C. What's going on? Are you okay? What's happening?"

"Tommy called. He's flying me to Las Vegas. Some insurance thing he needs help with. I canceled my clients, and he found a flight that leaves right away. He's sending a car. But I need your help with Bitsy."

"Seriously?"

"Seriously, Sam. You still have your key, right? Don't forget; she needs her monkey pillow and her blanket. Go get her now, okay?"

"Tell me again. What's going on with Tommy?"

"I'll tell you later when I find out for sure. He doesn't want you—he doesn't want anybody to know. For now."

"Celia," I started.

"I'll call you later, especially about feeding her. It's complicated, so you have to do exactly what I say. And don't forget—dogs can't have chocolate. Or sugar. Will you remember all of this?"

"I got it, C. I'll go get Tipsy and figure it out from there."

"It's not funny, Sam. Go get Bitsy. I'll call you from the road." A couple of minutes later I got a text full of instructions for Bitsy, including a complicated feeding protocol, followed by another full of thank you's and emojis.

This was not good. Celia's allegiance to her boyfriend was maddening, but this took it to a new level. Tommy was trouble, no doubt about it. He was ex-Navy, a fact he mentioned approximately every ninety seconds and I was certain wasn't true. They met when he charmed her at a tattoo parlor, and she ended up paying for the whole night, tattoos and all. She liked to tell their story: they started the night talking as strangers, chatting about anchor tattoos, and continued into the next day, talking about seamen. Tommy's mysterious nature had kept him dangerous in Celia's eyes, which appealed to her. But I didn't trust him, and he didn't seem to like me. Although Celia lived life spontaneously, this last-minute summons to Vegas affected her safety and, ultimately, me. I'd take care of her dog and then get her to come home. My "Come to Jesus" meeting now had a new agenda: convince Celia to jump ship.

HAPPY BABY POSE can feel both awkward and playful.
It can also connect us to our origins and a renewed sense of belonging.

CHAPTER 11

THERE'S A LUMBERYARD JUST NORTH OF MY HOUSE, and a group of men—and one woman—meet there most mornings. They remind me of crows congregating on the side of the road, but instead of fighting over stale french fries, they hold paper coffee cups and kill time storytelling and toe-digging. When large deliveries of wood are unloaded, I can hear the truck's backup alarms and smell the freshly cut wood drift through the neighborhood. The yard is seemingly untouched by technology, and its rough-hewn world feels like home.

On my way home from picking up Bitsy, who perched on my lap and held her head out the window with unadulterated joy, I passed the lumberyard. It made me miss my dad. When I was young, we had a life we could count on. Saturday mornings were chores, and Saturday evenings homemade pizza. In the afternoons, my brothers would take off on their bikes or cars to meet friends in faraway boy places. My dad donned his coveralls to work in the garage. His workbench was piled with dirty rags, tools, and rectangular wood pencils that he barely used but fascinated me. Sometimes I would steal one of the pencils and keep it under my bed to study it later. I spent a lot of time trying to figure out how it was made or how my dad kept it sharpened. I always meant to ask him.

While Dad worked, I would roller skate in the garage. Around and around in an oval, I created my own skate rink in the garage grit, dancing to music on the radio unless it was football season. The shelves that lined the garage held paint cans, which, when I went fast enough, blurred into the faces of spectators at my show.

As I got older, I graduated to inline skates and ventured from the garage. I rolled down the sidewalk, where more imaginary worlds awaited. We lived on a long hill, and at the bottom of the incline my speed increased, and the spectators, who had moved to the street, cheered maniacally. But my heart remained in the garage, where my dad tinkered and hummed and filled up the space.

I had been hoping that Ryan would be the same way, but he didn't seem like the garage or lumberyard type. Of course, he didn't seem like the restraining order type, either. I didn't know him well enough to know his type. Since our night together, he had texted me three times:

How is your day? Would love to see you again. Friday?

Don't want to bug you, but I feel like something happened the other day, and I'm not sure what. Give me a call?

Not a fan of ghosting, but you must have your reasons. I'm working second shift for the next few days, so I'm around if you wanna talk—even if it's only about Aaron Rodgers.

Truthfully? I missed him. It was time to learn more. I started with public court records and typed "Ryan Hobart." It occurred to me that I only knew his last name because of my snooping. What would my dad have said about that? Even thinking about how insecure and careless I'd been made my face hot with shame.

The database search produced one entry. Ryan L. Hobart was arrested for robbery in Manitowoc County in 2009.

My heart sank.

I scrolled lower to see that Ryan L. Hobart was currently serving time in the Oshkosh Correctional Facility. I felt lighter. Wrong Ryan Hobart.

Variants of his name didn't net anything else. I searched for him as a petitioner, and he wasn't listed there, either. There seemed to be no restraining order filed by him or against him in Wisconsin. Relief and hope started sniffing around again.

To be sure of my process, I researched court records for Celia's boyfriend, Tommy. Celia probably only shared a portion of his adventures with me, but I knew that he had some experience with the law. The night I went to dinner with him, Tommy visibly flinched when I mentioned that my brother was a cop. Although Celia tried to keep it under wraps, I could tell by her accidental comments that I made Tommy uncomfortable.

I typed in Thomas Elrod (yes, as you would imagine, Celia had a blast with that) and got an immediate hit. Misdemeanor charges had been filed two years earlier: "Invading a right to choose an insurance agent or insurer by persons engaged in financing." Although I didn't know exactly what that particular charge meant, there were other entries with similar charges. No jail time that I could tell, but clearly not the original Mr. Rogers, as he'd convinced Celia. This most recent case was dismissed for violation of due process, "failure to preserve apparently exculpatory evidence." I have no knowledge of the law, but it sounded like somebody was pressured to lose some evidence.

Tracking Tommy's adventures through the circuit court gave me the assurance I was looking for about Ryan. I had done my due diligence, and Ryan seemed to be innocent. Or at least he had no record.

Doing a general internet search for Ryan Hobart of Madison had more juice. There were a couple of stories about his heroics as an EMT and an interview in the local paper where he promoted a fundraiser for his friend with leukemia. I leaned back and took stock. By all accounts, Ryan seemed to be an upstanding citizen, and it was highly likely that I met a decent guy. *Wonderful. I had overreacted. Had I blown it?*

I knew he'd be at work, so I sent him one simple text: *Call me tomorrow?*

I watched my screen, hoping for an instant reaction. Nothing. It wasn't surprising, after the way I'd avoided him. I'd need to be satisfied that it was a start.

Next, I forced myself to research Ashley. Since Pen's call almost a week ago, I had been batting away thoughts of Ashley's murder, my familiar avoidance mode, but I owed it to her to find out what happened to her and make it real.

By all accounts, the end of Ashley's life was gruesome. Just reading about it made me nauseous, and I could only read a couple of lines before I shut my eyes. I stumbled through the news of her death that way, inch by inch, eyes open and eyes shut. She was stabbed multiple times by an intruder in her apartment and had died at the scene. A neighbor had called the police when she heard Ashley's screams. As of the last media report in March, there were no apparent suspects, and police were still investigating. There had been nothing in the news since then. Ashley's murder was overshadowed by the next news cycle, and there was no more commentary or apparent concern for a young woman's cruel demise.

I picked up my phone to call Pen, and it occurred to me how easy it was to be in her life again, even if Ashley's death was the focal point of our reconciliation. When I asked Pen if she had any more details about Ashley's murder, she asked if she could call me later. Her kids were in the car.

"I guess she was getting ready for a night out," Pen said when she called back. "My mom got details from her Omaha friends. Ashley's son, Dakota, was at a friend's house, and she was in the bathroom putting on makeup. Whoever did it got into the building by pretending they had a delivery for another neighbor. God, Sam, even talking about it is awful. It's not some crime podcast; it's *Ashley*." Her voice broke. "So this person let themselves into her apartment—apparently, she hadn't locked the door—and attacked her in the bathroom. They turned off the lights and stabbed her a bunch of times. Can you imagine the—"

I had been trying not to. We both cried, silent on the phone but together. Once we could speak again, Pen filled in with more long-form details: it didn't appear to be a robbery; there wasn't anything missing, and Ashley didn't have much anyway. The police had investigated a nasty ex-boyfriend, but he had an alibi. Because the attack was months old, each week that went by left little hope for answers.

The room started to swirl faster with each detail. I got up to pace, moving my body to be able to think. To remember Ashley, before.

Ashley might have been the first to instigate, but she wasn't entirely to blame. Pen and I had complied. On the rare occasions when I let myself remember it, my remorse over our cruelty was heavy, like a shameful fur coat. For years I wouldn't let myself think about it, and when I tried to forgive myself, I couldn't. It led to a pernicious layer of remorse I never addressed, except for the obvious job choice as a counselor with a crusade against bullies.

Becoming mean had an innocuous beginning. It started as bossy, which granted us unexpected power. It was fun to see what we could get away with, and we even adopted Ashley's slightly southern dialect. As a threesome, we became so insular that there were no checks and balances; everything we did was unobjectionable. As we started getting itchy and hormonal about life in general, we took it out on those around us. Gradually, as we moved from singing along with Celine Dion to blowing out our speakers with Black Sabbath, we gave each other permission. We preyed on kids who were weak. If they couldn't even make eye contact, we assumed they'd never tell.

We liked feeling notorious. People said our names without a breath in between—AshleySamPen. We even used our initials to create our own mascot, the ASP. Although I balked at the mascot, Ashley convinced me that a venomous viper was intimidating. We drew potential ASP tattoos on our notebooks as we planned our townhouse in New York City and a ranch in Santa Fe. We would be double maids of honor and name our children after each other.

If somebody had something we wanted, it became ours. The first time I saw this was watching the sad saga of Tina Lawler. I sucked in my breath at the memory. Ashley hated Tina Lawler. She was tall, thin, Greek, exotic, funny, and we could never say just her first name; it was always Tina Lawler. Or TL.

Ashley had Tina Lawler in gym class and took it as a challenge to make her life miserable. She stole makeup from the poor girl's backpack and helped her look for it when TL was distraught. On the day TL showed up for the swim unit with a new zebra-patterned bathing suit, I saw jealousy take hold of Ashley like a shock collar. Seventh grade was already a hormonal minefield, and TL's chest was farther along than most of us, so she brandished her swimsuit as proof. Ashley, with little kiwi bumps of her own, decided to take TL down a peg. She stole the suit and wore it brazenly the next day.

"Isn't that my suit?" Tina Lawler asked.

"No, I've had it *forevah*," Ashley said as she turned and walked away. It was such a combination of moxie and mean that I never forgot it. It was trivial—not even close to the worst thing we ever did—but I can still hear Ashley's voice gaslighting TL. I should have recognized it as a premonition, seeing how easy it is to be convinced of things you know aren't true.

Suddenly I was drained. I craved sleep. After Pen and I finished talking, I donned my most comfortable PJs, made a salty lemon water, and climbed into bed. Although the night air was cool and I could hear crickets calling to each other, I locked my bedroom window and turned on my fan so I could use the quilt Aunt Dorothea had made for me, a double wedding ring with a floral yellow and sky blue. It was no secret she hoped I'd go the traditional marriage/baby route, but like justice for Ashley, it was feeling more out of reach. Bitsy turned herself around and around until she found the perfect place against my leg, and we each burrowed into our comforts.

Bitsy's bark woke me after a few hours, pulling me from a nightmare about Ashley, her last moments, her red blood. She had been calling for me, and I couldn't reach her, no matter how hard I tried. Remnants of the dream faded slowly while I turned on my bedside lamp to ground myself in reality. I tried to distract myself with a book, and when that failed, I turned to late-night propaganda on TV. After a little while, Bitsy licked my face, and I turned off the television. It was a long time before I could turn off the tears.

I was making my bed the next morning when the doorbell rang. Bitsy barked and I jumped. From my bedroom window, I could see Ryan's car in the driveway. My heart raced.

"Be right there!" I yelled to buy a little time and put on a bra. I stopped in the bathroom to rub toothpaste on my teeth and wrangle my hair. My eyes were puffy from my restless night, and I splashed cold water on my face. It didn't help.

Ryan rang the doorbell again.

The morning air smelled fresh as I opened the front door but left the screen door closed. Bitsy hid behind my calves and staged a yippy, annoying bark until I picked her up. Ryan stood there in that damn EMT uniform, a bouquet of black-eyed Susans in his hands.

"Hey," he said without moving.

"Hey," I said.

He held up the bouquet of flowers. "I noticed you liked these when we walked by them downtown," he said. They looked fresh—and crudely cut—and I wondered if they came from the very terrace we had seen on our date. I started to ask him about it until Bitsy decided it was time to bark incessantly in my arms.

Ryan nodded his head to acknowledge the frantic dog.

"Who is this?" he said loudly to make himself heard over Bitsy.

"This is Bitsy." I moved her face toward him. I rubbed the top of her head to calm her down, and she finally quieted.

"I didn't know you had a dog."

"I don't. I'm watching her for my friend Celia."

He nodded as if that made perfect sense. "I know it's early, but I wanted to catch you at home."

"I'm—" I started.

Ryan jumped in at the same time. "So you got my messages?"

I nodded.

"I needed to see you again," he said. "I wanted to see what happened. Find out why—can I come in? I promise I'll only be a minute." He was still holding the bouquet of flowers.

I hesitated but then pushed open the screen door. Ryan moved through the foyer, set the flowers on the front table, and moved into my living room. He sat in the middle of my couch and perched on the edge like he was ready to bolt. Bitsy and I took the side chair.

"Look, Sam, I don't mean to be pushy," he said. His voice was soft around the edges, mesmerizing and gentle. *Stop*, I told myself.

He continued. "But I feel like something happened that maybe I can fix. We had such a great time the other night, and then it got weird."

I forced myself to come clean. "You're right. Something did happen. I've been embarrassed to admit it, but I found something when I was alone at your place, and it freaked me out."

"At my house?" He straightened up and tilted his head. Maybe still a little schnauzery, maybe a little vulnerable.

"Do you want some coffee?" I stood up to head toward the kitchen, forcing Bitsy to the floor.

"No. What did you find?"

I sat back down, grabbed a throw pillow, and covered up my torso. "I wanted something to put the fruit in, so I was looking through your cupboards. Just for the pineapple. I wasn't snooping."

"And?" He appeared genuinely clueless.

"And the cupboard closest to the fridge—that's where I started." I nodded at him, hoping he would catch on. Nothing.

"Where you keep your paperwork." Still nothing. This would be so much easier if he could read my mind.

"The lawyer's business card? About a possible restraining order?" I asked.

"Oh." That was it. An undecipherable "Oh." I looked to him for any nonverbal help. He grimaced, then shook his head, which didn't really help except to tell me that he was as confused as I was. The silence in the room made me ramble.

"It freaked me out," I said. "You don't have to explain it or anything, but it seemed like something that I should know. I mean, not that you should have told me—unless you wanted to—but it made me realize how little I know you."

Ryan slid back on the couch and put his hands on his legs. He looked ready to push himself up and out of this room, and I wasn't sure if that was what I wanted. The room was airless. Bitsy, who had claimed space on the floor, jerked her head up and looked at him with a canine understanding of the tension in the room.

"This explains a lot." He ran his fingers through his hair. "I wish you would have said something sooner. It makes sense now. You were a different person when I came to pick you up in the morning."

"I know."

"Did you think I was a stalker or something?"

"I didn't know what to think. Like I said, it freaked me out."

"And I assume you researched me?"

"Yes. You appear to be clean." I smiled.

"Squeaky." He sighed. "It's not about me, Sam. I'm helping a buddy of mine, and his ex-girlfriend is a psycho. Eugene—the lawyer—is on our softball team and is keeping me in the loop. It's my buddy's possible restraining order, his problem. It's also not his fault, either, but that's another story."

"So you have nothing to do with it?"

"Nope. And like I said, it's completely unfounded." He shook his head and then looked at me intently. "I wish you would have asked me about it sooner."

"I didn't know what to do. Also, I didn't want you to think I was snooping." Something else occurred to me. "But why do you have the business card? Why not your friend?"

"My buddy isn't comfortable dealing with all the legal jargon. I'm the point man, and then he wants me to explain it to him." His phone buzzed, but he ignored it. He didn't even take it from his pocket and look at it, which won points with me.

"But why—"

"Look, Sam, I'm helping out my friend. He got himself in hot water, and he's in a jam and every other cliché you can think of. But the truth is, he's not the brightest guy. Hell of a guy, but not very perceptive. Since I've seen a lot on my job, he thinks I'm smart. He and Eugene are including me in on everything."

His story seemed to make sense; my research echoed that he was indeed a Good Samaritan. At this point, I could either believe him or not. As I considered those eyes, those forearms, those hands that had been places—I decided to believe him.

"That does make sense," I admitted.

"It should. It's the truth." His eyes bore into mine with such earnest intensity that I had to look away.

"I'm really sorry," I said.

"I'm glad we could sort it out." He slid closer to me. "Is everything else okay? You look beat."

I nodded. "I am. I had a rough night. I found out recently that an old friend of mine died—was murdered. Stabbed numerous times, actually. I finally heard the details last night, and then my dreams were so vivid." I could almost feel the colors of my dream seep back into my brain as I talked. Ryan was suddenly at the end of the couch, and he reached for my hand.

"I'm having trouble processing it," I admitted. "I hadn't seen her for years, but my brain alternates between nightmares and denial."

"That's pretty common," he said softly. "Especially when you aren't used to brutality. That's the hardest thing about my job, seeing the aftermath. I'm always glad that most people don't know about the monsters out there and what they can do."

The image of Ashley as the young girl I remembered, bloody and frantic, flashed in my mind, and tears blurred my vision. "I keep wondering what it was like for her. Maybe you know. When people are attacked so violently, are they in shock? What were her last minutes like? Do you think she suffered?" I asked, not sure I wanted the answer.

"Usually, if the stab wound is in an organ, the body goes into shock immediately. I saw one guy—well, you don't need to know that—but with multiple stab wounds, death usually happens pretty quickly. And most likely, your friend didn't have time to register much pain. It probably all happened quickly. I'm really sorry, Sam."

"Thank you," I said, grateful he was here, grateful that he handled and hid the worst of humanity for a living. It was such relief to me that Ashley hadn't had a prolonged, painful death that my gratitude almost felt disproportionate. It was nice not to be alone. I started feeling a little better until he announced that he had to go.

"So," he said as he stood up. "Can we try again? Let's go out again, and you can bring a list of questions if you need to." He moved closer to me.

"I'd like that," I said.

"Tonight?"

"Perfect. I'll bring my questions; you bring your lawyer." I smiled, and he leaned in to kiss my forehead.

"You," he said tauntingly as he leaned back to look at me, "are going to be trouble."

<hr />

After Ryan left, I walked through the kitchen straightening paperwork and lining up my shoes with a restless energy. I skipped breakfast, slammed a sodium drink, and went to yoga.

The instructor was new, the class was unfamiliar, and the novelty felt like another fresh start as we started at the front of our mats, bent over in a gentle ragdoll pose. I started to loosen up and swayed back and forth without even comparing myself to the people around me. Indian sitar music played softly in the background with a reedy bass that soon melded into a Mariachi tune, upbeat but unexpectedly relaxing, and after a short while, my downward dog moved imperceptibly with the rhythm. I felt the release of whatever was pent up; the weight of uncertainty dissolved with each movement.

"Let your mind go where it wants," the instructor suggested, and I tried to listen to what my body was telling me it wanted: *Nachos*.

I almost laughed with my next inhale. We were still in a downward dog, but the dog was walking now, bending each leg and foot at a time.

The instructor continued. "Now that your mind has free rein, give it something else to focus on. Maybe center on making your spine long and tall. Maybe picture your hips higher in the air. What can you visualize right this minute?"

My free-rein mind provided an instant image: a frothy, frozen margarita with salt on the rim and a pink straw, long and tall, poking out the middle.

The Mariachi song ended, and a simple chant took its place. The instructor's cues were crisp and quick, and she deftly moved us into a spine twist, with our bodies coiled forward and our heads looking back. The sun was peeking through the slats of the blinds, and the student next to me had dirty white socks.

"As you twist, think of your spine as a series of hockey pucks," she said. "Try to keep the pucks stacked on top of each other in a straight line. Head tall. In between those pucks are soft pads that protect the vertebrae. They're squishy and cushioned, sort of like jelly donuts." She chuckled. "It's all hockey pucks and jelly donuts."

I looked toward the back of the room, trying to elongate my spine and ignore the soiled socks. My body was awake, but my mind couldn't stop its new mantra: *Nachos. Margarita. And now jelly donuts.*

I softened my focus and cut myself some slack. And when I got home, I made some scrambled eggs.

When Ryan picked me up for our date that evening, we both seemed unsure of how this reboot would look, so we started old-school with a movie and a drink. I had promised myself that I wouldn't sleep with him, that I would move us back to the beginning and ease into intimacy. I'd learn his middle name, the make of his first car, and his favorite pizza before he saw me naked again.

After popcorn and handholding, we stopped for a drink. The bar was a Madison staple, surviving waves of popularity over the years. Local bands who played for the love of the music drew loyal townies on Friday and Saturday nights. The dark wood paneling held pictures of musicians that had graced the stage over the years. The lights were low, and behind the din of clinking glasses and muted conversation, I could hear soft jazz. We sat at the bar, where Ryan ordered a hefeweizen with a terrible German accent. One mojito later, I was feeling relaxed and content.

"So. You promised me a deep dive into your past. No restraining orders, I know that. Any ex-wives to worry about?"

He laughed and took a long drink of his beer. The lemon slice bumped against his mustache, and he wiped it with the back of his hand. "Yes. Well, no. I did have a wife, but she has since 'moved on,' as she likes to say. I haven't seen her in years."

"Ex-girlfriends?"

"You could take them."

"Outstanding warrants?"

He slowly unrolled that crooked smile. "Just that incident in Amsterdam."

With that, a hand slapped Ryan on his shoulder, startling him. He twisted in his seat, and his closing fist almost knocked over his beer. He relaxed when he recognized the body attached to the hand, a man in a jean jacket a size too small.

"What the hell, Salinas?"

"Keeping you sharp, Ho. What are you doing in a classy place like this?" Ryan's friend Salinas was big, with shoes untied and a baseball hat on backward. He had his hand on Ryan's shoulder but tried to lean toward me to get my attention. He fell forward and caught himself on the bar.

Ryan reached over to steady him. "We're just getting a drink." Ryan looked at me, hesitating while apparently deciding whether to introduce me. The dining tables were arranged in a circle around a big fountain, and the noise of the water suddenly rose over the awkward pause.

"Who's this?" Salinas barged in, not giving Ryan a chance to decide, after all.

"This is Sam. Sam, Salinas." It was an abbreviated introduction at best. Clearly, "Ho" did not want this stretching out into any type of conversation.

Salinas moved around to stand between us and reached out his hand to shake mine.

"How do you know our boy here?" He kept hold of my hand as he motioned his head toward Ryan.

Ryan busted in. "It's a long story. Hey, Salinas, good to see you. Tell Frankie hi." Ryan moved his body slightly toward me, as if providing a small, nonverbal barrier, shutting Salinas out.

"Yeah, sure," Salinas slurred. "Hey, Ho, you wanna sub for the Marshfield tourney? We could use you. Bring Sam, here. She's a lot prettier than the last one." Salinas looked appraisingly at me and grinned. He smelled like he'd already played a doubleheader. Then he leaned toward Ryan conspiratorially. "That last one was a bitch, am I right?" Then just as quickly, he straightened as he remembered something. "Hey—whatever happened that night at Bindy's? Did the cops come?"

Ryan stiffened with more irritation. "Okay, Salinas. You better get going. I'll call Frank about Marshfield." He lifted his hand in a dismissive wave, and Salinas, bless his clueless heart, took the hint. He slapped Ryan on the shoulder one more time, gave me the finger gun salute, and headed down the hallway to the men's room. On the way, he bounced from one side to the other.

"Sorry about that," Ryan said as we watched Salinas ricochet. "Old softball buddy. I played co-ed three nights a week, and things got pretty crazy sometimes." He shook his head. "Looks like not everybody has moved past it."

"What happened at Bindy's?" I asked. No stone unturned from here forward.

Ryan shook his head. "I don't even know what he's talking about. He's obviously drunk."

"And who was the last one? The bitch?" My tone sounded playful, but I was a hound dog sniffing for details.

"Remember? I told you—sweet but psycho. Besides, you could take her. You could take 'em all." He leaned over and kissed me gently. With his lips still close to mine, he whispered. "I've never met anybody like you, Sam. You're smart, strong, and can hold your own. I don't think you've ever been treated right, and I want to do that. You're independent, but I want to show you how it feels to be cared for."

The words circled around me like I had chosen them myself. I was so tired. After losing my parents, my career, and the general upheaval in my life, it was a relief to realize I didn't have to do this solo. I could pass the baton. I kissed him again, pulling him closer with the crook of my arm. Behind me, the sounds of the bar were familiar; sportscasters on ESPN dueled with the bar's background music, people laughed, and glasses clinked. But here, right in front of me, was something new.

We decided to leave and wove through the crowd holding hands. At the door, I turned around to say something to Ryan, and behind him, sitting at the bar, was Salinas. Our eyes met. He raised his glass in a toast.

Outside, the night was warm. The quiet was refreshing.

"What now?" he asked as we headed toward his car.

"I need to check on Celia's dog. I don't know how long she can be left alone. But the invitation is only for a drink," I warned, playful finger-wagging.

"One drink," Ryan agreed.

Once we got to my house and let Bitsy out, he pulled me toward him, and I reached for him, even though I knew I probably shouldn't. It's like telling yourself you won't eat sugar anymore, then craving candy corn or those little orange pumpkins that show up each fall. He was a tasty, orange cellulose pumpkin, which I knew I shouldn't have—would definitely pay for later—but wanted in a passionate, unassailable way.

I pulled back a bit and put my hand on his chest. "You promise you're a good guy?" I dared those turquoise eyes.

"Promise," he soothed, hand on my face.

"Good," I said.

"Very good. I've missed you."

A small part of me still wondered if Ryan was for real, but the lonely, insecure part of me had more influence. Ashley's death was another stark reminder that life was short. I let Bitsy in the front door, gave her the nighttime treat, and we all headed upstairs to the bedroom. Ryan shut the bedroom door when Bitsy tried to follow. When I started to object, he kissed me. Sometimes you stick to your guns, your high-fiber, low-carb guns. But sometimes, when presented with a sweet pumpkin treat, you enjoy every bite.

Tuck yourself into **CHILD'S POSE** any time you need to recharge.
It can help you feel nurtured and restored when you're overwhelmed.
Find sanctuary when you need it, on or off the mat.

CHAPTER 12

A NEW NORMAL EMERGED. There were a handful of sunny days when I walked Bitsy twice a day and fell in love with my neighborhood. I had never noticed the numerous roof lines, turrets, and bay windows that looked out over gardens instead of garages. Each house was asymmetrical and ornate, polychromatic evidence of Madison's resolve to hold fast to the old while making way for the new.

Ryan called, texted, and lunched me. We made new recipes like pad Thai, and we made love. A little more love, a little less pad Thai. One day, after a particularly difficult power flow yoga class, I came home to find he had drawn me a bath. The bubbles were lofty, the wine was chilled, and I sunk into everything with an almost embarrassing desperation. Celia was in Las Vegas, my brothers seemed to be busy, and I preferred to ignore the fact that Ashley had been murdered. I appreciated that Ryan didn't bring it up, either. It was also easy to ignore the keying and the snake, which I convinced myself were coincidental. I was safely hemmed in by domesticity.

Bitsy helped in her own furry way. I learned that life with a dog is, I would imagine, like living with a toddler. Although Bitsy was considered elderly in dog years, she still acted like a difficult two-year-old. She didn't like to eat alone, so I had to stand near her while she ate her vittles. Except that they weren't vittles; they were specially prepared chicken breasts. Per Celia's instructions, I should entice Bitsy with peanut butter if she refused the chicken breast. She was high maintenance, but she made me feel useful. I'd always thought I would have children, but the door to that world was slowly closing. Besides, losing my parents changed everything. It was hard to imagine raising children without them around. Although Bitsy was an attention-loving, demanding, infuriating mop, she was a good little litmus test for my nurturing skills. I babysat Ella in her early years, but usually with disastrous results. Who knew it was so funny to hear a two-year-old say "ass"?

Ryan tolerated Bitsy. He admitted he wasn't much of an animal person, which bothered me. I usually don't trust people without pets or full bookshelves, and Ryan failed in both categories. On the other hand, those things were small potatoes. Just being touched again was gravy. He was interested in my family and laughed at my jokes and listened with an intensity that was remarkable. Pets and books could wait.

It was all wonderful until it wasn't. It started one day at the bank. Regina, the branch supervisor, called me in at 5:30 after I had balanced my cash drawer and helped my coworker balance his. She called me into her office and asked me to close the door.

"Have a seat, Sam." She motioned toward a chair facing her, palm up, in the way people do right before they fire you.

"Although you've been doing a great job here, I need to tell you that I got a call about you."

My skin suddenly felt itchy. "You did?"

"I did," Regina continued with a nod. "And it wasn't good. One of our customers, who wanted to remain anonymous, said he saw something when he was waiting in line at the drive-through."

The golden coins that Ryan sent through the tube. Was that against the law?

Regina sighed. "He thought he saw you put money from your drawer into your backpack."

I was stunned. These words she used made no sense. I tipped my head and stared at her. I thought back to my recent transactions. My cash drawer was counted and verified against the computer's data each night. I was on a roll, three straight weeks without one discrepancy. It wasn't unusual for tellers to transpose a number here and there or not count a penny or two, but I had been on a streak of good fortune, I thought.

"But—" I started to protest.

Regina held up that same palm. "I know. You haven't been off at all. Believe me, it would show up somewhere. I don't believe for a minute the customer saw what they thought they saw. But I wanted to give you a heads up that I'm required to document it."

I couldn't begin to formulate a response. This accusation and reprieve made me speechless. Regina's eyes softened, and she tipped her head. "Look, I knew this might be upsetting. But you and I both know you've been doing a great job. It's been gratifying to watch you settle into a routine after all you've been through. We've been so happy that you came to work here; your parents were such good customers. Good folks. Let's call this an unfortunate blip."

An unfortunate blip.

I doubted it.

Celia called that same night for her daily Bitsy check-in.

"How's life on the lam?" I asked her.

"Not funny, Sam. We're working our asses off during the day, then drinking and gambling with customers at night. And fornicating. Not fornicating with the customers," she laughed. "With Tommy."

"What kind of conference is it, again?" There was no "again" about it; Celia kept her allegiance to Tommy and didn't give me any details.

"Insurance. Boring. Except for the fornicating." She giggled, sounding decades younger than she should. "And how's Bits?"

"She's fine, Celia. No need to worry."

"I'm not worried; I just miss her. Put her on."

"What?"

"Put her on the phone. I want to talk to her."

"Seriously?"

"Seriously," she said.

I glanced at Ryan, who was checking emails on his phone at my kitchen counter. His buddies were on their way to pick him up for softball, and I was hoping he would leave before it got embarrassing with Celia and Bitsy. I went to look for the beloved diva and found her lying on my bed. More specifically, she was lying on my pillow. She woke up as I came into the bedroom and looked at me disdainfully when I put the phone up to her ear. She immediately pulled away. I got back on the phone.

"Bitsy's busy right now," I said.

"Try again." I reluctantly held the phone up to the dog's ear and could hear Celia's baby talk reverberate through my bedroom. It was weird. I let it go for a few more seconds, then got back on the phone.

"It's me now," I told Celia so she would stop. "When are you coming back?"

"Hopefully by this weekend. My clients are getting frantic."

Celia cut hair and waxed things for a living. She had a faithful following, but I imagine even her fans get impatient with her sometimes. Not to mention hairy.

"I miss you," she said. "Tell me everything. How is Cutie Ryan—is he legit? How is the sex? Do you still have that salt thing?"

This was refreshing, this long-distance, compassionate Celia 2.0. "It's all good, and the salt thing is under control. As long as I keep hydrated with sodium water, I'm good."

"Does Ryan know?"

"About the sodium? No. Why?"

"It feels like one of my little tests. Seems like something you'd tell him if you trusted him."

"I do trust him. But it doesn't have anything to do with him. It's *my* problem." Still, I got up from the bed to make sure Ryan wasn't listening. The bathroom door was shut.

"And you texted that the restraining order thing wasn't a thing. What happened?"

I gave her the entire rundown on Ryan, and she made me check Bitsy's availability one more time, then we hung up. I looked up and saw Ryan leaning against the bedroom door, and his eyes had a tightness that I hadn't seen before.

"What was all that?" he asked.

"Celia? She's hundreds of miles away and misses her dog."

"More like two thousand," he corrected me.

"Fine. She's far away. Nothing more than catching up with a friend. And why were you eavesdropping?"

"No, I just overheard. You told her about my buddy's restraining order?"

I nodded. "Is that a problem? It's not even yours."

"I just don't see the need." He readjusted his legs, but his eyes were still narrowed. "How long have you guys been friends?"

"Almost fifteen years. Why?" I straightened my back against the bed's headboard, which suddenly felt rigid.

"She seems a bit—I don't know—troubled," Ryan said.

"She is. She's had a rough life."

"I know, but what do you get out of the relationship? Seems to me like you're rescuing her all the time." He motioned toward Bitsy, the little furry example, who also straightened up with the rise in tension.

"Sometimes, but it's what we do. We trade off needing each other."

"Seems a little co-dependent. Maybe a little space from each other is a good thing right now." He seemed to recognize the harshness of his comments and softened. "I worry about you, that's all."

"That's sweet," I said. "But you don't need to worry. Celia and I have each other's backs."

"I'd rather she not know my personal details," Ryan said, still leaning against the door. But the casualness his body language portrayed was at odds with his tone. The effect was unnerving.

"You're wrong about Celia," I objected. "Plus, you have no right to listen in and question my conversations. Whatever I share with Celia isn't any of your business either. And next—"

Ryan's phone rang, and he answered it. It made me mad. I got off the bed, brushed past him in the doorway, got a drink of water in the kitchen, and gulped like it would cool me off. Ryan followed when he finished his call.

"That was our catcher. He's picking me up in ten."

I swung around to face him. "Perfect. And maybe you should sleep at your place tonight."

"What? Are you seriously that mad? It's not that big a deal."

"Yes, I'm that mad. It is that big a deal. I want a *little space*," I said with exaggerated air quotes, exactly like Ella would have done.

He rubbed his forehead, clearly confused. He tried coming at it one more time but left when I didn't back down. I paced the kitchen after he left, processing our back and forth. It had escalated quickly, but I was resolute in my firm defense of Celia. It also felt too early in the relationship for this level of drama. I was embarrassed for my part in the ramping up. The thought of an evening alone suddenly sounded lovely, and I was in my pajamas before he and the catcher pulled out of the lot.

Bitsy and I settled into our evening, which included chicken for dinner (for both of us) and root beer and RumChata (for me). We watched Comedy Central and ate in bed, and in solidarity and protest, we didn't even brush our teeth.

ffffff

The next morning's start was rough, remnants of my fight with Ryan hanging like cigar smoke in the air, so I went to one of Nena's slow flow classes to reset. On the drive over, I couldn't stop thinking about things I didn't want to think about. There was a long line at the reception desk, and BJ checked me in with a quick nod. When class began, left was right, I was wrong, and nothing worked as it should. It was a challenge to keep my eyes on the mirror and my mind on my limbs. We moved to an intense half-moon pose, where my leg shook and my arms started to flail before we were finally rewarded with a child's pose. My sweaty forehead melted into the mat. Acoustic guitar played softly in the background, a pleasant distraction from the thoughts that intertwined in my head like a rubber band ball. As I began to feel composed, the guitar solo wove into a soulful cello in minor chords that shifted me straight to melancholy. It happened that quickly.

Nena walked behind me as if I had summoned her there. She continued to give instructions to the class while she leaned toward me. *Was she calling me out? How could I screw up child's pose?* When she gently placed her palm on the middle of my back, I tensed. It was uncomfortable for me, and why would she want to touch my sweaty back? She kept her hand on me, a consistent light presence, and after a few seconds, I took an involuntary breath that forced me to relax. I had seen her assist other students from time to time. It was a thing. I made myself take another breath to stay open.

Let things happen, I reminded myself. The slight pressure on my back caused me to sink deeper into the pose and compress closer to my mat. Nena added her other hand to the base of my spine and pressed gently. Little bits of feelings unrolled themselves from the pinched grief I had packed like a little casket in my mind. Another buried inhale, another slow melt of my muscles, then she slowly lifted her hands. I still felt her there. I stayed flush against the mat, low and compact. Breath came from a deeper place in my lungs, and I exhaled loudly.

Sorrow was stored up in my muscles like scar tissue: layers of uneven pain from people who left, people who disappointed, strangers who scratched your car, sent dead snakes, and accused you of stealing. I took another long, slow, ragged breath and let it out, addressing what hurt the most. Ashley's death had opened the scab that covered up the loss of my parents. It was time to unleash some of that pain. Nena's touch had grounded me, and I suddenly felt safe enough to acknowledge the ache I kept stuffing underneath my skin. Taking a long pull of air, I twisted into the dark place where the grief had burrowed. Acknowledging my anguish literally made my chest ache. Although the last thing I wanted to do was cry in class, I soon realized it was deeper than tears; it was primordial. I stayed in child's pose and let the class go on without me.

I waited for some physical catharsis and was a little surprised that letting it out didn't kill me. In fact, feeling what I'd been trying to avoid didn't bring my parents' death to the forefront; it built a little fortress around their memory. There was comfort in finally feeling the pain and a sense of power in finally addressing it. It just took another person to draw it out.

Nena moved the class through the last series of poses, and I joined them. She continued to walk around the floor, carefully stepping between the mats, occasionally placing a gentle hand on an upended spine to soften the pose. "Open yourself up to everything you sense and feel within and around you," she said. "Notice, but don't judge."

What I noticed, but didn't judge, was how empty I felt. A good empty. Like a vessel that I would fill with the things of my choosing. My mood was brighter, and for the first time in a long while, I noticed that the thing that swirled within me was hope.

After class, I moved slowly and purposefully, like if I wasn't careful, I could spill the hope right out of me. I felt strengthened from the inside out. Standing in line for access to the cubbies, I had a sudden urge for ice cream. *Maybe even a sundae, although the hot fudge had a lot of sugar. Ice cream by itself was somewhat healthy, wasn't it? With all that calcium? Of course, it depended—*

"Sam? You okay?" I came out of my trance to BJ's voice. She was standing next to me, and I realized I had been frozen, mat by my side, not moving. *How long had I been that way?*

"I'm fine. A little spacey."

"You want to go grab a coffee? Looks like you could use some caffeine. I know I could." Her invitation caught me off guard. I started to make an excuse, then remembered my resolve to push myself past my comfort.

At first, I deflected. "Is it too early for a cocktail?" Then I pushed myself to say yes. "Sure. But right now, I'm looking for my keys. I swear I put them right here." I pointed to the painted storage compartments, all empty except for the one in front of me.

"I do that all the time. They probably got moved," BJ said as she returned to the reception counter.

"My flip-flops are here, and I know I put my keys in with them." I was a little angry that the people I had recently shared sweat with might be responsible for my walk home. I had always assumed my yogi brethren had an elevated code of ethics.

"What did they look like?" BJ came back over to look.

"They'd be hard to miss. They're attached to a charm my niece made for me."

"Sometimes people take the wrong keys and come right back. They probably grabbed yours by mistake. Somebody will get to their car and realize what happened."

We waited. After double-checking my car to make sure the keys weren't locked inside, BJ and I stayed until the last class cleared out of the studio. No keys. It was a replay of the night my car was vandalized. As I started to panic about the specifics of how I would function without keys, BJ had another idea.

"If you have another set at home, I could give you a ride," she suggested.

I started to decline, then thought again. Accepting help seemed to be the theme for the day. "That would be great. I better pass on the coffee, though. I need to make sure I have duplicate keys for everything that was on that ring."

"No problem. I'll run you home. And I'll leave a note for the staff to call you when somebody finds your keys."

We walked toward BJ's car, a blue Chevy Malibu with a gleaming exterior. She unlocked the door and leaned over the passenger seat to throw plastic bags into the back seat. The bags landed on a small hill of towels and notebooks. The interior of her car had that fake lemon smell, and empty water bottles covered the passenger-side floor.

"Sorry about the mess," she said as we pulled out of the lot. "Every weekend I think I'm going to clean out my car, and every weekend I find more important stuff to do. I'm taking a class right now, and it's kicking my ass."

"What kind of class?"

"Physiology. But I'm thinking of dropping it. I like doing research, but I get bored quickly. I've always hated school." She came to a stop sign and merely slowed before turning into her lane. "I'm more of a self-taught person."

"What kind of things have you taught yourself?" As she merged into traffic without looking, I wondered if she had taught herself how to drive.

"Lots of stuff. Painting, chemistry, anything I'm curious about."

"Were you homeschooled?"

She laughed, a cynical *pfft* that filled the car. "Hardly. I research things I'm interested in. The internet is a wonderful playground for people like me. In fact, now I'm going to research the concept of paradox that Nena brought up in class. That makes no sense to me."

"I must not have been listening to that part," I admitted.

"She was saying that two things that contradict each other can be true. Like if you really want something, you have to let go of it. I love Nena, but she can get a little weird. And she's also wrong: if you really want something, you go after it. Hard."

I laughed. "I know, it sounds weird. I've heard her talk about it before, but it makes sense to me. My own experience with paradox is that the more I try to control something, the less control I have. Pisses me off." We both chuckled until BJ made a quick lane change that pitched me into the door.

"Today Nena said, 'We can be both heavy and also light,'" BJ added. "Whatever that means."

"I kinda get that, too. Some days my body feels heavy when I come to class, but my brain and mood can be light."

"Wow," BJ said with a laugh. "Did you grow up in a commune?"

"Hardly. Nebraska. How about you? Did you grow up around here?"

"Nope. Another transplant. I don't know anybody who actually grew up here. Should I turn soon?"

"Sorry. Keep going on University and take it all the way to the cemetery. You're heading in the right direction, though. I forget—have I told you where I live?"

"You mentioned it was the west side," she said and then smiled. "I taught myself to be intuitive, too."

When we pulled into my driveway, I could hear Bitsy's hoarse bark through the open living room window.

"Is that your dog?" BJ nodded toward the fireball of fur in my living room window. Clearly not a dog person, based on her tone.

"I'm watching her for a friend. I had no idea she was this obnoxious when I was gone. My poor neighbors." I grabbed my yoga mat and started to get out of the car. "Let's hope I remember the garage code. I usually use my remote." I stood next to the open car door trying to remember. I'd chosen the code years ago, using something irrelevant and obscure, like the year that Judy Blume was born or my PR for the 400 meter. My mind was blank, and Bitsy started pushing on the window screen.

"Can I help with something?" BJ leaned over the console toward me. The barking intensified.

"I can't remember the code. I'm sure it's written down—inside." I started to panic, then my brain kicked in. "Wait. I remember. It's Ella's birthday."

"Ella?"

"My niece." I stared at the garage door, still not moving.

"You okay?"

"I'm a little creeped out," I admitted. "I've had some weird stuff happen lately. I'm just rattled." I readjusted my bag, mat, and resolve. "It's been a lot. I think I need some time alone."

BJ flinched.

"No—I'm sorry. I meant I need to stop and figure some things out. You know, 'notice, but not judge,'" I said, hoping the callback to Nena's class eased my clumsiness.

"What kind of things have been happening to you?" she asked. Bitsy had stopped barking, which was both a relief and a worry, but I wanted to continue this conversation with BJ. *Is this how adult relationships are formed, then? When there isn't work or school or practice to structure the building blocks, it was a gradual sharing of information and opening up?* I hadn't connected with new people in so long that I felt like an archaeologist, mining for what worked.

"I think somebody is messing with me. A couple of days after my car got keyed, I found a dead snake on my front porch."

BJ jerked her head back and touched her throat. "A snake? Already dead?"

"I know. It was gross. But I think it was a stupid prank."

"Are you sure it was dead? Who would pull a prank like that?"

"Definitely dead. Creeped me out. But it was still pretty tame compared to some of the stunts I've seen. I was a middle school counselor before—before this. I'm pretty sure this is the handiwork of one of the students I crossed along the way. They don't like boundaries."

I reminded myself to call my friend from the middle school. I still hadn't heard any details about Tyler.

"Sounds like more than boundaries. It's a tough age—"

My phone rang and interrupted her. I apologized and dug for my phone in my bag. It was Buck. Since he rarely called me, it made me nervous.

"Sorry, BJ, this is my brother. I need to take this."

"Of course." She waved me off, and I stepped away from the car.

"What's up, Buck?" I asked in a scramble, tripping where the driveway met the grass.

"It's Ella. She's in trouble."

TREE POSE combines a rooted standing leg with upper body ease.
Like a tree, your body needs to have a strong foundation
but be soft enough to sway. It's all a matter of trust.

CHAPTER 13

I SPRINTED INSIDE AND FOUND MY EXTRA SET OF KEYS, BJ drove me
back to the studio, and I raced to Buck's. I turned on the radio while I
drove, but the drivel compounded my anxiety; silence was better. My
car slowed on the gravel lane when I saw Finn's truck. *Shit.* If Finn was
there, whatever trouble Ella was in was serious. The police could even
be involved.

I hurried inside the house and found my niece, brothers, and
tension thick as cement in the living room. Ella sat on the couch, knees
together and pigeon-toed, which made her look even younger than
seventeen. Buck towered above her, hip cocked and finger loaded. He
stopped his tirade as I walked into the room, and they all watched in
silence as I sat down next to my shriveled niece.

"What happened?" I said. Buck's finger was still pointed at Ella as
he looked toward me. He tried to compose himself, and his lips moved
slightly, but no sound emerged, as if the words disintegrated when
they hit the air.

I turned to my niece. "Ella, what is going on?"

Ella dropped her face in her hands. She stiffened when I reached out to brush her bangs to the side. Her gray sweatshirt was so big it pooled around her hips on the couch. The sleeves were dirty, and she smelled like smoke.

"It's no big deal," she said quietly. And then a whisper. "I walked in the door, and he immediately made a huge deal out of this."

"Like hell," Buck shot back. "You were gone. No word." He gritted his teeth in the way he had done since childhood. His lips thinned and his anger amplified, and I gave him a look. *Let her talk*, the look said. Surprisingly, he did.

"Talk to me, El." I leaned into Ella, our legs touching and my hand on her back. A plaid throw covered the faded cushions and smelled slightly of dog.

"It was no big deal. A few of us went to the lake. All I wanted was to camp in a tent for once. Mom is out of town, and I knew he wouldn't let me go, so I didn't tell him. I told him I was at Paige's. He found out and freaked." She tipped her head toward her father each time she said the word *he*. The ultimate *he*.

"You didn't just 'not tell me,'" Buck argued. "You lied."

Ella didn't argue back, but her handwringing said it all.

"Tell her the rest." Buck's breathing was louder.

She hesitated, then leaned into me. "A few of my friends brought beer. They got loud and then decided to swim. Somebody must have called the cops, and then Uncle Finn showed up."

That added a new wrinkle. Standing behind my mom's old Queen Anne chair in the corner, Finn looked chagrined and uncomfortable, playing with the seam of the upholstery. My brothers could wrestle out any problem between them, but when it came to Ella, or any woman, for that matter, discussing emotions was torturous.

"Okay." I took a deep breath. "Look. This is obviously a big deal, Ella. Sounds like your dad was scared to death, and Uncle Finn saved your ass. But let's all calm down."

Buck clenched his teeth even tighter. "I am calm."

"I can tell. Where's Carole?"

"Mom's in Chicago. Board meeting," Ella sniffled.

I looked up at both of my brothers. "Can you guys give us a minute?" Buck looked full of stopped-up energy, and Finn looked relieved to be off the hook.

"Please, Buck," I nodded, affirming that I understood the gravity of the situation. He stared at me, looked at his daughter, and gave us an almost imperceptible nod.

"Let's go to your room," I said to Ella, hoping that a physical move would change the strain that throbbed in the little house. We moved to her bedroom and kept the door open while we sat on the end of her unmade bed. The blanket she'd carried around since she was in diapers peeked out from the tangle of sheets. I smoothed the fabric between us, then looked around the room to give me a minute to think. Her bedroom hadn't changed in years; it was too wholesome and girly for this conversation. She still had team pictures up from her elementary soccer team, and stuffed animals were squeezed haphazardly into the bookshelves. Laura Ingalls could move in and feel at home. I never had a girly room—never even wanted one. I was simply glad to have a room of my own, away from my brothers. As an only child, Ella never had to share much of anything. But as different as we were, I could still relate to the churlish complexity of being loved by Buck.

"What's going on, El? This doesn't sound like you," I said softly.

Ella leaned into me and whimpered. The whimper became a cry, which turned into all-out sobs. The sobs shook her body, and tears, snot, and fear built and released in waves until she slowed and took one long ragged breath. I handed her some tissue from the side table and waited out the storm.

"Oh God, Aunt Sam. It was awful. Mom kept telling me to check with Dad, but he was being such a jerk about it, and I wanted to have fun for once. If I've learned anything from Grandma and Grandpa—well, life is short." She took a ragged breath. "This all sounds worse than it was. It started so great, you know?" She paused. "And then it wasn't."

"I'm sorry," I said.

"And I don't get why they're freaking out," she said, nodding toward the living room.

I wasn't sure what to say. I was straddling an uncomfortable lane of loyalties, where I wanted Ella to feel I was in her corner but felt the need to defend my brothers, too.

"That's how your dad and Uncle Finn show their love, that's all. That's why they're so freaked out."

"That's a dumb way to show it," Ella said, leaning her head against my shoulder. I nodded.

"That's the best they can do. Sometimes I think we only have two speeds in this family: humor and anger. But you gotta be smarter about things, El. This could have been awful. I can tell it really scared your dad."

"I know. It was kinda scary, to be honest. All night I felt like we'd get caught or that somebody was watching us. Then those guys were wasted and could barely keep their heads above water. It took away any of the fun cuz I thought they'd go under." She continued to lean against me, and we sat like that for a while. I could see Buck's shadow from the hall where he was listening. We all remained like that, a sad little configuration, until Buck cleared his throat. Ella startled at the sound. We looked at each other, and she gave me a dour smile.

"But it's over now," she said. "This is probably the last time you'll ever see me. I'm going to be grounded forever."

I nodded. It would be a tense incarceration with no one but her father in the house.

Ella seemed to be reading my mind as she launched her next comment with a heavy sigh. "I wish I had a brother or sister." Since Buck was listening, I chose my words carefully.

"Funny. I always wanted to be an only child. My brothers, as you know, are a pain." She nodded in agreement, and I side-hugged her a little closer. "But I have to admit that sometimes it was pretty cool. Just when they would really get on my nerves, something would happen that made me know they cared. Once when we were skiing in Colorado, I wiped out on a black diamond slope. My ski started down the hill without me, and Buck chased that thing and brought it back to me by climbing up the hill sideways, almost inch by inch. When I started to thank him for what he did, he put his skis back on, turned around, and sprayed me with a wave of snow. He couldn't be too nice to the little princess, after all."

Ella laughed a little, then blew her nose.

"He really does care, El." She mumbled something, but I chose to ignore it.

"He does," I repeated. "If he didn't care, he wouldn't get so pissed."

Buck came back in and leaned on the door jamb. "My turn?" he said, looking toward me for the nod.

"Your turn," I said and kissed the top of my niece's head. "I'm gonna go. You guys talk."

"Thanks, Aunt Sam," Ella said into her chest. She remained on her bed as I got up to go. As I passed Buck, I tapped my hand against his flannelled, barrel-shaped chest, tagging him into the conversation. He sat on the bed where I had been, looking uncertain about what he was doing, too. The two of them put their heads together, re-creating the timeless depiction of father and daughter, one that would have made me feel better except for the shard of pain piercing me right where my own daddy used to be.

❦❦❦❦❦❦

On the way home, I replayed all the versions of Ella I've loved. She was growing up so quickly that I found I had to recontextualize from the toddler or terror or teen stages she inhabited fully. Now she was somebody new and unique, but I still saw pieces of myself in her. She was wry but naive and optimistic in a way that would eventually get trampled. She was toast and butter—a good, sensible girl. If she could remain strong when the rest of her angst-filled peers started tearing her down, maybe she could avoid uncertainty later in life. I wanted to protect her.

Ella's mom, Carole, was terrific and terrifying at the same time. She was an uber-successful copyright attorney and worked long hours for good pay. She loved Ella to pieces and assumed role modeling was enough for parenting. And what did I know? Maybe it was. Still, Ella had half of my family's genetic code, which meant she bled doubt. Carole didn't do doubt.

That's where I came in. "Aunt Sam, why is Dad so mad?" or "Will I ever have big boobs like Grandma?" I answered the questions she was afraid to ask her mom. She assumed I was wise, which I liked. She'd find out the truth soon enough. For now, I was a soft place to land, which was a good arrangement for me, too. And truth be told, being good to Ella helped me feel like I was righting some wrongs from my girlhood, too.

Back in my driveway, I checked messages. There was a text from Ryan: *I'm a putz. I'm sorry. Call me?*

There was also a message from Catherine. She had news about middle school Tyler and wanted me to call her, too. I knew that should be my first move, to get information to figure things out. It would be the smart thing to do.

I called Ryan instead.

He didn't try to hide his relief. "I'm so sorry, Sam. I don't know what I was thinking. Can I see you? I want to explain."

"I'm really tired, Ryan," I said. I only wanted an apology. After my yoga experience and Ella's escapade, I was craving another quiet night at home. "I need some time alone." But as I said it, I knew it wasn't true. Seeing my brothers had made me lonely.

"Only a drink. I promise," Ryan said.

I agreed. After running inside for a quick shower and taking Bitsy on a short but productive walk, I met Ryan at the Tavern, my neighborhood bar, which was surprisingly vacant for a Saturday night. We sat in the corner at a wobbly table that was stickier than it should have been.

"So. About what happened yesterday," Ryan said after we had been served our beers.

I held up my palm and interrupted. "Celia has been my best friend for years, and you don't know what we've been through. If she needs me, I'm there, no matter where. You have no right to judge." Although it was how I felt, the execution felt a little caustic once I said it out loud. I took a long pull from my beer.

He winced. "I know. You're right. I shouldn't have said what I did. Just because I don't understand it doesn't make it wrong."

"Thank you."

"I heard Dr. Phil say that last part," he said as he reached for my hand. "But I really am sorry." He looked so sincere that the anger inside me melted, little bits at a time, like an early fall snow. I knew it was something I should grab hold of, but it was watered down before I could even try.

"And your loyalty is impressive," he added. "Are you that way with everybody?"

"Probably not. But Celia was the first friend I've ever had without any preconceived notion of me. I had great friends from Omaha; we grew up together and were inseparable. They were like the sisters I always wanted. Then I came here to run, and people had expectations before they even met me. Running was my entire identity. I took a mindless job one summer to get away from the stress, and I met Celia. We hated each other at first." I smiled at the memory. "We were forced to work together and saw a whole different side of each other. Celia seems like she's all glow and sparkle. Once you get past the exterior, you see she's reflection and refraction."

Ryan looked confused.

"Once she lets you in, you find out she's lighter on the inside. I guess I'd call it transparent. I don't know many other women like that." I reconsidered. "Although I'm getting to know a couple people from my yoga studio that might have potential. I wouldn't mind having more friends that I can be myself with." I thought about BJ, who felt like she could be a drinking buddy, and Nena, who was intimidating but seemed to understand me.

"I'm learning a lot about who you are. But I gotta say that Celia doesn't seem like somebody you would choose to have in your life," he said.

"You need to get to know her before you judge her," I said quickly, taking back my hand. "How about that guy I met the other night?" I shot back. "Salinas? Is that the type of guy you choose in your life?"

Ryan laughed and drank his beer. "No. Salinas is a guy on my softball team, that's all. He's a teammate, not a friend. But speaking of my team, some of the guys are getting together tomorrow afternoon for a cookout, and I told them we'd come. I'd like you to meet everybody." It bothered me that he disarmed these charged conversations with a laugh and a dismissal, so I waded back in.

"How about I get to know your friends, and you really get to know mine? Celia has a heart of gold. I know it's hard to see at first, but I'd like you to give her a chance. She's a big part of my life."

He pursed his lips as if giving what I said true consideration. Then he put his hand on mine. "It's a date," he said. "Tomorrow. I promise you'll have fun, and I can't wait to show you off."

That didn't sit well with me either, but I was tired of talking. I let it go. I had reached my confrontation limit for the day. We finished our beers, watched the end of the Brewers game, and said goodnight.

My car was in the nearby parking garage on the second floor. I started to unlock the door when I noticed a white paper, folded in half, on the windshield. I checked the other cars, but none had anything similar. Inside, in big block letters, was written:

I KNOW WHO YOU ARE

I looked around the parking lot, trying to remember what cars had been nearby when I parked earlier. Finn always told me to notice my surroundings, but I was in such a rush to see Ryan that I hadn't noticed a thing. A car door slammed on the upper level, and I flinched. Bits of conversations from the street traffic below reverberated off the concrete while I stared at the note. *Was this a weirdly romantic gesture from Ryan? Or maybe somebody had the wrong car?* I knew it was all wishful thinking. This was the same phrase somebody had texted me from an unknown phone. After taking one more look around the parking garage, I carefully walked around the perimeter of my car, scrutinizing every inch. It was untouched.

It was suddenly too quiet. I opened the door and threw the note on the passenger seat, immediately locking the door. Leaning back against the headrest, I sighed. This was all too much to ignore. I called Catherine back—like I should have done earlier—and left a message, asking her to spill the info before we traded more calls. Now I was losing patience with confrontation *and* the unknown.

On my way home, I stopped at Celia's apartment for more supplies for Bitsy, and the disarray made me feel better. Things here were as they should be. Celia had left piles of possessions—thongs, bathing suit, hair scrunchies—like clues to her life, although I didn't see a sports bra anywhere. Apparently, our day at the health club hadn't inspired her.

The last time I was here, I scooped Bitsy and left in a hurry. I took it all in this time. Empty cereal bowls and wine glasses sat on her kitchen counter. The refrigerator held lettuce, green olives, and a few hard seltzers. In the living room, clothes draped furniture and shoes trailed from door to bedroom like the Rockettes had been there mid-show. Dusty pictures, including Bitsy in a glamour shot and one of Celia and me from New Year's Eve years ago, lined a dusty shelf. We looked the same but also different in a way that made me sad. We looked full of something like light that hadn't been dampened by shadows yet. The small curl of my bangs looked like sausage links (why didn't she tell me?), and Celia looked softer somehow.

Eager. That was it. We looked too eager. On the precipice of a new year, we wanted to hold on to what we believed was ours. If we hadn't been so eager, we would have seen that holding on was futile. Real faith comes in letting go.

Sometimes things get difficult. You may be expecting a simple chaturanga but are challenged with a **ONE-LEGGED CRANE POSE**. Cranes focus sharply on their prey through murky waters while appearing to have a sense of strength and poise. Look carefully through the murkiness of unexpected challenges; it's survival.

CHAPTER 14

WHEN RYAN CAME TO PICK ME UP FOR SUNDAY'S COOKOUT, I was running late. I had spent too much time focused on the garnish for my quinoa salad in a control-freak's attempt to impress his friends. It was also a useful distraction to focus on my preference between a lime twist or a playful cilantro sprig—rather than face the uncontrollable things that were orbiting my world.

"You'll be impressive no matter what you bring," he said, nuzzling my neck.

I leaned into him, soaking it up. "I'm so nervous," I admitted. "Maybe a glass of wine before we go?"

"You'll be wonderful. And I think I'll stick with beer tonight. Barchus promises to have the good stuff." He moved to the sliding glass door with his hands in his pockets, biceps expanding the sleeves of his tight white polo shirt. I cleaned up my kitchen counter but kept my eyes on him. *Perfect,* I thought.

"Perfect," he said.

"What?" *Had I said it out loud? The perfect part?* I needed to pull it back; it was too early in the relationship to be this infatuated. I still had things to figure out, including who left the note on my car. But I was smitten with this good man and knew there was no way he was the one who left it. I'd ask him later to be sure, but for now? *Perfect.*

"Perfect night for a barbecue," he repeated. "Can't wait for you to see this deck tonight. Barchus and his wife designed it, and the rest of us helped build it last summer."

"I didn't know you guys were good at construction *and* softball. Renaissance men?"

"Hardly. But we had a great time. It leans a little, but it's solid." He smiled as he looked over my backyard. "You have a great backyard. We could definitely put in a deck over here, maybe some more landscaping. Have you ever thought of planting trees along the lot lines?"

"Not really. I like looking out and seeing all of that." I nodded toward arches of light between the trees and an open expanse of sky meeting earth.

"A nice row of pines would really finish it off and give you a sense of security."

I laughed, and he turned quickly toward me. "Doesn't it bother you? People seeing into your world back here?"

"No need for security. I'm dating a renaissance man." I came up behind him and put my arms around his waist. He seemed to startle a little, then turned around and returned the favor.

"We better go," he said after a kiss. "And let's take your car. Mine is full of ball gear."

I opened the garage door, and Ryan got in the driver's seat of my car. When I raised my eyebrows, he smiled. I feigned a martyred sigh as I crawled in the passenger seat, perfectly garnished salad—lime *and* cilantro—on my lap, and we backed out of the drive. Tamping down my feminist irritation, I had to admit it felt good to have somebody else call the shots, even if it was old school. Sitting in my own passenger seat was also strange, but as we headed past city limits, it was a new perspective, giving me a chance to notice things. Traffic dwindled as we passed business parks with small ponds ringed with Canadian geese.

I decided to address the goose poop in the room. I grabbed the folded note from my bag and held it up for Ryan to see. "Did you leave this for me? On my car?" He glanced at it quickly before changing lanes.

"Nope. Wasn't me." He straightened in his seat.

"I found it on my windshield after we met last night, and after our conversation, it seemed like something romantic and mysterious. Something you would do."

"Intriguing. What does it say?"

"*I know who you are.*" I used my best seductress voice, and for one quick second, a scowl passed over Ryan's face. He recovered quickly, although it seemed a bit forced. I'd noticed his tendency to bat away compliments. This reminded me of how he brushed off my thanks for the chocolate coins in the drive-through.

"You're adorably famous," he said. "You must have an admirer. Another one." He turned to me and smiled, a crooked, sexy grin, which was such a romantic response that it felt like proof and admission.

Ryan continued to readjust behind the steering wheel until he finally moved the driver's seat back while he drove. "Never realized you had such short legs," he said.

"Yeah, but they're fast," I protested.

"Speaking of fast," Ryan said, pleased with his witty segue, "you don't talk much about your running days. Or even why you quit. I know about your collegiate career and the year before your injury, but what happened after that?"

"It isn't a big secret," I said, a little more defensively than necessary. "I tore my Achilles, and by the time I cycled through physical therapy and surgery, I lost my sponsors and my motivation." I turned to look out the window. "I basically quit."

He gave a quick whistle. "That had to be hard. Do you miss it?"

"Every day." I pulled the seatbelt away from my chest; it felt constraining in a way it hadn't before. I didn't like the reasons I quit running and I liked talking about it even less.

Ryan took a quick look at me and grabbed my hand. I was glad he sensed that it was a subject best dropped. As he pulled me toward him and rested our entwined fingers on his thigh, I considered how natural this felt—a road trip, a picnic, a day together. We drove in a companionable silence that was so rich that I didn't want to ruin it with music. These simple moments of touch and understanding were ineffable. *What was this feeling? Contentment?* A flash of guilt prickled my insides. *How dare I feel content when my parents will never feel that again? What about Ashley?*

Ryan broke the silence and my downward spiral. "Why are you single?"

I pulled back to look at him. "What?"

"Why haven't you been snatched up? I know you had one long relationship, but were there others? You never talk about them," he said.

"Where did this come from?"

"Learning about each other. The 'how we got here' discussion. Past relationships. Do you see yourself getting married?" he asked.

Whoa. This was some severe emotional whiplash. "I—I guess. It wasn't that long ago I thought I had found 'the one.' I kept thinking we were working out our issues and it would get easier, but it never did. There was very little romance, lots of conflict. I got tired of it being so hard."

"Did Juan cheat?"

"What? No. Nothing like that." The seatbelt was tight again. "Wait. How did you know his name?"

"You told me." He laughed, letting go of my hand to carefully steer past a slow-moving tractor.

I shook my head and took a swig of my electrolytes. "Really?"

"Really. At Bellatonia," he laughed. "I knew you were drunk."

"I wasn't drunk," I protested, but my cheeks began to burn. My memory of our dinner at Bellatonia was that it had been flawless. Effortless. I thought I had been lost in the moment, but was it because of alcohol? Once again, I felt weighty with guilt. *How could I be so casual with the thing that caused my parents' demise?*

Ryan reached over to me, brushing my warm cheek almost imperceptibly with the back side of his index finger. "I'm kidding," he said softly. I leaned into his hand, closing my eyes, feeling the warm connection between our skin. Damn. He really was irresistible. When we broke apart, I decided music would be nice, after all. The sun angled itself through the sunroof and made me drowsy, and the Rolling Stones were on the oldies station, telling me that I couldn't always get what I wanted, but based on how I felt at that moment, I knew the Stones were wrong.

Ryan, however, was right; Barchus and his wife had a killer deck. Their backyard gently sloped to a dock on Lake Kegonsa, where the weeds hadn't yet commandeered the shore and the water was a dark, mysterious gray—the kind of gray that would have tantalized my dad and brothers into believing it was flush with walleye. They spent a great deal of energy on the elusive walleye. For three straight summers, we made the trek from Nebraska to Minnesota to test a few of its 10,000 lakes. We rented a boat large enough for our family of six and spent quiet mornings and still evenings on the water.

I remembered it all. After dark, we'd grab our flashlights and spread out silently in the boat. Dad taught us how to shine the light in the water just right to catch a glint off the walleyes' eyes. Finn always loved that part of the day, but my favorite was the daily sunset cruise. Mom and Dad would bring their cocktails, and we trolled the outskirts of the lake. I'd drape my arm over the boat, letting my fingers skate the top of the water, and watch the lake houses perched on the shoreline. I made up stories about the people who lived there, wondering what life was like when you were a lake person. I imagined if you were a lake person, you had two dozen swimsuits and didn't have to clean your room. Thanks to this barbecue, I was about to find out.

Ryan and I followed the strains of Jimmy Buffett to the kitchen. A large farm table was full of bowls laden with picnic fare. Most of the party was yelling at the big screen in the adjacent den.

"We need Yount to come back," somebody said. "Cubs are too hungry this year."

"What we need is more beer," said a short man with wild hair and a madras shirt that made him look out of place in the bevy of Brewers fans. As he stepped away from the crowd and toward us, Ryan intercepted him.

"Barchus, this is Sam," he said, putting his hand on my back as if presenting the prized lamb at the fair. "This is the infamous Barchus," he motioned toward our host. "And his wife Colleen is over there." He pointed toward the kitchen to a tall brunette with wine in one hand and a wine opener in the other. She sauntered toward us, and I was reminded of a lynx: stealthy and sleek.

"Finally," she said, reaching for my hand but grabbing only the fingers. "The mythical Sam." She stood next to her husband, and he put his arm around her waist. She was tall and lithe, whereas Barchus was stout and rugged. As they stood together, I noticed that her waist almost came to his nipple line. Celia would've commented on that. Although they were decidedly unmatched, they seemed friendly and open as a couple, a trait I hadn't expected in lake people.

As I methodically met the rest of Ryan's friends, they all seemed to know more about me than I knew about them.

"I hear you're a Chiefs fan. Don't even mention them here," one friend chided, an unlit cigar in his mouth.

"Don't believe the story about the outhouse," said another as he handed me a beer. He nodded down at the mahogany-colored growler he held. "Lone Girl," he said. "New brew we're obsessed with."

"You must have made the cut if he poured from his growler," Ryan said.

We stood in the kitchen, and I met his friends between at-bats and bathroom breaks. No sign of Eugene, the lawyer helping with the restraining order, but it was an amiable group with a short attention span, and by the time the introductions were over, I had already finished the beer. It was light and hoppy, and I wanted another but resisted. As I went into the kitchen to ditch my plastic cup, I passed Colleen.

"What a beautiful home," I said.

"Thank you. It's a lot of work but worth it. I spent all yesterday weeding the small back garden. Go out and take a look. Nobody else seemed to notice."

Ryan was transfixed by the game, so I left the group and walked outside. The back garden wasn't a small plot at all; apparently, lake people liked everything grandiose. Colleen's garden was perfectly square, with straight rows that looked as if they had been combed. Staring at it made me happy. The lynx weeded well.

I walked down to the pier. The wind had picked up, and water lapped against the dock at uneven intervals. I took a deep breath to inhale the familiar smell of lake water and watched a pontoon navigate the swells. This would have been a perfect spot for walleye.

The smell of the lake algae reminded me of the last time we were all on vacation, back before my brothers' football schedules and jobs and girlfriends commandeered our family time. Eli and Levi stayed in the cabin, but Buck, Finn, and I went out on the boat with plans to fish and then swim. The boat's carpet smelled musty, so I kept to the front to breathe in the lake. Rocket, our black lab with the white whiskers, had hunkered on the floor of the boat. Dad loved speed, and we could always count on a race across the water to jump-start the ride. The wind, the water, and the waves all blurred as we sped across the lake. Sometimes we'd slow down to look at an interesting cabin, and other times we would fish in the shallows.

This particular day we stopped near the shore so Rocket could swim. The boys jumped off the side of the boat and threw a tennis ball for the dog. I fished with a bobber as Mom put her feet up on the edge and closed her eyes. Dad lowered the anchor, then grabbed a beer from the cooler. The sun felt warm, the boys were laughing, and I bargained with God: *Please make time stand still. I don't want to lose these days with Rocket swimming and Mom smiling and before Eli goes off to college. I don't want to grow up. Can't it stay like this forever?*

And, of course, it couldn't. Time never stands still, and life rocks the proverbial boat before we're steady. Finn and Buck started wrestling in the water, and Finn elbowed Buck in the nose. Rocket started chasing after a duck, and Dad had to yell to get him back. Buck climbed back in the boat and sulked, and Mom sighed and said we better get back. Dad backed the truck in the water three times before the boat was straight on the trailer, his jaw setting tighter with each attempt. We drove back to the cabin in silence, and I leaned out the window while the wind whipped my hair onto my cheeks. I never quite felt anchored in the same way again.

The pontoon on Lake Kegonsa was heading to shore, and as I watched from the dock, Ryan came up behind me and slipped one arm around my waist. He handed me a frothy margarita in a red plastic cup and nuzzled my neck again, his mustache prickling my skin. I pulled away slightly, and he laughed.

"Ready to eat? Everybody is hungry."

"Sure. And you better rave about the gourmet quinoa salad."

We moved into the kitchen, where people filled plates around the kitchen table. Red napkins matched the red and white bouquets in the center. The kitchen was spacious, but Ryan's friends stood in such a tight cluster that it made me slightly claustrophobic. Ryan stepped aside to let me go first.

He leaned over my shoulder as if to whisper. "Try a bratwurst," he said, louder than a whisper. Louder than necessary.

"No thanks. Not a big brat fan." I took a heaping scoop of my festive salad, noting that nobody else had taken any.

"They're really good," he added. "Barchus soaks them in beer." He pulled the foil off the heap of sausages as evidence, but they looked like a bowl of charred intestines to me.

"I'm sure they're great," I said, looking up, an edge to my voice. A woman across the table from me stopped heaping potato chips on her plate to listen. "I'm just not in the mood for a brat."

"But it's a cookout," he chuckled, playing to the crowd. A few people laughed stiffly; others took a sudden interest in the coleslaw.

"I don't want a brat," I said quietly, shooting him a look.

He covered the brats back up and reached for a bun. "Then you'll miss this," he said, handing me a bun. I kept staring. He continued to thrust it toward me. He finally sighed, opened the bun, and extended it even closer. Inside was a silver bracelet stretched out in the bottom part of the brat bun. The room grew quiet in that way that awkwardness cultivates. I reached into the bun and picked up the bracelet. There was one bead hanging like a charm from the bottom.

"See? See why I wanted you to have a brat?" Ryan raised his eyebrows, glancing at the kitchen crowd for validation, then looked at me like I was a tantrum-prone child who had finally ceased stomping around.

"It's beautiful," I said, unsure of how to react but feeling the pressure rise in my chest. "Thank you."

I looked around the kitchen, and the crew was smiling but seemed to want more. I leaned over and kissed him, which ratcheted the awkwardness up a level. He took the bracelet from the bun and fumbled with the clasp, finally getting it on my wrist. I held it up to the light and was rewarded with murmurs of approval in the background.

"Hey, Hobart, find that in a Cracker Jack box?" Barchus leaned his head back to laugh, and behind him, Colleen offered a drawn smile. Ryan put his hand on the back of my neck and squeezed gently. His friends soon lost their interest in us and returned to their food.

"Maybe I will have that brat," I said, hoping for levity. Ryan grabbed the tongs and carefully placed a plump bratwurst in the bun I had been holding, and we continued our travels around the food, my face as red as the napkins.

We sat on the same side of a cedar picnic table, facing the lake. I drained the last of the margarita, gambling against a brain freeze, and when none appeared, I took it as a sign I should enjoy another. Ryan got up to get us more drinks while Colleen skulked toward me.

"Mind if I join you?" She stood in front of me, and I noticed that her belt drooped in the front, a clear sign of stunning obliques.

"Sure," I said, gesturing toward the empty bench opposite me. With my palm upright, I noticed that I had dragged my forearm through guacamole, and a long smear of green was on my arm. *Nice.* Colleen noticed at the same time but took my hand to inspect Ryan's gift instead.

"Pretty," she said, twirling the bracelet around my wrist.

"Isn't it? I'm still in shock, I think." I smiled. Colleen smiled back, letting go of my arm. She lined up her fork and knife next to her plate as I quickly cleaned up the guacamole from my wrist and wiped my mouth for good measure. I reminded myself to relax. These were Ryan's friends, and there was no reason to be this anxious. Colleen suddenly pulled her shoulders back as if to contradict me, making me feel thick and peevish. She leaned in and lowered her voice.

"He's quite taken with you, you know," she said, looking at me sideways as if to measure my reaction.

He's quite taken with you? Was this a 1950s coffee klatch? I looked at her to see if she was joking, but she was stiff and proprietorial, with an added whiff of condescension.

"We have a great time together," I said, hoping to tie off the conversation.

"So I've heard." A smile landed quickly on her closed lips, then quickly disappeared. I took a sudden, intense interest in a carrot.

"A word of caution," she said. "Ryan has a painful history." She continued to fine-tune the fork-straightening.

"I'm aware," I said, my tone straddling anger and defensiveness as I realized I wasn't aware at all.

"And he falls very hard."

"I know that too," I agreed. I tried my own snarky smile; it felt more like a grimace.

"I've known him for a long time and have seen this before." Colleen glanced to the bar before her eyes landed on me. "Just be careful." She tipped her head at me and narrowed her eyes, a look that disappeared the moment Ryan returned. He handed me a full margarita, and I took an immediate drink.

"What did I miss?" Ryan asked as he looked from Colleen to me.

"Brewers' weak lineup," she said at once, beaming at him like a teacher's pet on conference day. I nodded, margarita still to my lips, looking over the rim at Ryan. *I either got threatened or warned,* I wanted to tell him, but he was focused on Colleen. The moment passed as Barchus came over to us, and the weak lineup was duly dismantled.

I looked down at the bracelet. It was too early for a gift like this, and I felt a rising irritation that the presentation was so staged. My emotional center was already sore from the earlier whiplash, but Ryan's manipulation was a new, uncomfortable strain. In the midst of new people, all I wanted were my old, familiar people. I set down the margarita—my judgment was cloudy enough—and calmed myself by listening to the background sounds of crickets and toads. My dad always told us that the toads we heard at night were males calling out for a potential mate, and each toad had his own song.

Two hours earlier, I had been arguing with the Stones. What happened? I looked out at the murky water, wishing to be home. Surrounded by people, by laughter, by the sounds of summer, I still felt alone. The solemn songs of the horny toads didn't help.

Restore yourself with a **SUPINE SPINAL TWIST**: shoulder blades grounded, arms spread wide, head facing away from your knees. As you switch sides, notice how much the view changes. Your perspective changes everything.

CHAPTER 15

TWO HOURS LATER, I WAS TRYING TO LURE a drunk Ryan out the door. The crew's energy had dwindled, and other than seeing Colleen and Ryan whisper to each other in the kitchen, there wasn't much for a sober person to watch. I waited until Ryan was alone before telling him I'd like to leave.

"Sure, Sam, sure. Let me grab a beer and tell Barchus we're leaving." Then he changed his mind. "Or we could stay here. I don't work 'til late tomorrow."

"Barchus is passed out on his couch. And I'll drive."

"Naah," he croaked. "I got it."

"Actually, you don't," I said, pointedly taking the keys from his hands. His eyes flashed from annoyance to irritation in a fractious second as he grabbed the air for the keys. *My* keys. I put them behind my back as he reached around my body, pulling me toward him and kissing me.

"All right, bossy," he said into my lips. "Take me home."

We waved a quick goodbye to the remaining crew. The lynx was nowhere to be seen, and I didn't go looking for her. We were barely on the road when Ryan brought up the bracelet. "So you really like it? I wasn't sure. Colleen helped me out. I don't have a clue about stuff like this. Colleen said I could keep adding beads to it, too," and he trailed off, eyes focused on the road as he lost his train of thought.

"I really like it. You and Colleen did good." I kept my eyes straight ahead. Darkness played with the edges of the road, blurring the straightaways into curves. Blinking to refresh my eyes, I rolled down my window for fresh air. The road was dark, the night thick, and I was tired. A quick drink from my ubiquitous water bottle made me cringe; taco dip and sodium-enhanced cherry didn't mix.

Ryan straightened up. "Aren't they awesome, Barchus and Colleen?"

"Yes, they are. You guys seem very close," I said.

"We are. They've seen me through a lot."

I let the silence fill the car, unsure if I should ask more or not. Before my brain made the decision, my mouth jumped right in.

"You and Colleen seem especially close."

"What do you mean by that?" Although he wasn't slurring words or sounding drunk, his voice had an alcohol-infused edge to it.

"The bracelet? Didn't she shop with you?"

He relaxed a bit. "Well, yeah, that. She's good that way."

"Does Barchus know how close you are?"

"What does that mean?" The edge was back.

"It means what it means," I said. I had no idea what it meant. But for some reason, I was getting sweaty.

"What is up with you?" Ryan turned his body toward me, and I could smell his beer breath.

"I don't like sneaky," I embellished the words like he was slow.

"What? Who the hell is being sneaky? Is this about the bracelet?"

"No. It's not about the bracelet." *Or was it?* I wasn't sure. "It's about you. And Colleen. Well, maybe not Colleen. But you."

Ryan sighed deeply and scrubbed his face with his palm. I realized that I was confusing both of us.

"Look," I said, "I'm not very good at this. But I know I'm pissed, so we should talk about it. Back there? Your playfulness with the car keys? That sucked."

He squinted for a second, and then I could see the lightbulb. "Your parents' accident. God, I'm sorry, Sam."

"Yeah. It sucked. The fact that a drunk driver—" My throat absorbed the words, and I couldn't finish. The anger I had been hoping to explain away took hold and made my hands shake. I focused on the road ahead of me, which was finally widening. *Who the hell lives this far out in the country anyway?*

"I'm really sorry," Ryan said and put a hand on my thigh. It felt too heavy. His voice was quiet. Empathetic. I let the silence sit densely in the car while I gathered myself up again. He hadn't been intentionally cruel or dense. Just ignorant. And unfiltered.

I sighed. "It caught me off guard, and I'm trying to get better about discussing things when they happen. Trying, anyway." I blew out a deep breath and took another swig of my drink.

"Aren't those bad for you?" He nodded toward my bottle. "You drink a lot of that. It's full of chemicals, you know."

"Doctor's orders, actually. I have a sodium imbalance. No big deal." I still sounded pissy. Ryan's face darkened with concern. "What kind of imbalance?"

I wasn't up for all of this. I wished he would either sit up taller or fall asleep.

"I went to the doctor after I passed out at the gym that day we met. I found out I'm low on sodium. That's all. One of these a day, and I'm back to normal." I held up the bottle and exaggerated a drink.

"Why haven't you told me?" he asked softly.

"Because, like I said, it isn't a big deal."

"I could have been helping you," he said.

"I don't need any help." I sat up taller.

He looked out the window, and I saw that the tag was sticking out of the back of his collar. For some reason, that softened me. He was trying. And this probably wasn't the best conversation to have on opposite ends of the sozzled spectrum.

"Seriously, Ryan, it's no big deal. The human body is an amazing beast, and we all need a little tweaking. I tweak with salt."

"I'll tweak you when we get home," Ryan chuckled, leaning over to kiss my cheek. He relaxed against the headrest and promptly fell asleep. An oncoming car lit up the interior, and then it was gone. The darkness the lights left behind was refreshing. I needed the quiet space to unravel what had happened with the bracelet and with my anger. Other than Ryan's intermittent snoring, I drove in silence.

When we reached my driveway, Ryan got out of the car and went inside. He took off his shirt and shoes as he walked to my bedroom, crawled under the covers, and fell asleep. Tweaking was out of the question, which was fine with me. As I plugged in my phone, I saw two voice messages waiting for me.

"Hey, Aunt Sam. Thank you for yesterday," Ella said. "I thought Dad would kill me, but we actually had a pretty good talk after you left. Shocker, right? Anyway, thank you. Love you." Succinct and sweet.

The second message was a study in contrast—an apology and good news from BJ all in one long breath. "Sorry to bother you. You're probably out doing something fun? But I wanted to let you know that your keys got turned in, just like I said. Somebody thought they looked familiar and dropped them in their pocket after their class. They brought them back today. I'll lock them in the desk drawer until you come back. Unless you need them. I guess I could drop them off. Whatever. Let me know if you need them? Nena's class is tomorrow— maybe you're coming to that. Okay, rambling done. See you tomorrow?" She ended the call, and I breathed as if in her honor. With the mystery of the missing keys solved, I finally went to bed next to a snoring Ryan.

In the middle of the night I awoke, clammy from a heavy, sticky, sweat. I had been dreaming of being chased in the desert, my legs trapped and useless in the sand. I snuck out of my snarl of sheets and went down to the living room, where the curtains trailed the wind like an afterthought, and I sat on the couch. Bitsy followed me to the top of the stairs and watched me as if it wasn't worth the effort to tackle the decline. My living room was refreshingly cool from the breeze, and I wrapped my arms around my legs and watched the night out the window. It was peaceful. Even though Ryan was asleep, his presence in my home somehow changed the air.

The bracelet was on my wrist, and I twirled it like Colleen had done. Giving me the bracelet had been a lovely gesture, but Ryan's approach bothered me. Why did he wait until we were surrounded by so many people? People I didn't know? Putting it in a brat bun was fun, I suppose, but also schmaltzy. A gift in a brat bun. Brewers-approved.

On the one hand, the presentation was romantic and theatrical. On the other hand, the gesture reeked of drama. It could have been a meaningful moment for us, alone. I understood that Ryan had only wanted to meld his friends and his "new girl" with one dramatic move; my objections about his delivery seemed petty. The man had given me a sweet gift, and I wished I could leave it at that. After all, I had been trying to be more spontaneous and adventurous. Doesn't a surprise gift fall into this category?

My new boyfriend was either amazingly thoughtful or an attention hound. Either we were working out the kinks, or it wasn't working. The anger that had been on a slow simmer earlier in the night confused me. Was it about being put on the spot with the bracelet, about drunk drivers, or about feeling alone? I wanted to talk to somebody about it and parse the feelings—or at least get another perspective. Celia was my primary confidante, but she was out. I would have tried Pen, but it was the middle of the night.

Turning on a nearby lamp, I curled up in the corner of my couch and reached for my book. Fiction was surely the answer, where I could retreat to a world without me as the fulcrum, but fiction wasn't enough to distract me. I turned off the lamp and watched the moon dance on the living room floor. The lights were turned off except the dome lights I always left on in the kitchen. Since my first apartment, leaving the lights on over the sink made me feel safe and watched over, like someone was waiting for me whenever I got home.

I decided to join the moonlight and crawled to the floor. Starting with child's pose, I moved slowly into downward dog. Deep breathing slowed my heart rate and dried the sweat that still glinted on my arms. I moved to a gentle pigeon pose to release my outer hips, which thanked me by opening up slowly and steadily. Then onto my back for a spinal twist, knees bent to one side and then the other. Moving through the familiar yoga poses was like melatonin for my monkey mind. After only a few movements, I felt better—more like myself, but tired—and tiptoed back to bed.

Monday mornings at work are the worst. And the best. The bank is busy so the time goes quickly, but after my eventful weekend, I could have used a slow day. I checked messages on my break and saw that Celia was trying to reach me. I called her over my lunch hour.

"Hi." Celia sounded hoarse and resigned.

"Are you okay?"

"Yeah. I'm ready to come home. We have a flight later tonight, but I really miss you guys. Can I talk to Bitsy?"

"Celia, it's Monday. I'm at work."

"Sorry. My days are mixed up. When are you going to check on her?"

"What?"

"Don't you go home on your lunch hour and check on her?" Her voice was getting higher.

"She's fine. She does great." Great might be a stretch, but there had been only a couple of accidents. And they were on the tile, so easily forgiven.

"I had a terrible dream about her, Peanut. I need you to check on her."

"I can't leave work, Celia. She likes watching the birds. She's fine." I tried to sound reassuring.

"She's NOT fine! She's probably lonely and confused and needs constant attention. You don't get it, Sam. Bitsy isn't as tough as she looks." Desperation was ramping up in her voice. This was about more than the dog.

"I understand, C, but I can't go right now. I have a meeting with the IT guys in a little while." There was silence on the other end, and silence with Celia never bodes well. "How about if I call you the minute I get home?" I tried.

"That's too long. I need to know she's okay. That dream was so real."

"Okay. How about this: I'll call Aunt Dorothea and have her stop in. If Bitsy seems like she's having trouble, Dorothea is the best one to have around. You know how she can be."

There was more silence on Celia's end as she gave this some thought. Dorothea was a nurturer. My aunt had an air about her that suggested warm cookies and cinnamon candles. Even her voice was soothing. It sounded like Celia could use some of that.

"Okay." She agreed. "Please make her a priority, Sam. She needs you."

"I know she does, Celia. I'm right here."

"I know," Celia said softly. "Call me the minute you hear back."

I thought about what I told Ryan, that Celia and I traded off needing each other. And although I defended her vehemently, I had to admit that her theatrics were sometimes draining. Hurricane Celia sweeps into a room, stirs up trouble—or fun—and leaves a path in her wake, and I usually pick up the pieces. More than once she has asked for a favor, calling from a pub crawl or cocktail cruise. While I stay home some nights to get caught up on bills and laundry, Celia is usually off on her next adventure and stops at Victoria's Secret to buy underwear along the way. She'd much rather buy it than stop and wash it. I get tired of being reliable and bland while Celia gets to be fluorescent.

But, as I told Ryan, she came through for me on the bigger things that mattered. I called Aunt Dorothea, and she agreed to check on Bitsy.

"No problem. I'm on my way to book club, so I'll stop at your place first," Aunt Dorothea said. "I wouldn't mind being a bit late. We're reading Jane Austen, and Marna is hosting. You know what that means;

she's more prudish than ever. She takes on the persona of whatever character we're reading. Last time she didn't even have wine. I swear, that woman wouldn't say 'shit' if she had a mouth full of it."

I laughed. "Do you still have my key?"

"Of course, dear. And I'll leave you a copy of the Mayo Clinic newsletter. There's an article in there about sodium I think you should read."

"Thanks. I owe you."

"Buy me a bottle of pinot," she said. "I'll give it to Marna."

Dorothea left me two messages while I was in my meeting. Had she known how to text, that would have been her next recourse. I couldn't imagine what would be so important to call twice; my aunt is not easily excitable. She wasn't prone to exaggeration, either. The second I heard her strained message, my heartbeat tripled.

"Sam. Oh, Sam. It's awful. Bitsy—oh dear—call me back." I didn't wait for the next message. I called her back instantly. She answered instantly, too.

"Oh, Sam. The poor thing. It's devastating. I need—"

I cut her off. "What is going on? What happened?"

Aunt Dorothea couldn't seem to catch her breath.

"What?" I gripped my phone frantically. "Tell me, Aunt Dor—"

"It's Bitsy, Sam. Come home. It's not good."

EXTENDED PUPPY POSE is a cross between child's pose and downward-
facing dog. It helps lengthen the spine and calm the mind.

As with most things, it can quickly go from playful to intense.

CHAPTER 16

I TOLD MY SUPERVISOR I HAD AN EMERGENCY, locked my cash drawer
in the vault, and raced home, hitting every stupid red light along the
way.

Dorothea met me at the door, cradling a towel-wrapped, lifeless dog
in her arms. Fear was pinned to my aunt's face. My stomach clenched
as I moved toward them. *This can't be happening. Bitsy needs to be okay.*

"Oh, Sam," Dorothea began. She shook her head and for a second,
I was cloaked in her compassion. It was familiar and soothing, a
reminder of all the times she looked at me that same way after my
parents' deaths. Inexplicably, it also pissed me off.

I interrupted her to avoid pity. "Is she—?"

"No. Not yet. But we need to get help. Now." As she spoke, something
clear leaked from Bitsy's mouth. It added to the acrid, sour smell that
permeated my kitchen, and as I looked past Aunt Dorothea, I noticed
puddles of liquid spotting the floor.

Aunt Dorothea continued. "We need to move quickly, Sam. What
clinic does Celia use? And we'll need another towel. The poor dear is

seeping through this ratty towel. Do you have an old sheet we can use?"

I was barely listening. I was still paralyzed with disbelief, a handy substitution for guilt. I gently pulled back the towel as Dorothea held the dog slightly away from her body. Bitsy's eyes were open, and one was covered with gunk. She had a far-off stare and was oddly absent, even for a dog. My brain started its circuitous monologue: *What happened? How did it happen? How am I ever going to tell Celia? I need to be practical here. I wonder if I can get Aunt Dorothea to call Celia. Wait—that was one of my good towels. Why did Dorothea call it ratty? What vet does Celia use? I know she told me. I didn't listen well enough. Celia shouldn't have trusted me. Am I this irresponsible? I wonder if I should grab a fitted sheet. Flannel? Which car would be best? Which one does Bitsy like best? If we wrap her in a regular sheet, what will I do with a partnerless fitted sheet?*

"Sam!"

Aunt Dorothea's acoustic slap worked. I focused. "Let's take my car, and you can hold Bitsy," I said. "You guys head out there, and I'll grab more towels." Then I remembered the lengthy instructions Celia sent me when she left. I pulled them up on my phone. In the plethora of texts Celia sent me regarding Bitsy's care, she'd sent her vet's name, number, and address.

"The clinic isn't far. I'm calling them now. I'll meet you in the car."

That felt better. I was back in control and hung on to the sliver of hope that my resolve would rouse Bitsy. I called the clinic and told them we were on our way with an emergency, then grabbed a stack of subpar towels from the closet.

We were on our way in less than a minute. "What happened?" I finally asked at the first stoplight after I caught my breath.

"I don't know," Dorothea said while gently opening the towel. She created a hood around Bitsy's face and stroked the top of Bitsy's nose. It was gut-clenchingly tender. "When I came in the door, she was flat on her side on the kitchen floor. There was so much vomit. I think she ate something, but this is all I could find," Dorothea said. She pulled a crushed aluminum foil package from her purse that had been resting by her feet. I was impressed that she thought to bring it. At least one of us was clear-headed in an emergency.

"What is it?" I said, sneaking looks while I tried to focus on the road. A cellophane label hung from the side of the package, curled and smudged.

"The label says it was four, sugar-free, banana nut muffins," Dorothea read.

"Where did those come from?" I asked Dorothea, almost accusingly.

"I assumed they were yours," she answered softly, kinder than I deserved. "It looked to me like she got into them while you were gone."

"But I didn't buy those—I've never even seen them before."

"It's what I found, dear," Aunt Dorothea said, replacing the mangled tin at her feet.

My phone rang. The veterinary assistant was calling, hoping to be better prepared once we walked in the door. I put my phone on speaker and started to give him the details I knew. Aunt Dorothea jumped in so often that I finally let her do all the talking.

"I'll pull up Bitsy's file," the vet assistant said. "Are you okay to stay on the line?" He put us on hold, and Aunt Dorothea and I looked at each other while a rendition of "Muskrat Love" filled the car.

After a few seconds, Dr. Brisbain came on the line. I was surprised to hear a female voice; Celia almost always chose men for every professional interaction that came her way. The vet had a slight British accent, which was somehow reassuring.

I described what had happened again, including information about the muffins. There was silence on her end, then a sympathetic tone when she finally started talking. "I'm sorry. What did you say your name was again?"

"Sam."

"Well, Sam, I'm glad you're heading here right off. We'll be ready for you. Can you tell me more about the muffins?"

"I have no idea where they came from—they suddenly appeared. I live alone, and I certainly never bought them. They look like they're from the local grocery store, and the label says 'sugar-free banana nut muffins.' Could it be the nuts? Can dogs be allergic to nuts?"

She sighed. "No, I'm afraid it was the sugar-free part. Likely xylitol, or rather, sugar alcohol. The muffins must have had xylitol in them to make them sugar-free. For a dog as small as Bitsy, a tiny amount can be dangerous. This information helps enormously. Can you tell how much she ate?"

"Quite a bit. But she threw up quite a bit, too."

"Oh, dear." Her accent made it sound like the most ominous "oh dear" I'd ever heard.

I dropped my chin to my chest. *This can't be happening.* I steeled myself to ask Dr. Brisbain the question I didn't want answered. "Will she be okay?"

"Bring her in. Let's take a look at our Bitsy Girl."

The nickname—and the compassion it bestowed—did me in. The back of my throat started to ache. I couldn't swallow. Of all the emotions I had suppressed to that point, kindness was the hardest to dodge. It's easy to rally against fear or rage. But kindness is a sucker punch that knocks the wind right out of me.

⁓⁓⁓

We got to the clinic in record time. Dorothea swaddled Bitsy and protected her like a football close to the endzone. I opened doors and an assistant in scrubs met us in the foyer, tenderly transferring Bitsy into her arms, rushing into the back room. The door slammed shut, and I jumped. It was too abrupt. After all the angst, worry, and smell, Bitsy was suddenly gone, and Dorothea and I stood helpless, staring at the closed door. The waiting room was silent. I closed my eyes and prayed; I'm certain Dorothea did the same. I was hoping she had more clout than I did. We looked at each other wordlessly, then sat on plastic chairs against the wall. Black dog hair had piled itself into a little rambling whorl near the door, and I watched another hair tumbleweed roll back and forth under an open window.

Dr. Brisbain finally came out to meet us. She was tall and severe-looking, and gazing up at her from my plastic chair emphasized the imbalance of our relationship. Since I really needed her deity-like knowledge and skill to keep Bitsy alive, I remained seated in supplication.

"Okay," she began with an exhale. "We've got Bitsy stabilized. The poor thing has been through it, right? Xylitol triggers a sudden release of insulin, which throws the dog's body into shock. I would suspect she went into shock within a half-hour of ingestion, but the fact that you found her so quickly is good."

"Do you think—" I started. She didn't let me finish.

"I think she probably experienced severe vomiting and seizures. That's hard on a body, so the next few hours are crucial." Her face softened and I chided myself for calling her severe, even in my head. "She's otherwise healthy, and I expect she's a fighter," Dr. Brisbain said.

"I was supposed to be watching her." My breath caught in my throat as I stepped into the confessional.

Her head tilted sympathetically. "Dogs are tenacious little beings and have nothing but time to get into whatever they want. You wouldn't believe the stories I've heard about what dogs do when they're alone. You simply can't protect them from everything."

I looked down at the floor while my brain rejected her words, choosing instead to trace the perfectly spaced stitches tracing the top of Dr. Brisbain's clogs.

"There's a reason it's called 'dogged' pursuit," she tried again. When that didn't work, she started to turn away from us, pivoting on her Swedish clogs toward her heroics. "Go home for a bit," she said. "We have your number. We'll call you as we know more."

Dorothea and I left the mauled muffin container with the receptionist and drove home. My guilt and fear fused into a wave of subcutaneous anger that I tried to hide from my aunt. None of this was Aunt Dorothea's fault. She tried to reassure me and I pretended it worked, and when she offered to come in and help clean, I sent her home with a hug and a promise to call.

Now I really needed to be alone. I needed to ground myself and try to make sense of what happened. I grabbed a bucket and sponge and got on my knees, literally grounding myself, and began scrubbing the kitchen floor to erase what had been done. As I scoured, I surveyed my kitchen. Other than the sugar-free muffins, everything looked the same. My pile of overdue paperwork was by the computer. Unopened mail next to that. A couple of dishes soaking in the sink. Everything was as I had left it, except, I noticed at last, the recessed lights over the kitchen sink were dark.

That one clue—lights turned off that I deliberately leave on—put me over the edge.

My insides grew hot and started to roil as I tensed. *Who did this? Who invaded my home and hurt Bitsy?* I scrubbed harder, concentrating on the only substantial clue; the sugar-free muffins. I didn't buy them. I didn't even eat them. The chemicals used to mimic a mediocre-tasting sugar did serious damage to my insides. Besides that, why wasn't this more well-known, that xylitol could be potentially fatal to animals? There should be somebody to blame. I scrubbed harder, trying to line up organized, rational thoughts on a fresh, clean slate, all while my heartbeat pounded in my ears.

Remember. Deep breaths. I tried to focus again. If the muffins were left as a gift for me, it was a lame gift. There was no note left, although, in the wake of Bitsy's binge, it was hard to tell what else she consumed. Dorothea and Celia both had keys to my condo but nobody else. *Wait. Except Buck. Maybe Buck stopped by. Or Ella.* After our interaction the other night, maybe the muffins were a thank-you gift. I'd check with them later. I'd come up with a list of possibilities as soon as I finished with the puke. I could be as dogged as poor little Bitsy.

I sat back on my heels. All my theories about the muffins were avoidance of the truth. Figuring out what happened was easier than admitting I was afraid. Deep down, I knew that someone was trying to hurt me, someone had now harmed an innocent pup, and I needed to consider that it could be Ryan. I just wasn't ready yet.

First, it was time to do the thing I dreaded the most—I needed to call

Celia. I toyed with the idea of not telling her. She would be home later in the evening, and besides, she would worry herself sick while stuck on an airplane. I pity the person who sits next to Celia during a crisis. Still sitting back on my heels, I bent over my knees to stretch and created a little rabbit pose. I tried to inhale and dizzied myself with the smell of the disinfected floor. As much as I dreaded this call, I knew I needed to make it.

My phone rang and I jumped. I prayed it was the vet saying that Bitsy was miraculously cured. Or would it be Celia, about to find out that her premonitions had been true, that Bitsy was in danger? I braced myself either way.

It turned out to be Catherine, calling from the middle school, jumping right into the conversation without a greeting. "At one point today, I had three kids trying to fistfight in my office. I didn't know it was even possible to get suspended from summer school. Are you sure you don't want to come back?"

"I'm sure. I'm hanging on to my one thread of sanity as it is. You obviously gave up on that. How are you?"

"Good. Crazy. You know how it goes. But I do have some information on Tyler."

My heart pounded again. "Share," I said. Was *he* the somebody I could blame?

"Our little angel has moved on," Catherine said.

"When?"

"Apparently, the family moved to Arkansas last spring. The new district requested his transcripts last summer."

"And do you know if he's actually going to school there?"

"Yep. I called their intake coordinator. Tyler is there attending classes. That's good news for us, right? Why are you checking up on him?"

"It's a long story, and I'll fill you in later. It sounds like you have enough on your plate. But thanks, Catherine. We'll catch up soon."

I stood in the same spot that Aunt Dorothea had rocked Bitsy and regrouped. Accusing Tyler of the stalking events had been a long shot.

Part of me had always known it wasn't him. But that was for later. First, I had a terrible call to make. A text message appeared from Ryan, but I ignored it. Celia came first. I took a deep breath, dialed her number, and paced.

"Hi, Peanut! We're at the airport." She sounded good. I was one sentence away from changing that.

"Hi, Celia." I tried to keep my voice even but serious, the first warning that bad news was coming. She got it.

"What's the matter? Why do you sound like that? What is it?"

"It's okay. Or at least it will be." Even if I wasn't sure, I needed her to believe it. For now. I started to doubt myself but needed to get it over with. Regardless of her reaction, I wanted this part done.

I dove in. "Honey, it's Bitsy."

"What? Bitsy? I can barely hear you, Sam. And hurry—my phone's about to die."

Background noise from the terminal rose with a boarding announcement. I wound up my voice and sidelined the dread.

"There's been an accident, Celia. Bitsy ate something that made her sick. She's—"

"What?"

"Bitsy ate some muffins with xylitol in them, and she's sick. She's at the clinic now, and Dr. Brisbain is with her." I winced as I said it, but it was done.

There was silence on the line, and I let it go. It was a lot for Celia to process. When it finally got uncomfortable, I broke it.

"Celia? Are you okay?" She didn't answer. I tried again. Nothing. When I finally pulled my phone from my ear, I saw that the call had ended, that her phone had most likely died. She probably didn't hear what I had to say. I hunched over the counter and closed my eyes.

※※※※※※

I looked up the flight time from Las Vegas. Three hours. I had three hours to pray for a miracle. I called the clinic and asked for an update on Bitsy and was told that Dr. Brisbain would return my call. *That must mean the news is bad. Otherwise, they'd give me an update right away. Or they're trying to figure out how to tell me the bad news. Should I wait for Celia to hear it? Maybe it would be better coming from the vet?*

I stopped myself with three slow breaths. Festering wouldn't help anybody. I turned to scour the floor again, and after two hours of cleaning everything from the tops of the cupboards to the crumbs in the silverware drawer, I got a call from an unknown number. It was Celia, on Tommy's phone.

"What happened to Bitsy?" She started. Her voice sounded far away. And frantic.

"She ate something that was poisonous to dogs. She's at the clinic now."

"Bitsy? You poisoned her?" She was breathing hard.

"I didn't poison her, Celia. Somebody left these muffins in my kitchen, and she ate them—"

"I told you to keep food away from her! I told you she needed constant attention!"

"I did! I kept all food away from her. Believe me, everything was put away in the cupboards or the fridge. And she wasn't left alone very long. It was these muffins—"

"Muffins? What the hell are you talking about?"

"I don't know where they came from." My volume was increasing with hers.

"I trusted you!" she said, and I could tell it was through gritted teeth. This was much worse than I anticipated, but I deserved each moment of discomfort. I waited.

"How is she? Is it bad? Will she—"

I needed to be honest with her. "It's possible, C." I heard a sharp intake on her end. "But Dr. Brisbain said we got her in early. Dr. Brisbain was hopeful."

I wasn't even sure that was completely true, but Celia and I both needed to hear it. Celia started to cry. It felt terrible to be so helpless over the phone. I wanted to hold her, to rock her, to comfort her. Watching somebody suffer is almost harder than suffering. When my parents died, so many people tried to help me through the process. Those with experience knew that it wasn't possible. People bring food because it's something tangible to do. The intangible—sitting alongside the bereft, in companionable silence, was sometimes too hard for people to do. But it was the best balm for me and my new wounds to have somebody close by as I waded through each new, painful moment.

At Mom and Dad's funeral, people lined up for a receiving line that was staggeringly long. It's unimaginable how many lives we touch. Waiting faces looked at me with such compassion that my chest felt twice as heavy with their pain. When I looked out the church doors and saw an even longer line, faces and sympathy and sorrow braided together until I became detached. I went into autopilot and accepted their condolences through a protective haze.

In the haze, I hugged, nodded, introduced. I thought I was quite convincing; in truth, I was quite numb. But when my work friend Catherine came through the line—bookmarked between my mom's coworkers and my dad's cronies—for some reason, I lost the anesthesia. I fell into her arms, she rocked me and sobbed with me, and I felt protected. She'd always had a soft spot in her heart, and I gratefully landed there.

I had a visceral need to provide that same comfort for Celia despite the fact that I was the one who caused her pain. Although Bitsy's poisoning was out of my control, it *was* my fault. I started to replay the events of the morning again, then caught myself. *Stop. It's about Celia now.*

"Is Tommy there?" I finally asked.

"He's here," she said quietly. "He's even more furious with you."

I hung my head. Even having Tommy mad at me was hard to bear. "Can you come here? Have Tommy drop you off. Going home might be hard," I said softly. "Bring your suitcase, come and stay with me, and we'll wait for an update together."

"I'm too upset."

"I know."

"With you," she said.

"I know." My throat closed up. "I'm so sorry, C."

There was more silence, and then in the quietest voice I'd ever heard her use, Celia said, "Okay."

I closed my eyes, and she hung up. There was nothing else to do but wait.

When Tommy's car finally pulled into the driveway, I went outside. Celia and I hugged and cried while Tommy glared at me with such venom that I closed my eyes. Once Celia and I pulled away from each other, I busied myself with lining up her luggage while she said goodbye to Tommy. He tore away without even a wave goodbye.

Celia turned toward my door, purse almost the size of a card table hanging from the crook of her arm, and sighed, like going inside my house was an act of courage. She started toward the front door, leaving me with her suitcases. I dutifully grabbed them and followed.

Inside, she moved from room to room with a despondency I'd never seen in her. She ran her hand across the top of the couch where Bitsy parked herself the most, picked up picture frames and looked at them without seeing them, and straightened books that were already so. I've watched Celia cry, sigh, and talk animatedly when receiving bad news before. But this time, there was silence. She looked out the window without saying a word and held silent poses that rattled me. I knew it was bad. Her love for her dog was an anomaly for her. She had loved unselfishly for perhaps the first time in her life.

We were standing in the middle of my living room when my phone rang. It was the clinic. I put Dr. Brisbain on speaker.

"Hello, Sam?"

"I'm here, Dr. Brisbain. And Celia is here too."

"I'm here!" Celia echoed, putting her mouth too close to the phone.

"Good. Glad you're there. I wanted to give you an update on our Bitsy Girl. She's on IV, and we have her stabilized—"

"Thank God," Celia said.

"—but she's still in critical condition," Dr. Brisbain continued. "It will be a long night, unfortunately. But we'll monitor her closely."

Celia's shoulders slumped. "Can I see her?"

"I'm sorry, Celia, but no. She needs her rest. I know it's hard, but we need to let her healing body do its work. I promise we'll take good care of her."

"I know you will," Celia said. "But she needs me."

"She needs rest most of all. You'll excite her," Dr. Brisbain said kindly. Celia let her head drop and backed away from the phone.

"Thank you, Dr. Brisbain," I said. "You'll call if Bitsy's condition changes at all?"

"Absolutely," she said.

Celia turned from the living room, unlocked my patio doors, and went outside. I thanked Dr. Brisbain again and arranged to call in the morning. Then I watched from the window as Celia stood on my patio, hands on hips, mouthing something. Prayer? Conversation with Bitsy? I turned away and gave her some privacy but hovered nearby to keep tabs on her.

While Celia wandered my backyard, I checked my messages. Two from Ryan. I deleted them before even listening to them. I was distrustful of everyone and needed to focus on Celia right now. Erasing the messages helped me compartmentalize my uncertainty about Ryan and pay attention to my friend's distress.

We had a long night ahead of us, so I invited Aunt Dorothea over for a late dinner. Worrying is cerebral and solitary, and doesn't give the hands anything to do, so Dorothea brought a few supplies, and we set out to make a sturdy spaghetti alla puttanesca. Dorothea fussed over Celia with all the nurturing I'd expected. She was perfect. Once Celia's tears abated, we all busied ourselves with culinary tasks while listening to Celia tell stories about Bitsy. Aunt Dorothea's favorite wine helped soften the edges. Celia was even able to laugh a few times, and I teased her about this being her signature meal since puttanesca translates to "spaghetti a la whore" in Italian.

Under the surface, blame ran rampant in my little world. Aunt Dorothea wished she would have come over earlier, and I felt guilty for leaving Bitsy alone. Celia even admitted that she blamed herself for putting us in this dreadful situation. Something had shifted in her since hearing the news; she suddenly had the ability to empathize, which I hadn't seen in her before and almost made it more difficult.

Aunt Dorothea left after we made—but barely touched—our spaghetti for whores. Celia and I still had the bottle of wine to finish, so we took our places on my couch and shared a throw. It covered our knees, and the soft chenille gave us something to grab onto. Because it had been a sticky summer night, I had the air conditioning set so low that it was almost chilly inside. As we sat huddled on the couch, I didn't want to ruin the moment by getting up to change it.

Celia's voice cracked. "My poor baby," she said for the hundredth time that night as she looked down at the throw and wound her fingers in the fringe. As I put my hand on her knee, my phone rang, startling us both. The ringer was loud and the timing terrible, and I scrambled to grab it from the ottoman. My heart was pounding as I looked at the number.

"Ryan," I said to Celia. I silenced the phone and tried to slow down my heart.

"That's ballsy. What time is—?" Celia started to ask.

She barely got the words out when there was a sharp thud on my front porch. Celia and I both jumped, and she grabbed my arm. Before fear could dull my reaction, I looked at the doorknob, praying it was locked.

It was. Fear spread through me, my own cold IV.

Celia started to speak, and we heard another thump. Louder this time.

A face appeared in the glass panel of the front door, framed by thick hands.

It was Ryan.

EAGLE POSE is a complex pose, requiring balance, twisting, and stretching of the shoulders. It takes concentration with a soft gaze and a gentle focus until your vision becomes clear.

You'll finally see what you need to see.

CHAPTER 17

CELIA YELPED AND PULLED THE BLANKET TO HER CHEST. I leaped from the couch and rushed to the door, the heat of my anger dislodging any remnants of fear. I unlocked it, pushed past Ryan to the porch, and slammed the door behind me, leaving Celia alone.

"What the hell, Ryan?"

"I was worried about you. You haven't been answering your phone, and I thought something was wrong." He reached for me. I held up my hand to stop him.

"So you decided to scare us? At midnight?"

"Us?" he asked, trying to move around me for a glimpse inside.

"Celia's in there. She's already a mess."

"Why? What happened?"

I looked at him. I couldn't see his features well in the dark, but I couldn't read him well in the light, either. I'd had enough.

"You need to leave, Ryan."

"Why? Are you still pissed about me getting drunk?"

I gritted my teeth like Buck. "No. Celia's dog was poisoned. There's a lot going on right now, Ryan. I need some time."

"But—"

"Seriously. I'm going in now, and I need you to leave."

I turned around, closed the door, and locked it. I watched from the window as he stood on the porch for a few seconds, then turned toward the darkness. Celia and I looked at each other, eyes wide.

"Are you okay?" I asked. She nodded. My heart was still racing, so I started to pace, too tired to make sense of things but too wired to slow down. I found a second bottle of wine and opened it with shaky hands. After a heavy pour to top off our glasses, I flopped back down next to C.

"What was that all about?" Celia asked.

"Ugh. There's so much," I answered. I hadn't kept her updated and didn't know where to start. I didn't want to start with Ryan; I was still too mad to give him airtime. I didn't want to scare her further with details about the stalking. Bitsy clearly was a victim of that. When I thought of telling her about Ashley, my chest tightened, and my vision blurred. I willed the tears away; I had no right to them.

"Tell me," Celia said with a small nod.

"Remember my friend Ashley?"

"I've heard a few stories."

"I found out she died," I said. I moved to pour more wine, but my hands were shaking. I tucked them under my legs.

"I'm so sorry, Peanut. I didn't know you kept in touch," Celia said.

"We didn't. I was about to reach out when I heard she died." I could not force myself to tell the truth, to use the word "murdered" with Celia. Knowing Bitsy might also have been a victim of cruelty was too much. There were boulders of guilt underneath all of this, and I wasn't ready to drill through the strata.

I looked at Celia. "You sure about this? It doesn't feel right to talk about it, considering what you're going through."

"I'm sure," Celia said, head down and a tissue balled up in her fist. "It's nice to be distracted for a bit. Go ahead. Let's make it all about you." She looked up at me and smiled, and I felt for the first time that Celia would survive this.

"Okay, then. You already know that my car was keyed during yoga one day."

"Bitch," she confirmed with a small grin.

I nodded. "The other day, while I was in another class, somebody took my keys. Luckily, the new receptionist found them and returned them to me, but the whole thing felt eerie. Especially now." I looked around the room and felt a chill.

"There was a cryptic note left on my windshield, and there's the whole snake thing," I continued. "Remember that? It felt like something one of my middle school students would have done. I thought I knew who was responsible but found out today I was wrong. Apparently, it wasn't Tyler, but if not him, then who the hell would send me a snake?"

Celia's narrowed eyes and tipped head urged me on.

"And Ryan. I'm so confused. It's like I've been so grateful for a boyfriend who takes charge that I've lost my cojones. I've been so desperate for comfort that I've been stupid. I'm going to tell him I need a little space right now so you and I can spend some time together."

Celia seemed to deflate a few degrees at the mention of her situation. I reached over and grabbed her hand. Her eyes filled, but she nodded with the "go on" signal, so I kept on.

"Now, of course, Bitsy. This doesn't make sense, C. I swear to God I never bought those muffins. I never left food out like that while Bitsy was here, and even if I did, she wouldn't be able to reach my counters. Looking back at what happened, I realized the light above my sink was off when I got home. You know me; I never turn that off. I asked Buck or Ella if they stopped by, and he said they didn't. You, Dorothea, and Buck are the only ones with a key. And I don't think anybody knows my garage code."

In the telling, I began to see the things that were happening to me as all of a piece. I paused, gearing up for what needed to be said. Celia nodded her encouragement.

"I've been denying the fact that most of this has happened since

Ryan came into my life. It all started right when I met him."

The look Celia gave me was the most accurate facial illustration of "NO SHIT?" I've ever seen. She tried to recover, widening her eyes as a cleanse, but I had seen it. And she was right.

"The only thing that doesn't fit is that I hadn't met him yet when my car got iced. Also—and this is a big one—he's a paramedic, Celia. Aren't they sworn to help? Why would he hurt another person?"

She rallied with her indignation. "Haven't you ever heard of those firefighters who do that? They know all about arson and start fires so they can be the ones to put them out. They want to be the heroes. Maybe Ryan has that complex and wanted to rescue you from the bad things that happened. Things that he created."

I considered that. I had been uncomfortable that he was such a "grandstander," as my dad would say.

"I can't figure out *why*," I said. I looked at Celia and could almost see her shutting down feature by feature. "But for now, let's get some sleep. Bits will need us tomorrow."

Celia nodded and checked her phone. I took our empty wine glasses into the kitchen and scrubbed the sink, losing myself in the physicality of it. When I went back to check on Celia, I found her asleep on the couch.

"Celia," I said, touching her shoulder. "Go sleep in the extra bedroom."

She sat up, yawned and stretched, causing the buttons on her shirt to strain.

"I will." But she didn't move. She stayed, elbows on her knees, lethargic, staring into nothingness.

I sat next to her quietly and waited.

"I'm afraid of dreaming about her," she finally said. She sounded so vulnerable that it made my throat hurt. "But here's the thing. I've been dreading something happening to Bitsy for so long, and now it's happened. And I am surviving."

"There's something to be said for that," I said.

She finally stood, kissed the top of my head, and walked toward the bathroom. I turned off the lights in the other rooms and adjusted the thermostat. I double-checked each door and window, which was my nightly routine, but tonight I was grateful Celia was here with me. I missed Bitsy. I could almost hear her little nails skittering down the tile floors, racing me to bed. Thinking about that innocent little body, hooked to an IV, by herself, made me cry. When I looked in on Celia in my spare room, she was back to sleep, a bottle of cold medicine standing tall on the nightstand.

I should have taken some, too. Frantic dreams punctuated intermittent sleep, and I was never sure what was real. I checked on Celia twice; the second time, I noticed a sleep visor askew on her face. It was a long night.

In the morning, she came to the kitchen wearing my robe, looking puffy and mottled. Her hair looked like a dandelion about to let go. She looked at me with raised eyebrows.

"Morning," I said as I gave her a side hug, which she didn't return. "I called the clinic already and left a message. No word yet."

She nodded slowly.

"How awful was your night?"

She stared at me. "Thank God for pharmaceuticals." Her voice was flat, matching her eyes.

"Can you sleep some more? It's still early."

She shook her head and grabbed a coffee cup from the cupboard. "No. And you're not exactly quiet in the morning," she groused as she poured herself coffee.

"Sorry. I'm used to being alone. I'm going to call my manager in a few minutes and take the day off."

She stared at me, took a long slurp of coffee, then got up and added milk. "Peanut," she said, her back toward me. "I think I want to be alone this morning."

It caught me off guard. She continued. "Nothing personal, but after being with Tommy in Vegas and now this—I want to deal with this alone, without you staring at me." She turned to measure my reaction.

"I get it. Sorry if I've been hovering. I've been worried."

"I know. And I know you feel terrible. But I need some space, you know? I don't want to go home without her, but I don't want to stare at each other until the phone rings, either. I need some time to process all of this. Is that terrible?"

Truthfully, it was a relief. I had already wondered how we'd spend the day other than pacing. If there was nothing we could do for Bitsy, going to work felt like a lovely distraction.

"It's not terrible," I said. "I completely understand. I'll bike to work so you can have my car. The minute either of us hears anything, we can call each other. I can leave work at any time." I cringed inwardly as I said it. Another emergency exit meant somebody else finished my work. But it was a no-brainer.

"I want to be strong. I want to prepare myself for whatever happens," she said. Then she cried just a little. I went to her, and she let me hug her—fully this time. I remained, recognizing the small remnants of sorrow that sometimes gather themselves up, burn themselves out, and give you more room to breathe.

"I found this quote," she said into my neck, garbled so I could barely hear. I pulled away. "I found it in the middle of the night. 'How lucky I am that I had something that makes saying goodbye so hard,' or something like that. It made me appreciate that although this sucks right now, at least I had her for a while."

"Wait. Celia, she might make it through this. She'll most likely be fine and back to her diva self."

"I know. But I'm trying to steady myself. To be ready. Maybe then it won't be so awful."

"You can't pre-grieve," I said softly.

"I know. But I've watched what you've gone through. It looks terrible. And she's just a dog." Crying again, soundlessly.

"It doesn't matter if it's a dog or a parent, C. The stronger the love, the more it hurts. But that quote is a good one, and it's true; the love is worth the pain. I've heard it before." I didn't mention that I'd heard it from Ryan. I shook away the memory of him reciting it for me at Bellatonia.

"Shakespeare, isn't it?" I asked.

She giggled. "Close. Winnie-the-Pooh."

✦✦✦✦✦✦

After assurances from Celia that she'd reach out if she needed anything, I got ready quickly and biked to work. It felt good to move my legs, empty my brain, and listen to the rhythmic sound of bike tires on the pavement. It was a cool morning, and I barely broke a sweat.

Before the bank even opened, my first call was to a locksmith. I left a message that I needed all my locks changed and asked them to call me back. After that, the drive-through lane was busy enough to keep me from my cyclical ruminating. Mostly. Mid-morning, my phone vibrated with a call from Celia, and I grabbed it immediately. A car pulled into the lane, but I ignored it.

"C? How is she?"

"Dr. Brisbain called. Bits is stable. I wanted better news than that, but that's all she would say. Stable."

"Stable," I repeated. I had no idea what that meant. *What is 'stable' for a dog? If she improved, would she have long-term effects? Could she get worse?* The ruminating started again, chasing its tail.

"It's not good, but it's not bad," Celia softly explained. She sounded exhausted, like putting together words was too much work. I felt terrible. *This is my fault. I should be there with her.*

"Do you want me to come home?"

"No."

I tried to walk the line between supportive and hopeful. "Okay, then I'm going to focus on stable. Stable sounds good. How are you doing? Do you need anything?"

"I'm fine. I like the quiet here." She agreed to call when she knew more, and we hung up. I helped my irritated customer while Celia's sad voice swirled in my head. Then I drafted a text to Ryan and read it dozens of times between customers, hoping to sound as neutral as possible until I figured things out. I finally sent it over my lunch hour:

I need to take a break, Ryan. Things are happening in my life that

165

need some attention. I appreciate all we've shared, but I need some space before I see you again.

He called twice that afternoon, leaving messages. I deleted them both. I deleted his texts asking for details, too. I felt so confused and listless—so unsure of anything—and the only thing I knew that would help was waiting at the yoga studio. Needing more movement and inspiration, I signed up online for Nena's next class.

At the end of the day, I biked home and checked in with Celia, who was waiting for another callback from the vet and a takeout delivery from Tommy. By six o'clock, I was on my mat. The warm room and Nena's encouragement lulled me into a soft concentration, something that felt manageable. "Breathe in, creating a full belly," Nena said. "Fill the basement of your lungs with as much good, fresh air as you can. Breathe out at a steady pace, emptying out the lungs. Empty out all that old, used air."

I closed my eyes and did as instructed. The breathing gave my muscles and heart some much-needed oxygen, and I started to feel better. After class, I stayed in the sweltering room and relaxed in corpse pose. I heard whispered conversations behind me and the heavy door creak as it opened and closed. When I finally opened my eyes and sat up, I could see in the mirror BJ and Nena huddled in the back of the room. As I rose to roll up my mat, I was unable to look away, captivated by their intimacy. BJ's posture and stance were almost subservient, and she didn't look like herself. Her hair was greasy, and she looked disheveled. Nena reached over and squeezed BJ's forearm, who flinched as she glanced toward me. I looked away, already feeling like I was seeing something I shouldn't. I put my head down, finished cleaning my mat, and quickly left the room.

When I got home, I found Celia at my computer, an opened bag of red licorice at her side. "How did it go today?" I asked.

She held up a finger, absorbed in something on the screen. I gave her some space and began unpacking my various bags from the day: lunch bag, yoga bag, purse. Some days I feel like I should pull a trailer. The kitchen counter was a parade of dishes Celia had used during the day. I joined her and tried again, standing behind her with my hands on her shoulders.

"What're you doing?"

She turned, licorice hanging from her lips like a sodden straw. "Shopping." She looked up at me, gray circles underscoring her green eyes. "It was a hard day. Dr. Brisbain asked me to stop calling."

She pointed to the laptop screen. "I decided that if the worst thing happens, I need to be prepared. I'll probably have Bitsy cremated. I shopped for caskets, but they were all ugly, and she deserves the best. Look." She pulled up another tab, a photo of a silver pendant with a tiny clear cylinder.

"It's a necklace for her ashes," she explained. "So she'll be with me all the time."

My shoulders drooped. I didn't know what to say.

"I could also have them sewn inside a Build-a-Bear. I've read about people doing that."

"Celia—"

"Let me do what I need," she told me. She straightened up and closed the computer and the subject. "I still haven't had my bath. Where is your loofah?"

I gave her a look. "I'm not a loofah girl. Besides, is that something two people should share?"

"Or maybe you should go first," Celia suggested, nose crinkled with disgust. "You reek."

I agreed with her. "Growth smells, my friend. I'll be quick. I want to do some more research on Ryan. I can't seem to let go of the why. If he's the one that did all this to me, I don't understand. Why?" I was glad Celia left my question unanswered.

Clean and fragrant, I returned to my computer for a fresh investigation into public court records again. I typed in Ryan's name, expecting a long process like my last search. But this time, Ryan's name showed up instantly. A restraining order filed against Ryan Hobart of Dane County. There it was—black, white, and obvious all over.

I slumped into the chair and closed my eyes.

"Do you have an LBD?" Celia asked, startling me. She stood in the kitchen doorway in my robe, hair in a towel, waiting for her tub to fill. She looked like she was about twelve.

I quickly closed the laptop lid, shame coloring my cheeks. "A what?"

"A little black dress. In case, you know, we have a funeral."

"Celia," I started to protest gently.

"Do you think Aunt Dorothea would come? I want mourners." She fingered the end of the robe belt.

I started another protest, but she cut me off. "I know how it probably looks to you, but she's my touchstone, Sam. Every little part of our day wound around each other. I've never taken such good care of somebody before, and I feel like our spirits are interwoven. Like I know that if she has to go, she'll come back and visit me. It's that intense. And even hearing myself say that out loud is embarrassing after all you've been through. All your friend Ashley went through, too. But she's been there for me. You have too, of course, but Bits and I are together constantly. I'm trying to prepare myself for what could be the biggest hurt of my life. Whenever it happens."

I didn't have the heart to tell her she'd never be ready for that depth of pain. But I admired her attempt at control. I nodded my acceptance, she turned toward her bath, and I turned back to my bad news.

I opened the laptop and dug in. The restraining order was filed against Ryan a few weeks after we met. The petitioner's name wasn't provided, protecting his or her (I was betting on her) anonymity, but the respondent was undeniably Ryan.

How stupid could I have been? I fell for the classic "it's for a friend" ruse. As I weighed this new information against the curious events of the last few months, I pieced together each strange thing that had happened, matching it to Ryan's whereabouts. The phone hang-ups. The snake. The note on my car. And now Bitsy. I couldn't deny it any longer.

My stalker was Ryan.

Anger spread like fire through my body until I stood up quickly, knocking the kitchen chair over behind me. The sound of wood crashing on tile matched my mood.

I grabbed my phone and followed up with the locksmith I had called earlier in the day, leaving a furious message about their lack of customer service. Then I found another locksmith with a 24/7 answering service, and they promised a technician in an hour. Expensive but necessary. I turned the upended chair back on its legs and went outside and reprogrammed my garage code using directions pulled up on my phone. I checked that the windows and doors were all locked. Then I stood in the foyer, wavering between ashamed and irate, a foot on either side of the line.

CAMEL POSE should be entered into carefully; it can be quite unsettling physically and emotionally. It stretches open the chest, exposing the vulnerable heart. Be gentle with yourself and what arises.

CHAPTER 18

I WAS BACK TO STARING AT MY LAPTOP when Celia finished her loofah-less bath.

"Find something?" she asked.

I nodded slowly, not looking up.

"Let me see," she said as she came up next to me and grabbed the mouse, clicking through the screens like a gamer. "I'm getting good at this judicial system thing. Tommy has me check up on his guys all the time. There it is." She pointed toward the same entry I had found. "Definitely a restraining order against your hero."

I had held out a tiny hope my earlier research was wrong, but Celia's confirmation squashed it. My heart sank. Celia—bless her—didn't say anything. She simply put her chin on top of my head. I stared at words on the screen until they blurred.

"I should have followed up on this earlier. More often. Maybe then Bitsy wouldn't be—"

Celia leaned closer to the entry. "Wouldn't have mattered. This is filed outside of Dane County and just recently. Those smaller counties don't always have the staff to keep up with the data entry. Sometimes they get behind."

"How could I have been so dumb?" I whispered. "Look what I've done."

"*You* haven't done anything," she said, but didn't say any more, and we stayed silent until my phone rang. It was the first locksmith, claiming he didn't get my earlier call but could be there in ten minutes. He sounded a little bit afraid of me.

"I hired somebody else," I told him tersely. "Somebody I can count on."

He issued a tremulous apology and hung up, leaving me with my much-too-obvious projection: I was clearly the one who couldn't be counted on.

Another knock on the door, another jolt through my system. This time it was the locksmith we could count on. After a cursory glance at his vehicle in the driveway and matching the logo on his uniform and the hat on his head, I let him in. Celia went to the guest room, and I cleaned up the kitchen while the locksmith changed the locks. He was professional and efficient, but having a strange man in the house was still unnerving. Although from my vantage point, even the familiar ones weren't trustworthy.

ﬆﬆﬆﬆﬆ

I didn't see Celia the next morning. I assumed she slept as soundly as I did, knowing Bitsy was still in stable condition and the locks were fresh. I numbly went through my workday until she called me as the bank was closing. We were too busy for me to respond, so when I didn't answer, she texted instead.

Celia: *When are you coming home?*

And five minutes later: *I talked to the clinic.*

My stomach dropped. It stayed there while I helped last-minute customers, trying not to throw up on a deposit slip. When the bank finally closed, I snuck a quick response to Celia's text.

Me: *On my way soon. What's going on?*

No response. I tried again. Nothing.

As soon as I balanced my cash drawer, I made a beeline home. Nausea had become a fist-sized knot in my stomach, and I rubbed it while I ran inside.

Celia stood at the kitchen island with a look I couldn't decipher. The knot pulled itself tighter. Music from *Les Misérables* played softly in the background. It felt melancholy, and I began wading into the familiar path of my own grief. *No. No. Please, no bad news about Bitsy.* I pulled myself back, waiting to hear what Celia had to say, still feeling my sadness in manageable little gulps. I breathed into the feelings rather than stiffening against them. It was true what Nena said in class: "You're going to need what you've learned here when you aren't on the mat. There's a reason it's called practice. You practice these skills so that it comes to you naturally when you are out in the world. When you need it."

I needed it. I braced myself as Celia moved toward me with her arms held out for a hug. Her body and her words shook me at the same time.

"It's Bitsy! She's going to make it!"

The embrace was tight; the news was good. The knot unraveled as relief made me weak, and I didn't fight the tears. Celia pulled away first.

"The clinic called and said she had a great night," Celia said. "Her vitals are normal again, and she's looking brighter. I begged them to let me visit her, but of course, they didn't want me to rile her up. But they said if she has another good night, I can get her tomorrow. Tomorrow! I have so much to do at my place. I want her homecoming to be perfect, you know?" She grabbed my hand, adding a little reassuring squeeze. "Bitsy is coming home!"

She was beaming and animated, and I was still processing in slow motion. I looked past her to the kitchen. Things were different. The dishes were done, and the windows were open. The humidity had dropped, and the summer breeze felt better than a fresh start. And something else; Celia was wearing makeup. It made me feel like things would be okay. Since Bitsy's poisoning, Celia had mostly stayed in her pajamas and stopped washing her hair, circumventing the natural order of things. Without her eyeliner and mascara, her face had been like a room prepped for a paint job, unfinished and unsettling. But now things could get better. The fake lashes were the proof.

I was opening a bottle of celebratory wine when we heard a knock at the front door. Ryan again? Celia and I shared another look, and I carefully looked through the pane. It was Finn. I unlocked the door as he came barreling through. He took in the wine bottle in my hand and Celia behind me and flushed.

"Oh, hi, Celia. I'm sorry to interrupt," he said with an uncomfortable nod to her. She returned the nod, although the rest of her body became unnaturally still. They stared at each other, not moving, until her fingers finally reached up and ran through her hair.

He pointed toward me. "We need to talk."

We headed to the kitchen, leaving Celia with the wine. "What's up?" I asked.

He perched on the edge of a counter stool and bounced his left foot. "I know you didn't want me to, but after this mess with the dog being poisoned, I looked up Hobart. It's not good."

"I know. I did research of my own," I said.

"Well, your research and mine probably differ. I have access to the responding officer's notes. Hobart basically stalked a woman and scared the shit out of her. This ends *now*." His eyes got big, like my mom's. It literally made my heart hurt. "I came over to make sure you were being safe. Doors locked, place secured." He looked around, taking it all in. He had always been a "noticer," but being on the force had only heightened his observation skills.

I pointed toward the door he had come through. "Locksmith was here last night." He nodded his approval. He paced the kitchen, eyes wild, winding down slowly.

"How's Celia?" He looked toward the living room, where we could hear the soft murmurs of a phone call.

"Why don't you ask her yourself?"

"I—I don't want to make it worse." For all his bluster when he walked in the door, he was suddenly mousy.

Wait. Don't tell me something happened between Finn and Celia. And I didn't know? "What's up with the two of you?" I asked.

"Nothing," he said defensively. "Completely out of my league."

"She's not," I said gently. "You'd be good for each other." *Much better for her than Tommy, for sure.* "You should spend more time with her—win her over. Start tonight."

He stood up taller. "We have enough to worry about with this Hobart issue."

"Chicken," I said.

Celia chose that moment to walk into the room. "We're having chicken? I am a little hungry." She smiled at my brother. "Are you cooking, Finn?"

He stood. "I heard about your dog. I'm really sorry."

"Thank you, Finnegan. But we found out she's going to be fine!" Celia's voice floated up an octave while she threw her arms in the air.

"That's great." He blinked quickly, feeling behind him for the safety of the kitchen stool.

"Finn," I interjected to save him, "would you mind taking Celia to her place? She's decided she's ready to sleep in her own bed, and I'd feel better if you took her home."

Celia agreed. "Would you mind, Finn?" Head tipped, her flirting techniques were back to normal, too. Maybe even over the top.

"Not at all. I have a call to make, and then we can load your stuff." He shot me a look that somehow combined panic and possibility at the same time. Finn was the opposite of a player; he'd only had one meaningful relationship in his life, one that devastated him when it ended. We had both loved her. She ended the relationship abruptly and took us both out at the knees, and Finn's confidence with women was obliterated in the wreckage. But tonight, he was on his own.

We packed up the things Celia had spread over my house during her stay, and after hugs and goodbyes and Finn's final tug on the door to make sure it was locked, they were gone. And then, as much as I had been craving solitude, it was suddenly too quiet. Celia's and Finn's voices reverberated in the stillness, crowding out thoughts desperate for their own time. But I wasn't ready to face them. In an old, familiar move, I called Pen to distract me. I realized I hadn't heard from her in a while. Although she didn't answer, the familiarity of her voice in the greeting reoriented me in a small way.

Calls to Pen for distraction, validation, and commiseration were once the norm. I hadn't been that vulnerable with anybody since. Living with Celia underscored how guarded I am, regardless of how much I love her. I accept her but don't rely on her. I try not to rely on anybody and as a result, my friendships haven't ever been effortless. Somehow it's easier for me to compete with women than be close to them. In my running days, I had always admired the sprinters, outgoing and fun, laying their cares and sweat and vulnerability on the track until the next race. They only moved forward. As a long-distance runner, I gravitated toward being a loner, and my collegiate runner friends were the same. My last true intimate friendship was with Pen, but we were childhood friends, so life had happened to us simultaneously. There were no secrets to challenge us.

As an adult, I had created a protective layer that required heavy lifting from anybody interested in me. *Was I too much? Not enough?* I wore a coat of self-consciousness that kept me constantly questioning myself. It kept people I valued from seeing who I really was—the coat massaged the message. It was draining carrying it around. The only time I took it off was during a run. But it was useful. It was protection in case people like Ashley turned on me.

And now Ashley was dead. Memories of her looped on a reel in my head, spliced by the knowledge of her murder. I paced, trying to make sense of things. I couldn't stop the circular thoughts from draining me.

I finally called Aunt Dorothea.

"Wanna grab dinner?" I asked lightly, even though my need was heavy.

"Sam! Everything okay?" she asked. I could hear birds in the background, and she intuitively heard what was behind my call, too.

"All good. We need to celebrate Bitsy's good news."

"Gladly. I was so happy to get your text. I can't wait to hear the details. Let me spruce up a bit first."

I knew she was already spruced. "I'll pick you up in a half-hour," I told her.

We went to her favorite Italian chain restaurant. She wore a lavender cardigan over a long-sleeved shirt, which seemed much too hot and made her skin look pallid. We each ordered a margarita, and she took a hearty first taste.

"That's so good," she said, licking her lips. "They add amaretto to these to make them Italian." She pronounced it *Eye-talian*. "So why isn't Celia joining us for this lovely dinner?"

"She went home to prepare for Bitsy's homecoming." Aunt Dorothea smiled. Then I gave her the rundown on Bitsy, and she delighted at every turn. "So this is a celebration and a thank you for helping me with Bitsy," I said. We toasted to Bitsy's health. I had to admit that the amaretto was a good touch.

She waited until our food was carefully placed in front of us before whispering. "Did you figure out who left the muffins? That's been concerning to me," she added.

I bought some time with a straw full of margarita. I couldn't tell her about Ryan. Not yet, anyway.

"She hasn't answered my text yet, but I'm betting on Ella," I said, hedging before a quick change of topic. "And although I feel terrible about the reason, it was nice having Celia around. I got used to it. Now that she's gone, it's too quiet."

"I'm quite familiar with that problem," she said. "Too much time and quiet to think." She circled her fork with an abundance of fettuccine and savored the first bite.

"How do you do it?" I asked, voice cracking. "You've lost more people over the years than I have. Sometimes it's overwhelming. Does it get easier?" This was territory I hadn't intended on slogging. I took a breath to steady myself so I didn't sob while eating *Eye-talian*.

Aunt Dorothea wiped her mouth but still had a smear of grease on her chin. "I don't really know, honey. Sometimes the pain is so sharp I can't help but experience it. After your uncle Rich died, every so often I had to pull the car to the side of the road to yell and cry," she admitted. "I don't know when that stopped, but after a while, the yelling went away." She looked up at me. "I still cry. I miss him every day. But I do know the more I avoid the pain, the worse it becomes."

She reached over and patted my hand. "I know you've suffered more than your share," she said. "Losing your parents this early; it isn't fair. There's no getting over that. But it is possible to go around it. I see so much of them—both of them—in you. They're going to live on in you."

She grabbed her napkin to wipe her eyes. I did the same and then reached over and wiped her greasy chin. "Things are never what you think they'll be," I said softly.

"I know. But you'll get through it. You're an amazing girl, Samantha," she said.

"With an amazing aunt," I added.

She smiled at me weakly and reached for her margarita. "I must have spilled mine," she said sheepishly. "Are you supposed to be drinking alcohol with your sodium issues?"

"I've got it under control, Aunt Dorothea. I've been taking care of myself. Don't worry."

She took another big drink and licked the salt from the rim. "I do worry. I can't help it. Any word on that private school job?"

I blanched as I remembered my fake job interview. It felt like such a long time ago, that lie. "No. For now, I'm happy at the bank. I'm thinking about taking some classes, though. I might want to coach." I surprised myself again with the things that rolled off my tongue when I was with her. I had been thinking about coaching. It was a new idea that I hadn't parsed yet, but as I said it out loud, it sounded good. And if I wasn't going to be honest with Aunt Dorothea about Ryan and his stalking, at least I could share this.

"I'm so glad. That's a good sign." She grabbed a straw to inhale the few remaining droplets from the bottom of her glass, slurping loudly until she consumed it all. "That's a very good sign," she repeated. "You sound like you're handling things. Maybe now would be a good time to start going to church?"

When the waiter wasn't looking, Aunt Dorothea shoved the extra breadsticks into the ziplock bag she had hidden in her purse. I drove her home and gave her a long hug before saying goodbye. She grabbed her leftovers, seemingly unfazed by the alcohol, and turned to me.

"Thank you for supper." She held up the bag. "Leftovers and love. I made out like a bandit!"

Once home, I tried to shut down my brain as I shut off the lights and went to bed, a sweating glass of ice water on my nightstand for cleansing. I needed to do better on so many fronts, including my electrolytes, but decided to cut myself a little slack for the night. Restless sleep was punctuated by dreams where I yelled for help, but people couldn't understand me because I was mummified in heavy fabric. I was grateful for my alarm in the morning so I could finally go to work, where quarters and dimes were separated into discernible trays, and the inside of a roll of coins held exactly what you imagined.

Try **REVOLVED CRESCENT LUNGE** when you struggle with pent-up emotion.
A deep immersion into this twist can cleanse the liver and release anger.

CHAPTER 19

THE MORNING WAS GRAY, SO I TURNED ON THE NEWS for the noise.
Even Gayle King's cheery pragmatism couldn't nudge me from my
inertia, without Celia's chatter or Bitsy's patter. And now that Ryan
wasn't who I thought he was, I couldn't stop looking at my future
through the shroud of loneliness. Things improved when Pen called
back that night, excitement in her voice.

"Hey—I had a great idea. I have a conference in Omaha next week.
Could you meet me? For the weekend?"

I thought about all the reasons I shouldn't: more time off from work,
being available to Celia in case she and Bitsy needed me, and, of course,
the most salient; what if whatever Pen and I had wasn't the same?

"I really miss you," Pen tried persuasion in a sing-song way.

"Let me check on a couple of things," I said. But I knew I'd make it
work. The chance to see Pen was served with a side dish of synchronicity
and it would be perfect timing to get the hell out of dodge. We hung
up, and I walked around my living room thinking about logistics. As I
glanced out the front window, I noticed a red pickup parked across the
street that seemed out of place somehow.

I looked closer at the driver. It was Ryan, looking straight at me. Our eyes met, and I slowly backed away from the window. Those same aquamarine eyes that had captivated me were now hardened and hawk-like. I double-checked the lock on the front door and called Finn. Then I moved to the kitchen, not sure what to do with myself or how I should feel. Memories of Ryan lined up like a grainy video—his boat shoes and picnic basket; his hand on my neck, pulling me closer; his eyes, laugh, smell.

The slam of a car door brought me back. Finn was in my driveway in less than five minutes, an impressive blur of dark blue hustling from his squad car to my front door.

I barely unlocked it before he lurched inside. "Where is he?"

"He was there." I pointed to the empty spot across the street.

"When did he leave?"

"Right after I called you. He was in a truck I've never seen before."

Finn stepped around me and moved through my rooms like a detection dog, quivering nose on high alert. He grabbed for the mic on his lapel as if he were going to radio in, then stopped himself. The protocol for being a brother wasn't as clear as it was for being a cop. It was unnerving to see him this rattled. I moved back to the kitchen island and sat, hoping he would follow.

"How long was he out there?" He looked at me before his eyes darted around the kitchen.

"I don't know. I called you the minute I saw him. But Finn—he didn't actually do anything. He was just sitting there across the street." I wished I didn't sound so defensive.

"Yeah, and that's how it starts, Sam. If he's anything like the rest of the creeps in the world, it will escalate into stuff you can't even imagine. We need to take care of this. Now." He kept his hand on his holster.

"I know," I said. "I have no clue what I'm doing. What should I do? I haven't officially broken up with him or anything. I told him I needed space."

"No more contact with him. Period. Has he been calling?"

I nodded.

"Texting?"

I nodded again.

"Save everything. Ignore him, but save every contact he makes with you. No talking to him, responding to emails, nothing. Understand?"

"I got it, Finn. No contact."

He paced around the room like he had before. "You also need to write everything down. All the things that have happened to get you to this point. We need a record of it all. Write down everything you can think of that is pertinent. And keep track every time you see him drive by." He walked around my kitchen perimeter, pulling up the back of his duty belt. Finn had always hated tight belts or tight clothes, and the uniform must've driven him crazy. "I'll call you later today when I'm on duty, but for now, make sure you are careful."

"Okay. I promise—and thanks for coming over. There's one more thing," I said, waiting a beat. "I've been thinking of going home."

He looked at me the way only brothers can, like I'd grown a beak or announced I was marrying a wombat.

"Home?"

"To Omaha. Pen Edmonton's going to be there and wants to meet up. I'd love to get away. I also want to see our old life." It sounded strange when I said it, but it was the truth. "Don't give me shit, but I want to remember it. Or reconnect with it." I shuffled uncomfortably, waiting for him to, indeed, give me shit.

He didn't bite. "Pen? What's she up to now?"

"I found her again. She lives in Maine but will be in Omaha next weekend. I know it's last minute, but any chance you want to come with me?" I pouted a tiny bit, a tactic that always worked on my dad.

Finn watched me through squinted, cynical eyes. It was becoming his face's resting pose.

"But what do you know about Pen now?"

"Stop. It's Pen."

"You never know," he said, shaking his head.

"Do you want to go or not? Or wait—did something happen between you and Celia the other night? Maybe you're *lovahs* now, and you don't want to be away?" I stretched out the word *lovahs* in such an aggravating way that I worried I pushed too far.

He sighed. "Funny. So are you admitting your driving sucks, and you need somebody to take you to Omaha?"

"No, I'm asking my annoying brother if he'd like to accompany his sister, who is slightly freaked out and could use a friend."

He was quiet for a while, and I could see him give it serious consideration.

"Actually, the timing works pretty well," he admitted. "It would be good to get you out of here, and I have a couple of days off. Maybe I'll look up a few of my old buddies, too. But I get to drive."

"Then I choose the music."

"Deal."

And that was it. With brothers, the less said, the better. I could have told him that I appreciated him, felt safe with him around, and loved him, but that would have made him retreat wherever boys go. It was enough that I asked and enough that he said yes.

Finn waited until he heard me lock the door before he walked to his car with one last belt tug. I watched him leave, noting the familiar cowlick that curled at his collar. It swirled to the right and had prevented him from achieving the Leonardo DiCaprio haircut he wanted in his teens. It somehow made me feel better that not everything has to change.

My phone rang and I jumped; I hadn't even realized it was still in my hand.

"What's wrong?" Ella said when she heard my voice. I must have a telling hello.

"Nothing. Tired. What's up?"

"I'm babysitting. Soooo bored. Then I realized that I need to get some new volleyball shorts, and Mom is gone, so there's no food at my house, so I'm going to the mall tomorrow after work. Sheriff Dad has finally released me from my jail sentence. Wanna come? Any more hot dates you need to shop for?"

I hesitated, not sure I could compartmentalize the events of the past few days well enough to pull off a lighthearted shopping trip. I wanted to shield Ella from knowing the details of life's depressing realities. On the other hand, it might be fun. And how many more times would Ella ask me to accompany her like this?

"Hello?" she whistled.

"Sorry. Actually, I could use some yoga clothes."

"Cool. I'll pick you up tomorrow, probably around six." Which meant she'd be there at seven.

Hearing the animation in Ella's voice buoyed me a bit. I realized that another night at home, watching for Ryan and feeling hinky, sounded terrible. If I hurried, I could make it to an evening yin class, so I threw on some passable yoga clothes and rushed to the studio, adrenaline and suspicion fighting to ride shotgun.

As the last one into the studio, I took the last space closest to the door. There was no time for my requisite stop in the bathroom, which gave me another layer of worry. *Will I make it through these next sixty minutes? What if I suddenly have to go? Has anybody ever left in the middle of class before? At least I'm close to the door.* Even as I obsessed, I knew it was my brain's way of avoiding the big things by focusing on the small.

I floated in and out of attentiveness in class. I followed instructions, shutting off my brain except for physical cues until the instructor—a short woman with a pixie haircut and dangling earrings that looked like fish lures—reached inside my scared, angry, pained heart.

"Open it all up on the mat. It's safe here. Let your body relax and unroll some of those fears. Or the anxiety. Or the pain you feel. It might seem huge to you, but give it a boundary. It can be contained right here on your mat. Picture it enclosed in this space so it isn't overwhelming."

That seemed manageable. I conjured up all the terrible things that had been happening around me: my parents' deaths, Ashley's murder, Bitsy's poisoning, Ryan's betrayal, and the rest of my screwed-up life. I pictured it as one big, ragged tumbleweed—large, dry, dangerous. Then I imagined myself kicking it. I watched as I angrily rammed my foot into the corpus, breaking it into thorny pieces. I pictured taking a baseball bat to the pieces on the floor, crushing them into a fine dust that had no power. I knew I'd still have to sweep up, but it was on my terms now. I had gained purchase on the events that were out of my control, and I never even left my mat.

That night I slept with such depth that it almost made me tired. And in the morning, the world looked new.

※

The next day Pen left me a message with details about our meetup in Omaha. Her voice sounded tempered; all her enthusiasm for our trip was gone. I tried not to take it personally and hoped it was the usual minutiae of life. Ella picked me up after work, only a half-hour late. Her driving skills were improving, but she was still easily distracted. Amid a diatribe about Paige (current nemesis) and Miranda (current bestie), I looked in the passenger-side mirror and saw a small, dark, two-seater a few cars back. It darted in and out of traffic, almost copying our movements. My stomach lurched. *Was it Ryan? Was it his car? Or his license plate?* I stopped listening to Ella and focused intently on the car's driver, who was clearly a single occupant, definitely male, but I couldn't tell if it was Ryan. I leaned closer to Ella's side mirror as the sports car disappeared from my view.

"What is up with you?" Ella said loudly.

I held up a finger and turned around in my seat to watch behind us. The car found an opening in traffic, pulled into the lane next to us, and sped up. I quickly faced forward and looked at the driver as the car flew past.

Not Ryan. Not even a male. A woman with enormous sunglasses and attitude, based on the look she shot me.

"Seriously. Are you okay?" Ella asked, moderately annoyed with me.

"Sorry. I thought I saw somebody I knew."

"That's random."

"I know." As if on cue, my phone buzzed. It was a text from Ryan: *Thinking of you.* With flower emojis. I didn't open it but turned back to Ella. "What were you saying? Miranda said what?" The Miranda-Paige saga continued. I tried to listen to what seemed trivial while tamping down my anger and rubbing the tension from my neck.

Ella rushed me through the mall until we reached a store with a wall of cologne at the entrance and an overcharged bass in the back. She moved through the store like a hawk, scanning the sales rack like it was a field of mice. She looked up at me mid-pounce.

"Aren't you going to try anything on?" she asked.

"I feel like I'm too old for this store," I said, looking around. "Plus, I'm not thrilled with how my body has changed since I stopped running," I admitted quietly.

She heard it and stopped the hunt. "Why are you always so hard on yourself?" she asked, tipping her head. "You say that kind of stuff all the time."

I didn't have an answer for her. In fact, her question caught me off guard. As I struggled to respond, a sales clerk approached, offering us a dressing room, mercifully giving me some time. Ella gathered her arm full of hangers and followed. When she got to the dressing room, she held the door open with her butt and turned around. I hovered, not sure if I should follow her inside. She waved me in. "You need to tell me how these look."

I sat on the cheap chair in the corner and held her bag. How many hours had my mom spent in changing rooms with me? She would perch in the corner and I tried on clothes, never self-conscious. I figured she grew my body inside of hers and had the right to see it change through the years. My mom and aunts never hid their bodies from me, either. Their transparency had been a gift. I saw how naturally the female body changes. Trying on outfits alongside my mom always felt like the before and after of things.

If she wasn't trying on clothes for herself, my mom would take on the dual roles of consultant and maid. The gift of having her there was lost on me at the time. I'd try something on and then hand it to her when I was done. Only once I started trying on clothes by myself did I realize what a luxury her undivided attention had been.

In my mom's honor, I tried to be Ella's consultant and personal assistant. Ella seemed oblivious, narrating and preening and handing me the discards. While in the throes of a volleyball play-by-play, Ella was interrupted by sounds from the dressing room adjacent to ours.

"Mom! That looks so stupid. I already told you that!"

Ella and I looked at each other, eyebrows raised. I was glad to see my niece's shock at somebody's vitriol toward their mother. I knew Ella and her mom had issues, but I couldn't imagine her speaking to her mother that way.

"NO. I said the blue one. The BLUE one!"

We couldn't hear the mother's response, but it sounded like a muted apology.

"I need a smaller size. They're over by the jeans." The daughter sighed dramatically. "Forget it. I'll go myself." She threw open the dressing room door, let it slam against the opposite wall, and marched back out into the store. I was up and out of Ella's dressing room almost before I knew what I had done.

She was jerking hangers on the rack, looking for her size. I came up next to her and pretended to be shopping, sliding hangers in the same way but without such angst.

"I heard you in the dressing room," I said to her, not looking up.

She stopped moving. "What?" She sounded incredulous in the way only teenagers can.

"I heard you in the dressing room," I repeated. "Is that your mom?"

"Yeah. So?" Her hip jutted out, and she went back to her hanger yanking.

I faced her. "You need to show her some respect. She gave you life, a roof over your head, and food to eat. She's shopping with you now. You know how many girls would kill to have their mom take them shopping? You know how lucky you are to be in the same room with her?"

She backed away, scowling under eyebrows that had good practice.

My voice dropped, and my pulse rose. "Someday, you'll be shopping and would give anything to have your mom close enough to touch."

I looked at her straight-on. "You don't even know how much you're going to miss her," I said.

I turned around and left her speechless. Out of the corner of my eye, I saw someone sidestep away from me toward the camouflage of a display, probably afraid of me. I didn't care. Ella stared at me when I joined her again, where I resumed my spot in the corner and hung clothes in silence while she tried on another pair of jeans. She looked a tiny bit afraid.

She was probably justified. Grief looked different from day to day, and apparently, unexpressed rage was the special of the day. Every so often, reality would sideline me. My parents wouldn't see Ella graduate, wouldn't meet Finn's wife (if he ever got one), and would never see the fruition of things they'd started. Nothing would ever be the same. Someone had taken all that away from me, and my anger was unpredictable and impartial. I was learning that grief is a formidable and quiet companion, but anger is sneaky and erratic, striking without warning.

"You okay?" Ella asked softly, for the second time that day. I was staring at the carpet, clothes twisted on my lap.

"Oh, yeah," I said with a low laugh. "It pisses me off when people take things for granted." Ella watched me for a second, and I could tell she wondered if I was referring to her. I waved her off and told her the jeans were perfect. She slowly began talking again, chatting about the upcoming school year, kids in her grade, and how clueless they were. She was thinking about joining forensics. Maybe get a job. She was dreading geography, but English would be easy.

"Last year, Brandon was in my English class," Ella said. She caught herself as a flush spread across her cheeks. "If I tell you something, promise you won't tell?"

"Depends. If it's bad, that puts me in an awkward position with your dad."

"It's nothing like that," she said quickly. "But Brandon finally asked me out. Officially. We're going to Devil's Lake next week."

"On a 'date'?" I said, exaggerating the air quotes.

"No. Just 'hanging out.'" She returned my gesture with a wry smile and faced the mirror, smoothing the fabric over her flat abs. "But let me be the one to tell Dad."

"Of course," I said.

And then I made myself shut up. I wanted to lecture her about being careful, to warn her about being so charmed by attention that she could make ridiculous choices and lose a part of herself along the way. I wanted to caution her about ignoring signs she's too smart to miss. But I didn't say a word. I watched my niece, hopeful and naive, and hung discarded jeans in the corner. I was learning that we each had to figure out some things on our own.

Sometimes, it's essential to return to the basics. **CAT-COW POSE** is comprised of two counter poses; move between them with your breath, inhaling with cow and exhaling with cat. Bring awareness to how you're grounded. Appreciate your roots.

CHAPTER 20

FOR THE NEXT FEW DAYS I WAS VIGILANT about my surroundings, double-checking locked doors and watching for Ryan. I saw him everywhere, and yet I didn't. The fact that things were so quiet seemed to prove that he was behind the disturbing events of late, trampling the tiniest remaining bud of hope that he wasn't responsible.

Finn picked me up early Friday morning. Before we left the city limits and put some road between current events and past, I called Celia to check in on her and Bitsy. They were both happy as clams, according to Celia. "And not the naughty kind," she said with a throaty chuckle. I replayed my freak-out at the mall with Ella, ignoring the side-eye from Finn. The conversation sewed up the loose edges of one portion of my worries and felt good.

And then we were Nebraska-bound. It had been years since we had been there. There were few occasions for us to return home, which left me living a life that always felt slightly out of context. I never saw people from my past or ran into high school friends at the grocery store. Having reinvented myself as an adult, I always felt like the lines of my new identity blurred a bit without the outline of who I used to be.

Finn was a good diversion from my nerves about seeing Pen. Straight from the sibling handbook, he was quiet, didn't ask many questions, knew my history, and understood my familial shorthand—until he changed the rules after an hour on the road.

"We haven't had a chance to talk much about Ashley," he said. "Are you okay?"

"I'm trying to be. It's so horrible, Finn. I hadn't talked to her in years, but I did really care about her. She has a son. Had a son. And now he won't ever be the same. The stuff that happens to you as a kid lasts forever."

"True," Finn said. "I didn't know it at the time, but we had it pretty good."

A rusty truck pulled into the lane in front of us, accelerating with a thunderous rattle and a dark plume of smoke. The driver seemed oblivious to the chaos he caused behind him in the passing lane. *Why didn't people pay attention? It shouldn't be difficult: Slow traffic on the right. Lock your doors. Don't drive drunk.* I tensed, anger settling in my jaw.

"Why are people so clueless?" I blurted.

Finn looked at me questioningly. I pointed to the truck. "Asshole."

The sun was behind us, creating a haze on the horizon. The roads meandered through hilly moraines, flattening as we left Wisconsin. It felt good to get away from the upheaval of my life. I closed my eyes.

Finn's tapping—fingers on the steering wheel, off the beat but annoyingly loud—roused me from my unintended nap. Everything had been so exhausting of late. I opened my eyes and looked at him. He seemed irritated, or sad, or something else I couldn't read.

"What's up with you?" I asked, nodding to his tapping hands.

"Nothing." He squinted at the road and then seemed to override himself.

"What the hell, Sam? Why didn't you see through this Ryan dude from the start?" His intensity was startling. I repositioned myself in the seat and looked away. My eyes were still blurry from sleep, and the dairy cows were mere black spots dotting the farmland.

I cleared my throat. "I don't know why I couldn't see it. I've been asking myself that same question."

"You're smarter than that," he said. "And you have no idea the evil that's out there." I knew Finn had seen things on the job that he never talked about, things that generally corroded his view. "Has he been calling?"

"The first few days, it was every couple of hours. He left messages, but I didn't even listen to them. Now he calls twice a day. The calls are easy to ignore, but I can't avoid reading the texts. They're on my phone when I turn it on in the morning."

Finn sighed. "Did you bring the list of events we talked about? Everything that happened?"

"I did," I said, but I didn't pull it out of my bag. I found myself contorting my body away from him like I could twist away from the truth.

Finn didn't seem to notice. "Good. I want to pull together the facts. We're too busy at the station to have somebody on it, so email me the document so I can have Derek in the office file it for me." He waited a beat. "And you didn't instigate any contact?"

"No." *But I wanted to.* When I thought of him, my first inclination was to remember the Original Ryan—Mustache Man—not this new, alarming version. I missed the Ryan that I knew. It had started with such promise at the beginning of the summer, full of pad Thai, chocolate coins, and beverage napkins. The fact that he knew details about my running career made me feel relevant again. The relationship had unfurled easily, and I didn't want to remember its brown and ugly demise. I was embarrassed that I had been so blind and desperately placed too much hope in one person's lap.

"I don't get your attachment to him," Finn muttered.

"I guess I was lonely," I finally said. "There's something about being part of a couple that feels safe."

We were driving through Iowa, wholesome and flat. A car passed us like we were standing still, and Finn cringed. "Do you ever think about their last moment?" I asked him quietly.

Silence.

"Were they in the middle of a conversation? A fight? Or lost in their own thoughts?"

"Jesus, Sam."

"I know. But these are the things that keep me up at night." Some nights I woke with a clear vision of the accident, the physical altercation of car hitting car. I could hear the sounds of metal crushing and tires screeching. *Did they yell? Were there words? Did my mom grab my dad's hand and squeeze it, knowing their time had come?*

I started to cry, little tenets of sadness that had accumulated for some time. Finn reached over and cupped my shoulder, perfectly placed and awkward at the same time. But it loosened him a little, and I noticed his breathing changed like he was holding onto something, too.

I watched the cars on the road, moving around each other as if choreographed, and then I watched my brother at the wheel, wondering if we were both destined to be alone. *At what point do people accept that their chance for love has passed? There must be some point at which it is prudent to give up. Maybe this was it. I'd need to do better at being single. I should probably start going to restaurants by myself more often to get used to it. Maybe buy smaller bags of tortilla chips. Wine comes in individual bottles; that might be a good start. Or boxes of wine. I wonder how long those would last. A good math problem: If Single Sam buys one box of wine and drinks two glasses per night, how long will the box of wine last?*

"Sam?" Finn looked my way with his head cocked. "You okay?"

I smiled. "Fine."

"Where do you go when you do that?"

"You don't even want to know."

"Celia told me you do that a lot," he said.

"Oh? This was during your trip to her house? Pillow talk?"

He ignored me, taking the next exit toward a truck stop. To the right were eighteen-wheelers parked in rows, facing out. "We have more to discuss," he said as an explanation. "But if I'm going to deal with you all the way to Nebraska, I need caffeine."

We reached the Nebraska state line, crossing the Missouri River, which put you on notice that things were about to change. Everything seemed different. And familiar. It was just like we left it and had also changed enormously. Cornfields on either side of the road welcomed us like a runway toward the tiny suburb we once called home, where there was a comforting symmetry in the placement of mailboxes, lawn chairs, and striped-green hostas. Once in a while, there was a surprise—maybe a potentilla or deflowered peony—but mostly, there was a secure nod to keeping things the same.

"Remember mowing the Pestellini's yard?" Finn said. "Wait, you never did. It was only me and Buck." He laughed. "Those kids were such brats. They'd throw stuff at us while we were mowing. I swear they were only two years younger than us, but there we were, mowing their lawn while they were inside watching TV. Buck used to taunt them to get them outside, then try to mow as close to them as possible."

"I was always babysitting. Remember the DeMain girls? All they wanted to do was hang out inside. Steve Cosgrove lived right next door, and I was sure he had a crush on me. I knew my life would change if I could move those girls outside."

We continued deconstructing the past through adult eyes until we parked on our old street. Everything looked shabby and a little sad. The steps to the Herman house, which I could take two at a time and Finn could manage three, were cracked and sagging to the right. The Conways had been meticulous about their lawn, but now it was overgrown and full of weeds. Each house wore the past twenty years. The trees were bigger, but the neighborhood was strangely quiet. No more bikes thrown haphazardly on the corner, no sprinklers in front yards, or swing sets in the back. A ghost town.

As if on cue, two kids in helmets biked up the street, barely skirting Finn's truck. I jumped. They were gone in an instant, and I watched them, tennis rackets peeking out the top of their backpacks, while I tried to catch my breath, mad that I had contaminated this moment of childhood nostalgia with my adult-like fear. Finn pulled away from the house, and I didn't look back.

We met Pen at Faust's, the same bar where we had first used our fake IDs. I had persuaded Finn to stay; I needed a barrier to my nerves. I was afraid that my memories of Pen would be wrong. I was hoping that she hadn't morphed into somebody I didn't like anymore or somebody I wouldn't be friends with now. Mostly, I didn't want to find out that she had been more important to me than I was to her.

My fear dissolved the second I saw her. She was sitting at the bar, facing the mirror. As we got closer, I could really see her; it was still twelve-year-old Pen, but muted. Her caramel hair was longer and highlighted. Age had softened her edges so that she looked approachable and happy. I recognized how she went from straight-faced to smiling instantly and tucked her hair behind her ear because she was nervous. I was instantaneously twelve again in her bedroom with the A-frame roof, listening to Annie Lennox on her stereo.

Pen saw me in the bar mirror and swiveled around. She was off the bar stool and in my arms before I knew it, and then looked over my shoulder and saw my brother.

"You brought Finn!" she said, much too loudly, in my ear. She hugged him tightly. The top of her wavy hair tickled his lips, and he made a face. I couldn't tell if he was pleased with her affection or, like back in the day, irritated by the both of us.

But he hugged her back. When she pulled away, she appraised him, still holding on to his arm. "Damn. I knew I should have married you," she said to him.

"I don't recall asking you," he shot back.

"You wouldn't have been able to handle me."

"Wouldn't have wanted to."

And we were off. Pen and I sat at the bar and faced Finn, who stood. While negotiating our space, acclimating ourselves to each other, and ordering a round of light beer to commemorate the past, I stopped to watch Pen and Finn. A familiar warmth spread through my chest that I hadn't felt in a long time, and watching these two—my earliest and truest friends—I felt secure. These two people were the footing for my heart.

"Hey, Dork, did you hear me?" Finn said, looking at me.

"She still does that?" Pen laughed. "That spacey thing?"

"Word on the street is that it's even worse these days," Finn added. He leaned past me to catch the bartender's attention, putting his hand on my shoulder. Maybe Finn was feeling it, too.

Conversation was easy. We talked about Pen's life in Maine, circled around to my life in Madison, and shared details of the years in between. After a couple of beers, I felt courageous enough to venture into the important, nosy stuff.

"When did you get divorced?" I asked.

"A couple of years ago. He was an asshole," Pen summarized as she took a long pull from her bottled Miller Lite. That hadn't changed either.

"You must have been too much alike," Finn teased, and she stuck out her tongue at him.

I kept digging. "How is it really? Having kids?"

"It's both exhausting and excruciatingly heart-warming at the same time," Pen said. "The twins are five, so sometimes that happens all in the same minute. I still can't believe that I'm trusted to care for human beings."

"Wait until they're teenagers," Finn said. We looked at each other as Ella came to mind.

"I'm dreading it," Pen said. "When they're little, you worry about them falling, choking, the mistakes you're making." She looked at Finn and rolled her eyes, knowing he'd have a comment. "But when they're older, the mistakes will be scarier."

"I can't imagine. I feel the pressure with Buck's daughter—" I started.

"Wait—Buck's a dad?"

"Yup. Ella is sixteen and always going through something. It's hard enough being an aunt. Can't imagine being a mom."

Pen sighed with what sounded like resignation. "I feel like I'm making it up along the way. Luckily my mom is a huge help. Wish I would have listened to her earlier."

"Like about Ron Ramsay?" I reminded her, and she laughed instantly. The shared memory required a glass clink for an upperclassman who went from classy to clingy in one quick date.

Pen and I were finally digging into the meat of things, so I was ready to excuse Finn from his chaperoning duties. "Speaking of losers, weren't you going to look up Riverton tonight? I don't want to make you late," I said to Finn.

"Nope. This is fascinating, TP," he said.

"I can't believe you still call her The Pain," Pen laughed.

"Right now, he's being the pain," I agreed. "You're harshing our vibe, Finn." He grinned at me over the top of his beer, and I realized he had been waiting for me to get to this point for a while. He finished his beer, set the empty on the bar, and looked at his phone. "They're picking me up in a few minutes, and then I'm staying at Riverton's. You two will walk to the hotel?" Always the safety monitor. We agreed to call him in the morning, but not too early. He leaned over to kiss us each on the cheek, another anomaly.

"Be good," he said and headed toward the door. I noticed he didn't even offer to pay.

We spun our chairs toward the bar. "I hope that's okay," I said to Pen. "I have no desire to see his friends, do you?"

She shook her head. "Not at all. Remember what a jerk Riverton was to me? I have no interest in seeing that creep. Speaking of bald, have you seen a recent picture of Tim Witherspoon? He used to be so hot. Still thinks he is. The kids who were so cool in high school never seem to get past that stage."

"I haven't seen pictures of anybody. That's part of the reason I wanted to come back. Once I left town, I really left town. I feel guilty that I haven't kept in touch with anybody since I moved away and started fresh. But since my parents died, I have this need to—I don't know—reconcile myself. To figure out who I was. Maybe that will help me figure out who I am."

Pen was quiet. *Too deep too soon?* She twirled her beer silently, watching it swirl from side to side. I started to change the subject, back to neutral ground, like the weather or dissing ex-cheerleaders, when Pen spoke so softly that I had to lean in to hear.

"I'm so sorry about your parents, Sam. I adored them." The twirling bottle slowed. "I wish I could have been there for you. I can't believe they're both gone." She looked at me with such earnest empathy that the room stilled. It was a tender moment sitting down and claiming space in a loud and raucous bar. Pen reached over for a hug and still, after all these years, smelled the same, a mixture of Pantene and something homegrown, like parsley.

"They loved you, too," I whispered and took a shaky breath. We sat linked like that for a short while. The bartender, who had been making his way over to us, quickly walked away. "Gee, your hair smells terrific," I whispered in her ear, hoping to hearken a memory and lighten the mood. It worked. As we readjusted and drank more beer, it occurred to me that our night together was a microcosm of the years we spent as best friends—laughing one minute and crying the next, undercurrents and over-sharing knocking into each other as they ran their course.

"I have serious regrets about so many things, Pen. I can't believe I let you slip away. We make these decisions when we're young and have no idea how they're going to play out. Do you ever think about all of that?"

"All the time." She nodded. "Especially now that I see how mean girls are to each other. I don't ever want my kids to treat people the way I did." She snuck a look at me. "The way we did."

I reached into my wallet and found my niece's school picture. "This is Ella."

She took the photo tenderly and studied it. "Very pretty. Buck's a good dad?"

"You wouldn't believe it. But whenever I spend time with Ella, I get a rush of memories about being that age."

She shook her head and handed the photo back. "What happened to us, Sam? We were 'good girls.' We did confirmation. We made hot pads by hand. How did we end up so mean?"

I shook my head. "Even if Ashley was the trigger, we should have done something about it."

"Can we blame her?" Pen looked sheepish. "Especially now?"

We were both silent, staring down at our drinks. It was the first mention of Ashley, and it stopped time.

"I don't know," I said. "Maybe it was all the Slayer we listened to. I'd like to think that something took hold of our brains. Ashley started that whole mess with the cafeteria ladies; I know that. It started out funny, then morphed into mean."

Pen nodded. "I know. And Larry Jacobsen." She shook her head.

"I feel awful that we were so mean to him. He's one of the people I thought I'd try to find while I'm here. I really want to apologize."

Pen swiveled quickly to face me. "You don't know?"

"Know what?"

"Larry Jacobsen is gone. Suicide."

I stared at her long enough to make her uncomfortable. She said it again. "Larry Jacobsen is dead."

"When?"

"A few months ago. Actually, it was around the holidays."

Pen's words felt like ice on my skin. The bar got louder. The bartender picked up my beer bottle to replace the napkin, and I watched him move in slow motion.

"I had no idea," I whispered.

"I assumed you knew. Apparently, he used a gun. His little sister— what was her name? Barbara? She was the one who found him. There was no dad in the picture, and their mom was in jail or treatment or something. I think there was a brother, but I'm not sure. Poor Larry." She motioned for another beer from the hovering bartender. When he looked at me, I shook my head.

"I can't believe it." I dropped my head and tried to absorb it. First, Ashley's murder and now Larry's suicide. It was too much. It would have been a good time for some yogic breathing, but the news was even too disturbing for that.

"I know," Pen said. She put her hand on my arm. "It's all awful. Look, let's go for a walk and get some air. They've redone the entire Old Market, and I want to show you. We'll figure out the rest later," Pen said. She left her full beer on the bar, paid the tab despite my objections, and we headed out the door. She put her arm around my waist, and I laid my overloaded head on her shoulder.

We walked together, the dark barely a sliver between our hips. Pen's long dancer's stride reminded me of Nena in the yoga studio; they both wore such natural gracefulness that I felt like I was constructed of chunky sweaters. Thinking of my new yoga world while deeply entrenched in my past was unnerving. I tried to pull back thoughts of either world and live in the moment, even silencing my phone.

The night air was sobering as Pen and I walked downtown. Uneven walkways and exposed warehouses were a perfect backdrop to our meandering, past renovated storefronts, and darkened, empty apartments.

Along the way, there was a lengthy series of striped, cement parking blocks with spaces in between. My body needed movement. I hopped on top of the narrow blocks, teetering from foot to foot, trying to balance while I moved.

Pen reached up a hand to steady me, but I moved away.

"I got this. I'm a yoga pro now," I said.

Pen laughed. "You seriously haven't changed, Sam. You've always needed to prove you can do it on your own."

"I have? Even back then?" I asked, hopping off the blocks to hear what Pen could tell me about myself.

She nodded. "Remember when we did that walkathon in fifth grade?

It was like twelve miles or something. Mr. Oz organized it and walked with us, and whenever we got tired, he gave us a piggyback ride. You were the only one who didn't accept a ride, Sam. You had to do it all yourself. Classic Sam."

I remembered. I wouldn't admit how sore my legs were and went home to a long bath. Mom woke me up in the tub, bubbles deflated, and the water tepid. That heady feeling of being faced with a challenge and pushing myself to prove my strength was the fuel that kept me competitive during my running career. It's what I relied on for years; now, it was one more thing that was lost to me. I was realizing how many things I needed to grieve.

And then, like I had hoped, Pen and I took turns presenting our tarnished past to each other, bringing each memory back out in the open and polishing it in the telling, trying to understand it in the context of adulthood on brick walkways and under gilded streetlights. There was a natural tenor to our movements, and I realized that the core of our friendship was still intact. We finally wore out and returned to the hotel, each climbing into a bed, whispering in the dark like in the old days.

The next morning my mouth felt like the inside of a fuzzy slipper owned by somebody with athlete's foot. Pen and I went out for breakfast, and I tried not to throw up in her rental car.

"I almost forgot," she said at breakfast that I didn't touch, "when I called my office today, they said I got a strange call on Friday. Seems weird." She took a bite of hash browns while I stifled a gag.

"Why?"

"My assistant said it seemed like someone was trying to get my itinerary. He asked when I'd be in Omaha. She didn't give out any details, but when they hung up, she did a reverse phone search. She's always got my back, swear to God."

"Who was it?"

"Some guy named Tommy Allgood? Alrood? I wondered if it sounded familiar. You know, with all the weird stuff going on."

Tommy Elrod. Celia's Tommy. A creeping sensation moved up the back of my neck. I took a deep breath to calm down. Another benefit from time on my yoga mat—learning how to calm the body's fight-or-flight response until the mind can decide if the danger is real.

"Have you heard from him since then?" I asked, fidgeting with my fork.

"Nothing since. Do you know him? Do I need to worry?" Pen stopped eating and wrinkled her forehead. Her divorce had already emptied her trust bucket. She was just building it back up and I hated to dip back in, but I wanted to keep her safe, too.

I tried to keep my voice steady, neutral. "It's my friend Celia's boyfriend. I'll call her today and find out what's going on. He's an entrepreneur who doesn't sleep, so I'm sure it's some new idea. But I'll make sure."

Entrepreneur. That was being kind. Why the hell would he call Pen? How did he even know about her? Tommy had some explaining to do.

Pen had an afternoon meeting, so we said a tearful goodbye after breakfast and promised wholeheartedly we'd stay afloat in each other's lives. I called Celia and left a message, trying not to let my irritation with Tommy infiltrate my words. I wasn't very successful.

Finn met me in the hotel lobby. He carried my suitcase while I carried my hangover, and we set out to spend the day exploring. I did my best to put aside thoughts of poor Ashley, adult Pen, and underhanded Tommy so I could sink into my history. Our history. We drove past our old elementary school, the church parking lot where I kissed Scott Secada, and the pharmacy where Buck got caught stealing a Mounds bar.

"If you're going to steal something, why the hell would you steal coconut?" Finn laughed. We pulled across the street to our old high school. Renovations had added another wing and about an acre of parking, and it barely looked the same. We climbed out of the truck toward the stadium entrance. The track lanes were faded, but the stripes and hash marks of the football field were crisp and straight, spruced up for the start of the school year.

Finn and I reminisced about Saturday mornings when we rode to the track in the old Buick Skylark. We'd run laps or race Dad, working up an appetite for breakfast at Little Pete's Diner. All my brothers except Buck ran track at this school, and we often joked about how much Jameson sweat sprayed the asphalt over the years. Eli had run a lightning-fast 800 and still held the school record.

"I could take him now," Finn said as we walked toward the track. "Maybe I'll run it today. You'll take a video."

But as we followed the sidewalk edging around a row of arborvitae, we were confronted by a new, sturdy gate. A massive fence closed off the track that was once open to the community. Although the stadium was dedicated to a beloved football coach who gave everybody a chance, the implication was that not "just anybody" was welcome there.

"Bummer," Finn said. "But tell Eli I ran it, okay?"

We looked through the bars of the railing to the charcoal-colored track. It looked smaller than a 400 meter, although I remembered days when the straightaways felt like miles. Alumni money had been well-spent on new bleachers, insignia painted on the football field, a sky box, and banners. It was the same foundation but prettied up. I thought I'd be moved by my past, but I realized that the life I left behind had already moved on. Instead of standing still while I was gone, it went on without me, with a better trajectory.

"Mom and Dad spent a lot of time on those bleachers. Did they ever get to see all these renovations?" I asked Finn.

"No idea. It all looks so different."

"Everything is different," I agreed, and then we were silent. "Mornings are the worst," I ventured.

"I know."

"There's this millisecond before I open my eyes when I'm not conscious of anything. They haven't died yet, and there won't be pain when I wake up. It's just a blank slate. And then I open my eyes, and I feel it all."

"Makes it hard to get out of bed," he agreed.

"And then I start piling on. All the mistakes I made, all the times I was a little turd."

202

"Most of the time, you mean?"

I ignored him. "Specific memories pop into my head like my brain has been storing them up. The other morning I remembered how Mom made my prom dress, and I was so impatient with her when she wanted to hem it. The woman spent hours on it. I wish—"

"I know. There are so many things I wish I could redo. But we can't do that to ourselves, TP. They wouldn't want us to."

"I wish I had a chance to close things up. It's like I can't move on." I looked at him. "I'm tougher than this. I should be able to handle it better."

He turned toward me. "You have experience losing both parents at once?" It was kind, the way he said it.

"I expected more of us," I said. Finn leaned over and put his arm around my shoulders. The track and all the memories we laid down on the asphalt felt farther away than ever. "I'm not sure I can do this, Finn. Go on without them?" I was crying softly now. We were both silent for a while until I pushed myself to say what I was thinking. "Will it ever get easier?"

"I don't think so."

I looked at him. He had beard stubble, and in the sunlight, I noticed a little gray. He looked tired and sad and vulnerable, and I hated it.

"It's true," he said. "I've done some research, and this doesn't just go away." He pulled his arm from me uncomfortably and stared straight ahead. "We gotta learn how to live alongside it."

He held on to the railing with both hands. A motorcycle revved behind us, making Finn's words feel like gravel. We faced the track for a few more minutes, then turned toward the car.

"Where now?" Finn asked.

"Let's go back to Wisconsin," I said.

"Good. I have a massive headache, and I wouldn't mind sleeping in my own bed," he said. It meant, of course, "I'm done being the good brother but want you to be the one to call it." We turned the car north and headed for Wisconsin.

About twenty miles outside of Omaha, Celia called back.

"Where are you?" she asked.

"On our way home." I had no patience for small talk. "What's up with Tommy calling Pen?"

"I asked him," she said. "And it's legit. I told Tommy all about your insurance friend coming in from Bar Harbor. I didn't even think he was listening. He's been wanting to open an office in Maine and thought you'd be a good connection. He may think you're nosy, but I guess you're still good for networking." She half-laughed but stopped when I didn't reciprocate. "When I told him you and your friend were in Omaha, he was thinking about combining a trip he needed to take there, too. That's all, Peanut."

"Why didn't he call *me?*" I asked, cutting her off.

"He said he tried." She was starting to sound snippy, too.

"I'm sorry," I finally said. "I'm still pretty freaked out by what's been happening." I hadn't fully processed the last couple of weeks, all the pieces that didn't fit, but couldn't seem to pull it together. I was perpetually on high alert to danger, but it was a visceral reaction rather than a reasonable one. Is that what Ashley's memory would mean to me now? A reminder to be fearful, a bramble of shame? She deserved more than that. We all did.

"I'm sorry," I said again. "Thanks for checking. Bitsy's good?"

"She's great. Wanna say hi?" The baby voice was back. This time it was reassuring.

"Give her a hug from me," I said. "Hugs to both of you. I miss you. I'll check in later."

"Sounds good," Celia said. "And based on your mood, good luck with that hangover."

The wheels of Finn's truck slapped the highway in a comforting rhythm, and I fell asleep an hour outside of town. I woke up when we stopped for lunch, and then we filled the last five hours with companionable silence, talk of Brewers, and Kenny Chesney's latest song. There were no cars following us and no reason to be afraid. For the first time in a long while, I was relaxed. We ate enough malted milk balls to make me nauseous, and when we finally pulled into my driveway, I was drained. Finn came inside with me to check things out.

"Do you want me to stay?" he asked.

"No. I'm fine. I think it's probably over."

"There will be plenty of eyes on your place. I put out the word."

I reached over to hug him. "Thank you," I said into his shoulder. "For everything."

He had apparently used up all his words standing at the track because he had nothing else to say. He hugged me tightly, and I watched his cowlick as he turned to go.

The sun was barely up the next morning when my phone rang. I was so groggy I fumbled the phone, dropping it on the floor. I finally answered and it was Pen, clearly shaken.

"Sam. I'm so sorry to wake you—I know it's early. But I needed to make sure you're okay."

I sat up in bed, concerned by her tone. "I'm fine. Why? What's up?"

"I'm still at the hotel in Omaha. I was about to head to the airport. When I went outside this morning, I saw—Sam, it's been vandalized. Somebody spray-painted it. After what you told me about the weird things happening to you, it can't be a coincidence."

"What got spray-painted? Your car?"

"My rental car. Somebody used bright red paint and completely covered the driver's side. It's gross."

Even though I was barely awake, I tried to reason my way out of my fear. *Maybe somebody had the wrong car. Maybe a marketing stunt?* But as I batted away each ridiculous thought, the truth was becoming clear. Chillingly clear.

Pen continued. "I'm scared, Sam. After all you've told me, I'm really scared. The visual of that red paint freaked me out."

I remembered that feeling with my own car. My body retained the sensory memory of seeing such a vile display of hatred. And now it happened to Pen.

"What does it say?" I said softly.

She took a breath and dropped her voice.

"It says, 'YOU'RE NEXT.'"

CHAIR POSE looks simple, but there's a reason it's also called fierce pose. It tests different parts of your body at once, requiring balance and intense core strength.

Maybe it's here that you'll discover your power.

CHAPTER 21

"YOU'RE NEXT."

Pen repeated it. My heart bounced like it was running loose in my chest.

"Who would do this?" Pen asked. "I looked around the parking lot, and no other cars were tagged." She lowered her voice. "It *has* to be related to Ashley."

I rubbed my eyes and sat up straight, trying to think. *Was she right? Or was it—more likely—related to Ryan? But why would he go after Pen?* I shook my head, hoping to loosen some clarity. My brain cells were still asleep, but the part of my brain that processed emotion was awake and lit. Guilt raked my stomach, and I felt terrible for coming back into Pen's world and leaving my pile of chaos.

"I'm so sorry, Pen. I'll call Finn right now," I said.

"Okay. Let me know what I should do. This is awful."

"I know. Promise me you'll be careful, okay?" I felt like I was begging.

"Promise. Ditto."

I called Finn but he didn't answer, so I texted him instead, asking him to call me immediately. I tried to corral my thoughts, wild things that wouldn't slow down. I could only focus on Pen's voice: *I'm scared, Sam.*

I didn't know what to do with myself. Luckily, Finn called back right away, telling me he'd contact the Omaha police and Pen directly. The rest was out of my hands. I cleaned and paced until Pen notified me that she was safely on her plane and in the air, and I tried to shake the guilt from my tensed-up spine. Fear tightened my chest, and my whole body ached. I tried to rub out my sore neck muscles and tendons, reaching my shoulder blades from all angles, but it was a lost cause. There are just some things we can't do for ourselves. Massage and forgiveness, for example.

I pulled up the yoga studio's schedule and saw that Nena was teaching a flow class in a half-hour. I could stretch my road-weary muscles, wring out the junk food and beer from my system, and work on a little mindfulness. Maybe even unearth some self-compassion. I found some yoga clothes that passed the sniff test and went to the studio.

The studio itself didn't pass the sniff test. Based on the accumulation of smells—something like BO mixed with hash browns—it had been a busy weekend. I was early to class, so I relaxed in something similar to corpse pose with my eyes closed and listened to the sound of other students coming into the room with their combination of whispered conversations and place-making. I tried to make sense of my trip home: rediscovering Pen, Larry's suicide, Finn's comfort, and the violent threat to Pen. It was all too much.

Nena walked through the door and welcomed us while she lit votive candles around the room. It was a small class, and her voice was soothing and soft. "Let's take a few breaths in child's pose," Nena said. "I'm guessing that we all had full weekends. I understand that sometimes it's good to forget about what happened before you walked into this studio. But whatever happened really happened; there's no denying it. And what occurs after class is part of you, too. So don't deny the before and after, but maybe loosen your grip on it."

I tried to take the "loosen your grip" attitude with me as I left the studio, returning to it whenever I started to freak out. That night Pen texted me, repeating her reassurance that she was fine. On Monday, after no updates from Finn and a frustrating day at work, I pulled into the garage and looked at my bike. If it had fingers instead of spokes, it would have curled the index toward me. Time for a ride. After a quick wardrobe change and a pit stop for my requisite sodium drink, helmet, and clip shoes, I was out the door. When I got to the bike path near my house, I surged. Old railroad tracks converted to bike trails traversed the area, and their long, straight lines called to me. I needed the length of things, the feeling of an unobstructed road ahead of me, where I had control over how fast things flew by. Although I loved distance, I still had a need to sprint my way through things simply to prove I could. Once the trail got hilly, I realized that with all my gym time and yoga classes in the last few months, I had made headway in one area of my life: cardio. I was sweaty and satisfied when I got home.

It was after eight when I got a text.

Ella: *This blows.*

Me: *What?*

Ella: *Supposed to be on a hike, but people are acting stupid.*

Me: *Lot of that going around. Are you okay?*

Ella: *Yup. But don't want to stay very long. S'posed to come home with Heidi later. Any chance u could come get me? We're at Devil's Lake again.*

Me: *What is it with you and that place? But I'll def come get you. Where should I pick you up?*

Ella: *The parking lot by the lake entrance. Thank you so much! I owe you.*

Me: *No problem. C U soon. I'll text when I get close.*

It wasn't exactly "no problem." Devil's Lake was nearly an hour away, and I had an early morning meeting at the bank. It bothered me that

Ella was out there again after the trouble she'd been in before. But I knew she wouldn't ask for help unless it was serious. I briefly thought about updating Buck, but first, I wanted to get on the road.

Before I got on the interstate, I stopped at a small gas station with a grimy convenience store. Ella would call it "sketchy." As I was in line to pay, I looked up and saw Nena walk in the door. My first impulse was to ditch the Funyuns and Dr. Pepper (a reasonable treat after a long ride) I was about to buy, but she headed directly toward me before I had a chance. *Why is it that nobody sees me when I'm at Whole Foods?*

She wore normal clothes—nothing yoga-ish about her—but still looked regal. Her hair was tucked up into a short-billed baseball hat, and she smiled as she approached.

"Sam!" she said pleasantly. I wasn't even sure that she knew my name.

"Hi, Nena. Funny to run into you here," I said, trying to move the bright yellow bag to my side.

"Even yoga instructors need gas sometimes," she said. And then she winked. Nobody winks anymore. But she pulled it off, a nice combination of old-fashioned and intimate, like we were in on the same quiet joke.

"I mean, it's ironic that we're both here, leaving Madison at the same time."

"My friends and I are canoeing down the river tomorrow. I'm meeting them at the campsite," Nena explained.

"Sounds fun. I'm picking up my niece from Devil's Lake," I said as I handed the cashier my credit card. Nena turned toward the refrigerated section of the store.

"Wait for me," Nena said, with a finger in the air. "I want to ask you something."

I waited outside near a pile of firewood, almost nervous about what she'd say. The interstate traffic roared, and the smell of stale cigarette smoke permeated the air. People rushed to their cars with cases of cheap beer and hot dogs from the roller grills, and when Nena came out with her kombucha, she was decidedly out of place.

"It's good I ran into you," she said. "I want to surprise BJ after class next week for her birthday, but I can't remember if it's Tuesday or Wednesday. I know you guys are probably going out to celebrate."

"Me?"

"She mentioned that you two had plans." Nena cocked her head, mirroring mine.

"Not that I know of," I said.

"Maybe I misunderstood. I thought she said something about you and your brother. I feel like she's been struggling lately."

The pavement was hot from the day's sun, and I could feel it through my shoes. It was the only thing grounding me as this surreal conversation was taking place. I started to ask a question as my phone rang. It was Ella.

"I'm sorry. I need to get this," I said to Nena.

"Of course."

When I answered, Ella sounded breathless. "Are you close?"

"About twenty minutes out. What's wrong?"

"I just want to leave right away. Can you hurry?"

"I'm on my way. Are you okay?"

"Yeah, I'm fine. I'm glad you're almost here. Do you know where we are?" Her voice was getting higher.

"I think so. By the beach, right?"

"Yeah. I'll watch for you."

"Hang on. I'm on my way." I hung up and dug for my keys. My brain went into overdrive, picturing Ella hanging off a cliff or cornered by a bear or a boy.

"Everything okay?" Nena asked.

We were standing near my car, and I couldn't seem to find the right key. "It was my niece. Something's up. Sorry, but I better run."

"Absolutely. Can I help with anything?" She put her hand on my arm.

"No—I'm sure it will be fine. But thanks."

"Be safe," Nena said. She walked to her Prius, gave me a quick wave, apple in hand, and I drove to get Ella.

Devil's Lake is a teal lake ringed by craggy cliffs, sentinel pines, and rounded oaks. The bluffs are popular with nature enthusiasts and rock climbers, and the beach is popular with everybody, as the water is free of the weeds that frost most area lakes.

I had been on these roads many times before, but in the twilight, they were unfamiliar. Ominous. Night was closing in, and the humidity hung in the air like fog. Signs past the unmanned ranger station pointed toward the beach parking lot. I followed them as the road funneled to little more than a single lane. As I turned a corner the wind picked up, blowing leaves across the road. The sudden movement jolted me, and I slowed down. Two more twists of the road and my headlights shone straight ahead into dark green foliage. I turned on my high beams, trying to see what was ahead.

In the glint of my high beams were two golden eyes, glowing.

I squinted, trying to gauge what I saw. Human? Animal? Ella's immature friends? I slowed to a stop, trying to think over the sound of my heart pounding in my ears. I watched the eyes, and they watched me.

Suddenly the eyes blinked. Almost as an afterthought, I tapped the car horn three times to end the stalemate. The night seemed to bristle at the noise, and the eyes turned to the right. A tawny deer skittered across the road, frantic. Too young to be alone, so Mom would be near. I watched for her, but the fawn appeared to be solo.

After a few minutes of careful breathing, I started up again and turned into the beach parking lot. It was empty except for one lone minivan parked in the far corner. I pulled up next to the van, still wary of high school pranks and skittish animals, but the interior was dark, and no one was around. With my keys in one hand and my phone flashlight in the other, I got out and peered into the van's windows, where car seats and floaties convinced me it didn't belong to any of Ella's friends.

I got back in my car and tried to call Ella. I was confident this was where we agreed to meet, but she and her friends were nowhere to be seen. Ella didn't answer, and my call was disconnected before I could leave a message. Poor cell service. *Damn.*

Now what?

Maybe I misunderstood our meeting place. More likely, she misunderstood her location in the park; geography wasn't a solid trait in our family. I waited a few more minutes, then drove toward the camping area. Hopefully, Ella would stay put and let me find her.

Ten yards up the tree-lined road, I saw headlights in the distance. I relaxed, realizing that the kids had probably been driving around looking for me. As I started to pull over, the other car shot around the corner, headlights on high, accelerating toward me.

"Stop!" I yelled as if they could hear. I pulled to the edge of the road as the car raced past my car—ironically close to my side panel where "Bitch" had once been—and disappeared toward the parking lot. As it blurred past me, I could see it was a black BMW. While it circled the parking lot, I practiced my rant to the young, reckless driver. The car came back out of the lot, pulled behind me, and stopped. I idled, waiting for Ella to get out, but there was no movement. I checked my rearview mirror. Buck would want to know who it was, but it wasn't one of Ella's friends. Despite the tinted windows and the hat pulled low, it appeared to be a male, older than a teen. *Was it Ryan?* Whoever it was seemed to be alone in the car. My heart started to race. Nothing about this felt right, and I locked my doors.

I edged forward. The BMW moved with me, so close to my backside that I couldn't see its lights in my mirror. I pulled on to the road and cautiously headed back toward the main gate with the BMW following every move I made. When I sped up, he sped up. I braked, and he came closer.

"I can do this," I whispered to myself, realizing the danger of my situation. "I can." Crouching closer to the steering wheel, I decided to punch it.

The acceleration felt good. I felt strong. It was no different than any competition I'd ever run in. The roads started looking familiar, and I punched it again on the next curve. I could hear Coach Fulsom's husky voice: "Surge on the corners!" as I leveraged some distance. As I finally made it back to the two-lane road, the BMW picked up speed behind me. Coach was in my ear again. "Pass wide, Sam." I pulled closer to the middle of the road, taking up space and claiming my lead.

As I started to gain some confidence, the BMW thrust forward, coming up behind me and barely missing my back bumper. Then it accelerated. It moved alongside my car, matching my speed. As much as I wanted to look at the driver, I didn't feel safe taking my eyes off the road. The car edged toward me, and I screamed, knowing I was about to be hit.

My body took over before my brain could react, and I slammed on the brakes. I dropped behind the BMW as it swerved in front of me and sped away. I pulled to the shoulder, shaking, heart pounding like thunder.

It was the first race I ever lost on purpose.

I sat on the side of the road, waiting for my heart to slow down and my breathing practice to take hold. As the BMW's taillights disappeared and the sound of my blood stopped pumping in my ears, remnants of the speed and sounds of the night echoed in my head.

This clearly wasn't an accident. Somebody had tried to run me off the road.

I needed to find Ella.

I pulled back on the road. The night seemed darker, and I headed back toward the camping area to be out in the open. A half mile past the park entrance, there were tented villages with campers curled around fires. Campers are notoriously good people, so I found a place to park nearby. I texted Ella, hoping for a response, and realized I hadn't ever called Buck; nobody knew where Ella and I were. Bugs circled the incandescent lights as I put my forehead on the steering wheel to get a grip. I was starting to calm my breathing when my phone rang.

I jumped.

"Aunt Sam? Where are you?"

"In front of the bathroom in the campsite. Where are you?"

"I know where that is. I'll be right there. Don't leave. Please. Stay there."

I checked my locked doors and scanned the area while I waited. She was at the passenger door in less than a minute. I unlocked the door, and she opened it, throwing her backpack toward me as she heaved herself into my seat. She slammed the door. Her hair was down, and her hairband had slipped so low it was almost on her eyebrows.

I locked the doors again.

She let out a groan. "Let's go," she said. "I'll tell you everything in a minute. But let's go."

I pulled away from the guardian campers and turned on my headlights.

"All right," I told her. "Buckle up."

There are times in life when you'll need to trust yourself. You'll be called to use your strength, flexibility, balance, and concentration all at once. **DANCER POSE** can help you prepare for that.

CHAPTER 22

"I'M SUCH A LOSER!" Ella covered her face with her hands. Away from the campfires, the dark roads bore an eerie calm. I tried listening to Ella while tuning to the sounds of another revving engine, but my senses were overloaded. It reminded me of the way Bitsy's ears turned independently of each other toward whatever sound she heard. I channeled Bitsy Girl, becoming hyper-alert at my surroundings.

"It's so stupid. I can't ever see those people again. I'm going to ask Mom and Dad to move. Or can I move in with you? For sure, I'm going off the grid. Maybe I'll be homeschooled. I know! You can teach me! Can I do it online? Can I homeschool myself? Mom will never go for it. You didn't tell Mom about tonight, did you? She's gonna kill me. At least if she kills me, I won't have to face these guys again."

"Slow down, El. What happened?"

She waded in, a meandering story interrupted by a series of "like" and "right?" "There was a ton of booze, again. Jake even promised me there wouldn't be any liquor. How can I like these people so much when they're so clueless? Sometimes I feel like switching entire friend groups."

It would have been a great time for auntie advice, but I lost the thread when we passed through an intersection and the black BMW was there, parked down a side lane.

It looked low to the ground, lights off, crouched in the dark like it had haunches. As we passed through the intersection, its amber parking lights popped on, making the car look like it had come alive. It had a face now, with menacing, glowing eyes.

And it was headed toward me.

My heart rate doubled. It was one thing to mess with me, but this put Ella at risk.

Not today, creep.

I adjusted myself in my seat, grabbed the steering wheel a little tighter, and prepared for battle. First, I needed to prepare my passenger. I didn't want to scare Ella, but our problems were now bigger than Jake getting jealous. I sprung into the middle of her tirade.

"Ella, I need you to call 911."

She jerked toward me. "Why? About Jake?"

"No. There's a car that's been following me tonight. It's back."

"Where?" She twisted around, wet hair whipping against the seat.

"Listen to me. Call 911 and tell them we're being followed."

She pulled out her phone, fumbling with the grip, then dropped it. It slid between the seats.

"Oh no!" she yelped.

"It's okay. We're fine." I knew we were far from fine, but I needed to be strong for Ella.

I looked in the rearview mirror. The car was keeping a reasonable distance at this point, which felt even worse.

Trying to keep my voice modulated and my eyes on the road, I turned to Ella. "Get my phone from my purse and dial 911. Password is Grandma's birthday. Then put it on speaker." It felt like she was moving in slow motion, and my heartbeat was so strong I could hear it. When she finally dialed the three digits and handed me the phone, I turned it face down on the console to mask the light.

"9-1-1. What's your emergency?"

"I'm driving, and I'm being followed. He's been following me all night and tried to run me off the road."

"Are you okay?"

"I'm fine. But my niece is with me now, and—" Part of me wanted to explain how anger had altered the fear.

"And where are you?"

"We just pulled out of the camping area of Devil's Lake."

I drove toward the main highway to more lighting and a better chance of being seen. The BMW started creeping up behind me slowly. I sped up. In the meantime, Ella grabbed her phone from between the seats and in a mature and self-sufficient move had pulled up our location.

"He's coming closer," I told the operator.

"Keep calm and drive safely," she advised. "Are you sure it's a male?"

"From what I can tell."

"And do you know this person?"

"I'm not sure."

Ella swiveled toward me. I could feel her stare but ignored it.

We came to a small clearing and another intersection. It gave me choices. I turned right and was rewarded with a road that headed toward traffic. My hands were sweaty and sore, and as I started to ease my grip on the steering wheel, the BMW suddenly bolted up behind us. Ella grabbed my bicep. The operator repeated her "keep calm" mantra. I tried to breathe.

The car came so close behind us that I couldn't see its headlights again.

And then he hit our bumper. Ella slouched farther down her seat. The car backed off for a moment and then came up quickly and bumped us again.

Ella screamed.

"Ma'am? Can you tell me what's happening?" The operator's voice, coming from Ella's lap, felt like a lifeline.

"He's hitting us!" I yelled. This time the nudge was more solid and the reality of the situation made me sick. This was no longer something I could handle. I was almost ready to match Ella's screech when I saw a gravel turnaround ahead.

Bless these Wisconsin roads.

"Hold on," I said.

I swerved onto the shoulder. The black car seemed to stutter in hesitation, then juked to the left, barely missing my bumper. He overcorrected and headed toward the opposite shoulder.

Just as he was past us, I slammed on the brakes. Gravel roiled under the car frame and sounded like buckshot against a road sign. My wheels locked and strained against the friction of the move. We skidded past the turnaround and were barely at a stop when I reversed, slammed it back into drive, and pulled back onto the road in the other direction. We fishtailed, then straightened. Every muscle in my leg helped force the gas pedal to the floor.

I looked in the rearview mirror. The BMW had righted himself back on the road, and the sight of his taillights moving away from us was a quick—but dubious—relief. My mouth was so dry.

The neon sign of a convenience store rose in the distance. Through our closed windows, I heard the faint peal of emergency sirens. I focused on the road in front of me.

The convenience store parking lot heralded bright fluorescent lights. I pulled in, parked the car, and immediately leaned over to Ella. We grabbed each other for a long, tight hug, as close as our two seat belts would allow. Ella was shaking, but neither of us said a word.

"It's over. We're fine." I yelled toward my phone on Ella's lap. "We're fine," I said again.

It wasn't long before red and blue lights strobed against the side of the building, and we pulled away from each other to see a patrol car park behind us. As a woman with a black uniform got out of the vehicle and approached us, I lowered my window.

"Is everybody safe? Are both of you okay?" Ella and I nodded. "I'm Sauk County Sheriff Deputy Garcia. Let's get you out of the car and get some fresh air." She stepped back while I opened the driver's side door and gave me a sympathetic smile. "I'll give you a minute here, and then I'll take your statement. Sounds like you guys have had quite a night."

Ella and I extricated ourselves from the web of seat belts and got out of my car. The night was quiet, but the commercial lights in the lot made everything feel theatrical. As I told Deputy Garcia our story, she took notes. At first, Ella listened quietly, allowing me to do the recounting, but as she regained her composure, she became vocal and animated and began inserting her perspective. Deputy Garcia seemed to take it in stride.

"And you said there were no license plates on the car?" she asked.

"No plates that I could see."

"Were there any identifying marks on the car?"

"Nothing. A black BMW. Tinted windows."

I looked at Ella, who seemed to be deflating as the minutes wore on. She looked pale, and I was starting to feel dizzy, which meant my hormone levels were careening, too. The Dr. Pepper and Funyuns weren't going to help. I asked Ella to go into the convenience store and buy me a sports drink and handed her some cash. She walked slowly toward the store.

When Ella was out of earshot, I turned to the deputy. "I think I might know who did this." I talked quickly, and Deputy Garcia nodded her understanding. "I've been having trouble with an ex-boyfriend. I think he's stalking me." I told her about Ryan's phone calls, texts, and the restraining order that started it all. I told her I'd already contacted my local police department, and they had started a file.

"That changes things," Deputy Garcia said, her tone heavier than before. "Once I'm finished here, I'll contact your municipality and add to their file. They'll contact the subject and most likely question him. We take harassment and stalking seriously, especially when something like this has happened. After we're done, I want you and your niece to head for home very carefully." As she finished, she leaned back, her voice lighter again. She nodded over my shoulder to where Ella stood, a plastic bag of food at her side. Ella looked at me with such disappointment that I had to look away.

The deputy returned to her vehicle to finish up her report. Ella stood with me, leaning against the car, facing the road. She handed me my electrolyte drink, and I downed it all at once. We were silent, watching bugs fry under the bright lights.

Deputy Garcia came back and gave me a case number for the report she would file, closing out her official capacity for the evening. And then she stayed with us. She listened to us and chatted amiably, walking us back from being overwhelmed by the night. She even got Ella to laugh. Like nurses who hold your hand during an injection or a teacher smoothing your hair after a recess fall, she was proficient but, more importantly, kind.

After we felt better and thanked Deputy Garcia, Ella and I got back on the road. She set two apples, string cheese, and a king-sized candy bar on the console between us.

"I'm starving," she explained.

"No problem. Glad you went healthy."

She looked out the window. Pointedly. She was mad. She pulled the string cheese apart the way she'd always done, making it look like tentacles, an octopus of calcium. I drove the posted speed and felt adrenaline leave my body, fatigue in its wake.

"Do you want to tell me the rest of the story?" I asked her. "What happened with Brandon tonight?"

"It's Jake, not Brandon. That seems so long ago. And not important anymore, considering what happened tonight." She waited a few beats, then unleashed it quickly. "Why didn't you tell me that you were being stalked?"

"I guess I didn't want to worry you," I said.

"But I tell you everything. And you don't tell me anything."

"I tell you stuff," I replied, sounding like the adult version of teenage whiny.

"Not the important stuff. You tell me the surface stuff but never the important stuff."

She had a point. She had always felt like somebody I should watch over, like Aunt Dorothea watched over me. The thought that Ella could be trusted and resilient was a new notion. At the very least, she deserved the truth, as much as a sixteen-year-old could handle.

"I'm not sure what is going on," I admitted. "Remember that guy, Ryan? You helped me pick out clothes for our date. I really liked him. And then I found out stuff about him that made me question his character, so I quit seeing him. But he didn't give up that easily." I tried to gauge how I was doing with a quick look at her. I wanted to be honest but not overwhelm her, considering what we had been through, but her face was devoid of clues.

I went on. "This could have been him tonight. I don't know. Uncle Finn says I need to document everything, so I thought I better make sure we filed a report. But I didn't say anything because I didn't want to worry you."

She was quiet, holding the wilting octopus.

"And I didn't mean to exclude you."

It took her a long while to respond. "Why don't adults think that we can handle anything? How are we supposed to learn if you don't trust us? You're just like Dad. He gets upset sometimes, I can tell, and when I ask him about it, he gets quiet. I'm not stupid. I see how sad he gets."

This was news to me. I hadn't seen much emotion out of Buck since the day of our parents' funeral, and even then, it was more anger than sorrow. "What do you think he gets sad about?"

"Grandma and Grandpa. Usually it's after a song or seeing somebody that looks like them. When I try to bring up memories about them, his body gets still. I miss them, and I want to talk about them. It's like he doesn't want to remember them, but he can't help it."

Keen observations for somebody that needed watching over.

"You all think I'm too young to handle any of this, but have you considered that I miss them too? I miss Grandpa's stupid jokes and Grandma's oatmeal cookies. I miss when we were all together. I lost them, too, you know? But nobody talks about it with me."

She took a big bite of the cheese stick. I let her words sink in. I wanted to respond with something wise and wonderful but had nothing. I could see that she was done being placed at the kids' table. I nodded, took her hand, and gave it a squeeze. That seemed to be enough, and she turned on the radio. The music was a welcome reprieve. She returned to life on her phone, leaving me time to consider what she said.

So Buck was struggling. And during our trip to Omaha, Finn had admitted he was having trouble, too. Seemed that we were all discovering that the aftershock of death was as painful as the first explosive tremor. But lonelier.

After that, Ella's adrenaline seemed to leave her body, too. She slouched in the seat, and her head bobbed as she fought sleep. When we finally pulled into her driveway, her mom came rushing out the front door in a tightly belted bathrobe. She headed straight toward Ella.

"Thank God!" Carole said as she opened the car door to assess her daughter. She cupped Ella's cheeks and ran her eyes over her daughter's face, searching for something.

"Aunt Sam's a beast," Ella said. My sister-in-law glanced at me, but the look was indecipherable. Ella had texted her mom about our evening on the way home, so I didn't know how it was framed. Maybe, in deference to me, she had underreported and kept it mild. I took my time moving toward them, waiting for the verdict.

Carole turned toward me. "What the hell happened?" So much for a mild framing.

"It's a long story," I said. I motioned toward the house. "Can I tell you over a beer?"

She nodded, put her arm around her daughter, and headed toward the front door. I followed behind. I looked for Buck's car in the open garage and was grateful to find it was gone. I didn't have it in me to fight that battle, too.

Their kitchen was clean, sparse, and dark except for the light over the sink. Ella disappeared after another long, rocking hug from Carole, who grabbed two beers from their fridge, a stainless-steel beast with no magnets or schedules on board. She produced a bowl of sliced limes from the refrigerator and slid them toward me. Tendrils of gray hair rimmed her face. Apparently, even intimidating lawyers couldn't outsmart the aging process.

"What the hell happened tonight?" she asked.

Over the kitchen counter and a Corona Light, I gave Carole details. It was a relief to tell her; I needed to talk about it to make it real. A couple of hours later, it felt like a dream.

"And I'm guessing you know who it was," Carole said.

"I don't know for sure. I'd rather not say until I'm sure, Carole. But I'm on it. So is Finn."

She nodded. "But you realize that Ella can't be with you until you straighten this out."

"Of course." I acted like it was a reasonable consequence, but the thought of any distance from Ella made the back of my throat ache.

We took long drinks of our beer, and I'm sure we were both thinking of Buck and what he was going to say.

She cleared her throat. "Thank you," she said softly.

"For what? I didn't really think you'd be thrilled with this evening's escapades," I said.

"Well, of course not," she agreed. "But if you wouldn't have gone there to give Ella a ride home—to get her away from a bad situation— this could have been much worse. I want to thank you for that. You're always accountable, and I appreciate that. Your brother could take lessons."

I raised my eyebrows, then busied myself with a lime. Nobody wants to hear about their brother's failings. But better his failings than mine.

"I'm getting tired of his inconsistency with Ella. Sometimes he's overprotective, and sometimes he's almost absent. Tonight was a good example. I had a meeting. And he didn't have a clue about where she was or what she was doing. I don't know what we'd do if she didn't have you to count on." She took a long drink of her beer. "Ella thinks her father and I are unreasonable and idiotic, but she'll tell you things she won't tell us. You listen. And you can say things to her that we can't." She grabbed a sponge from the sink and scrubbed the kitchen counter as if wiping up the invisible dirt would help uncover the right words.

"She trusts you. And I'm grateful for that." She kept wiping but looked up at me. "Of course, I wish it was me she trusted, but at least it's somebody with a semi-decent head on their shoulders." It wasn't the best compliment I'd ever received, but I took it.

Carole went upstairs to check on Ella, and I took to my phone. One voice message from Pen to see how I was doing and report that nothing new had happened on her end, and one missed call from Ryan, but he didn't leave a message. His call came in at nine o'clock as I was practicing my Nascar technique in Devil's Lake. *If he had been in the BMW, did he call me from the road? I never even heard the phone ring.* For one quick second, I watered that dying small hope that maybe it wasn't him in hot pursuit after all. Although the idea that it could be someone else was even worse.

Meanwhile, my nervous system was fried. The night had been one long siege, relying solely on my fight-or-flight response, and the cortisol was starting to wane. My body began to shut down, system by system, starting with my brain. Emotions came next. I could have easily cried. Part of me wanted Carole to come downstairs and find me lost like this. Even a little head pat would do.

I decided to spend the night at Buck and Carole's house, so I opened another beer. Because I'd spent the night numerous times before, I had my own designated pillow and Scooby Doo blanket folded and waiting for me in their linen closet. As I stretched out on their basement futon, I finally started to relax. I closed my eyes and even practiced a little yogic breathing to calm myself down. My plan was to fall asleep quickly before Buck got home and be out the door in the morning before he woke up. I doubted he was going to be as gracious as Carole had been.

Swaddled by Scooby and overcome with exhaustion, I set my phone alarm for early morning. It would come quickly. Although I was safe and secure in Buck and Carole's house for the moment, I couldn't help but wonder what the next day would bring.

Sometimes, in the middle of acute tension, we need to find ease.
WARRIOR II helps us find power in our strength
and peace in the moment.

CHAPTER 23

IN THE MORNING, I FOLDED UP SCOOBY and snuck upstairs, hoping to avoid Buck. Just as I had planned, I missed him. He was already gone but had left a note for me near the coffee maker: *Call me asap.*

Carole was gone already too, and I crept into Ella's room to check on her. She slept soundly. I wanted to touch her face; it was innocent and unlined, and she looked like the six-year-old I wished she still was. She didn't deserve any of this spillover from my chaotic life. Whoever was trying to mess with me crossed a line when they endangered her.

Pen, too.

This had to stop.

I drove the familiar roads home from Buck and Carole's with my window down; the combination of fresh air and mundane route helped shore me up. Even in the midst of all this, the smallest routine helped me return to myself. I sat in my driveway for a few minutes to survey my front door. Nothing seemed off-kilter or out of order, nobody lurking in the bushes.

Everything inside seemed secure, too. Still no word from Finn, but

I called the police department and left a message for the officer in charge of my case. When I checked my email, there was a notification that my early meeting at the bank had been postponed.

I felt stifled and stale and without any control over my life, so I started with the best way I knew. I found my running shoes.

Other than the few minutes on the treadmill the day I met Ryan, I hadn't been on a run since before my parents' funeral. There was the initial injury: a nasty Achilles tear. My physical therapist had developed a rehab program with walk breaks and cross-training, but it felt weak, and I lost motivation to follow through. Then, when I officially gave up on the idea of becoming a professional runner, I was too weighed down by shame to hit the road. Once my parents died, it was out of the question. Running has always been at my core—and is the only way I'm able to process things—but after all the years of my parents' support, it felt like a betrayal to try again. For the first time in my life, they wouldn't be on any sideline.

I had been doing every possible exercise as a substitution, but I craved the motion, autonomy, and resolve. My body needed to run. I knew going out by myself wasn't smart or safe, but it was all I could think to do. Finn wouldn't like it, but I'd stay on busy roads and be hyper-vigilant. I was taking back my life.

I started with a slow jog, turning from my driveway onto my tree-lined street. The oaks were full of green acorns, and a few littered the road. I instinctively tiptoed around them to avoid a rolled ankle, grateful for the agency to finally dodge some trouble. At the stop sign, I stopped to stretch my tight calves, dropping my heels off the curb. The last time I had stopped here was on a walk with Bitsy when I let her choose the path. This time I was choosing the path. Thinking of poor Bitsy added another layer to my anger, and I awkwardly started my jog. Having my phone in my pocket made me feel even more off-balance, but I didn't want to miss Finn's call. I still needed to call Buck, too, but dread kept me from it. I wanted to avoid his wrath, of course, but it was deeper than that. We hadn't connected for so long; I was nervous about having a real, honest conversation with him, and now we were entangled in something that was my fault.

As long as I was beating myself up, I took responsibility for the mess my family was in, too. Something like this—whatever *this* was—should have made us "stand shoulder to shoulder," as Aunt Dorothea would say. We were failing and flailing. Without our parents, we were untethered. I hadn't seen Eli and Levi since the funeral, and our contact was dwindling. Finn and Buck were obviously struggling, too. Apparently, I had no proprietary claim on unexpressed grief. It was hard to admit that we had let ourselves become this distant. Mom and Dad would have been disappointed. I started to pick up my pace, forcing anger toward the surface, picturing a finish line where angry spectators blurred and dropped away but my family was safe and secure. I sprinted until I couldn't breathe, gasping for air and emptying my lungs. Coach would never let us stop after a race, arms on knees and bent at the waist, but I reveled in it this time. After a few minutes I straightened up like I was taught, officially blessing my diaphragm with oxygen, and jogged back home. I had a scowl on my face but purpose in my gait.

I knew what I needed to do.

Finn called back as I was stretching.

"I heard about Devil's Lake," Finn started. "I can't believe what happened. Are you and Ella okay?"

"We're fine. What did Buck say?"

He ignored my question, filling in with his own. "Why didn't you call me?" His voice was edged with impatience.

"It all happened so fast. And yes, we filed a report."

"Was it Hobart?" He jumped on the end of my words.

"I doubt it. He actually called during—"

"Are you still talking to him?" His voice got tighter.

"Finn. Stop. I was going to say that when I finally got cell service, there was a missed call from him. I'm not responding to him. You can see my phone—"

"I believe you," he humphed.

"That's good. And I'm sorry I didn't call you. It's been overwhelming."

He responded with silence. I knew this dance well. He would need time to chip away at his anger; nothing I could say would change that.

"Look," I finally said. "I need to get to work. Can you call me later? Maybe during lunch?"

"Fine," he said. "Be careful."

I made it to work with thirty seconds to spare, which left me feeling rushed all morning. Whenever I had a spare moment, I made notes of all the events that had happened since our trip to Nebraska on an old withdrawal slip. I still couldn't make sense of anything. Maybe it was time for shoulder to shoulder after all.

When Finn called back, he wasn't mad anymore; he was in "official capacity" mode. He caught me up on the parameters of the investigation, which would include questioning Ryan, but it hadn't been assigned yet.

"Thank you. Seriously. I appreciate it, Finn."

"It's okay," he mumbled.

He seemed amenable, so I waded in. "Are you doing anything tonight?"

"Zoe Saldana wanted to stop by for drinks, but I told her I'd rather hang out with you," he said sarcastically. Then he lowered his voice and got serious. "I thought I'd stay at your place until this gets resolved."

"Thank you, Finn, but it isn't—"

"Yes, it is," he said authoritatively.

Relief and gratitude softened my shoulders. This time I wouldn't fight the help. "Okay. Supper is on me tonight," I said. "And I was thinking about having Buck come over, too."

"Let me guess," he said. "You haven't talked to him yet?"

I didn't answer.

"I imagine he's pretty pissed. You probably want me there for backup."

"Partly true. I haven't had a chance to tell him my side of the story in the Ella adventure. But I also feel like the three of us need some time together." I took a small breath, winding up for the pitch. "I thought maybe I'd cook."

As expected, Finn laughed, an annoying, cackling laugh.

"Fine. I'll order in," I said.

"Now you're talking. What time?"

"Let's say six," I said. "And I'll call Buck."

I chickened out and texted Buck instead. He responded immediately.

Me: *Can you come for supper tonight? We'll talk.*

Buck: *Yes. Carole and Ella too?*

Me: *Let's make it siblings for now. You, me, Finn?*

Buck: *K. We have a lot to discuss.*

After work, I ordered the pizza (meat for my brothers, veggie for me) and made a salad. I also pushed the good beer toward the back of the fridge and the Miller Lite up front. When they arrived, Finn grabbed a Miller Lite. Buck, whose only greeting to me had been a deep grunt, reached in the back for a Lake Louie.

"Figures you'd go for the expensive stuff," I told Buck as I walked into the kitchen. He stiffened when he stood up from the refrigerator and turned toward me. We were in for a good one.

"What were you thinking?" he said loudly. "You think you live in this vacuum and can do everything by yourself." He started in and I let him rant, his voice shaky, his eyes sunken, and his beard shaggy and sprinkled with gray. I felt like I was seeing my brother in a new way— old and puckered—as if grief, fatherhood, and the daily worry about weather and crops were eating away at him.

Finn was quiet. We had both been through this cycle before. Buck started with a litany of things you had done wrong, then forgave quickly. He merely needed to run out of steam.

"I know I shouldn't be mad at you," he said, rubbing the place above his nose where his eyebrows faced each other. "But you put Ella in danger. Because of the situation you're in, with this frickin' stalker, Ella could have been hurt. Or worse." He sighed and rubbed the forehead spot faster, like he was powering up the thoughts before his mouth could spit them out.

"But I also realize that the only reason you were up there is because Ella called you. And dammit, she shouldn't have been up there." He took a breath and added quietly, "She should have called me." He looked at me. "But that's a whole different subject. The most important thing is that she called you for help and feels like she can trust you. I'm glad you were there for her."

"Buck," I waded in softly, "Ella is amazing. I know it probably hurts that she didn't call you, but really, who calls their parents when they think they've screwed up? Did you call Mom or Dad when you thought you might be in trouble?"

"Are you kidding?" Buck said. "I was afraid of Dad, straight up. And Mom, well, I never wanted to disappoint her. You know how she could make you feel bad with just a look? I would have walked home from Devil's Lake before I called them."

"Right. It's natural. And here's the thing I learned last night: Ella is resilient. She followed her instincts and kept her cool until it was the right time to fall apart. She's amazing, and you guys are doing a great job with her."

"With your help," Buck said. "And I know she screws up sometimes. I don't mind that. It's how she's going to learn."

"It's how Mom and Dad were," Finn added. "They let us fail. It's helped us each get where we are. I think they'd be proud," he added, almost sheepishly.

"But they'd be pissed that we aren't seeing each other more," I said. I looked at each brother pointedly. "We need to do better. Ella needs it, and so do we."

My intense eye contact made both brothers look at the floor.

"Especially now," I added.

"So what is going on with this stalker creep?" Buck asked. We finally sat, curving around the kitchen island, and I started from the beginning: the car keying, Ryan and his restraining order, Ashley's death, the snake, Bitsy's poisoning. Finn, who could have added side comments but didn't say a word, got up and paced the room. It took another round of beers to unspool it all and dampen my embarrassment.

"When I texted you about the muffins, I was in the middle of it all," I explained to Buck, wanting him to understand how I had missed so many signs. "I was in so deep I never stopped to see the big picture.

I'm still trying to make sense of things." I remembered the notes I had made at work. "Hold on," I told them. "I'll be right back."

I grabbed the withdrawal slip ruminations from my bag, a handful of words that looked insufficient for the damage that had been caused. It was a little too "on the nose" that I had composed a list of withdrawals the stalker had taken from my life. When I came back into the room, it was obvious my brothers had been talking about me. Buck looked pissed again.

"Finn told me about Pen Edmonton's car," Buck said. "This keeps getting worse."

It was all making me lightheaded. I wobbled a little and held on to the back of a chair. After I grabbed a sodium drink from the refrigerator and sat back down, they glared at me.

"Okay, I'm also having a little hormone issue," I added. The kitchen was stuffy, Finn narrowed his eyes, and Buck crossed his arms over his chest. I knew the word *hormone* would shut them down, so I focused on words like *electrolytes* and *sports*, and they were suddenly sympathetic.

"But dammit, Sam," Finn said while Buck shook his head. "Why didn't you tell us?"

"I thought I could handle it," I said weakly. "But I'll admit it now. I'm scared. I could use your help."

They both watched me. My kitchen would have been noiseless except for the undercurrents of tension and strain.

Buck finally raised his bottle of beer, which was almost empty. "Okay. I'm here. I know Mom and Dad—the accident—I know that changed things for all of us. But I'm here. From now on." He looked at me and nodded. His eyes looked a bit brighter, and I felt a rush of gratitude for his pivot.

"Me too," Finn added. "Unless Zoe Saldana calls." He lifted his beer, I raised my sodium water, and a series of little breaths escaped from my pent-up heart. I tried so hard not to cry. I hugged each brother, one at a time, and felt grounded and safe for the first time in a very long while. Then we ate pizza and watched the Brewers, who were playing the Angels. Every so often, I stole a look at my two brothers and saw a familiar softness in their faces that made me homesick. Even with the Angels up by three, things felt good.

⚜

When I opened the living room blinds in the morning, a little blue Datsun was parked across the street. The sun angled over the windshield so I couldn't see inside. Finn was taking a shower, and as I started to yell for him, the car pulled away from the curb. Barely a minute later, a patrol car drove by, slowly. Finn had probably commandeered help from every cop in the county. I told him about the Datsun before he left for his shift, and he lectured me about being safe, varying my routine, and staying near my coworkers whenever I could.

"You aren't going to like it, but I don't want you alone until this is resolved," he said. "We're on lockdown."

"Whatever it takes," I said. I decided not to tell him about my run the day before. "Except—can I go to yoga tonight?"

He turned around and stared at me. His lunch cooler swung from his arm, and he looked like he did when he was twelve, headed for school, mad that he had to ride the bus. He sighed. "Can somebody go with you? How about Celia?"

I laughed. "Celia? Yoga? Big no on that one. Plus, she's focused on Bitsy right now, based on her daily updates. But I'll go straight from work and park in front of the building. I'll come straight home, too."

He reluctantly agreed. And then he shook his head and left. I locked the door behind him and finished the rest of my adult preparations for the day, wishing for the simplicity of a school bus ride again.

DOLPHIN POSE increases circulation to our face and our brain, which can stimulate our true vision and intuition. It's important to see things clearly.

CHAPTER 24

"HAVEN'T SEEN YOU IN A FEW DAYS," BJ said to me as I walked into the studio that night. I kept my promise to Finn and had parked in the first row, closest to the building, and was early for the night's yin aroma class. The class made promises, too: a gentle release with long holds, targeting connective tissues and fascia. I had been looking forward to it all day. BJ stood at the reception desk, folding small white towels into piles in the middle of the clutter. The towels would be infused with things like citrus or lavender and handed out when we were done. We'd leave class flexible and fragrant.

BJ smoothed each towel with a straight palm, her olive skin a sharp contrast to the bleached cloth. "Were you on vacation?" she asked.

"Sort of. I took a little road trip back home."

"You didn't miss much around here," she said. "A lot of people are away right now. It's a good time to get away." She sounded different. Wistful, maybe.

She shook out a towel and snapped it crisply. "Must have been nice to spend time with your brother that way."

"It was," I said. And then it occurred to me: *How did she know I was with Finn?* I looked at her, replaying our most recent conversations, trying to remember if I had mentioned him. And then my last conversation with Nena flashed in my memory, too. *"BJ said you and your brother were taking her out for her birthday,"* Nena had said. I had been so distracted by Ella's drama that I had written it off as a miscommunication, but now I wasn't sure.

"Wait," BJ said, pursing her lips. "Was Nena not supposed to tell me about your trip with your brother? You have a weird look on your face."

"No, it's no big deal. I'm getting paranoid, I think." I didn't remember telling Nena about the trip either, but I couldn't keep track of it all. I shook my head. I needed a break.

BJ shrunk a little, like she was hurt. I had been so wrapped up in myself that I was probably missing cues. The last thing I wanted to do was bruise this new relationship. Even if I had concerns, I didn't want to judge things too quickly. I tried to recover. "Didn't you tell me you had brothers? Do you get to see them very much?"

"Just one," BJ said. "And no, I don't get to see him. He's far away."

"That's got to be hard," I said.

"It is. I really miss him." Her eyes filled with tears, and as she wiped them away, she smudged her thick eyeliner. Just one eye, which made her seem even more vulnerable.

"Hey, we never went for that coffee. Want to try again?"

"That would be great," she said. "We should do it soon, though. While there's still time."

I looked at her, confused.

"This summer. Before the fall gets busy," she said, motioning around the studio with her index finger.

We agreed on Saturday morning, and I was almost late for class. In my rush, I left my water bottle at the front desk. I decided to get it after class. It wasn't water or sodium I needed; it was stillness.

My sense of unease was compounded when the only spot left in the room was at an odd angle. My classmates' mats weren't parallel, and I wasn't aligned with anything around me. "Catawampus," I could hear my dad declare. I stuck out like a sore, uncomfortable thumb. The instructor handed me a large, rectangular pillow and an encouraging smile, and I rolled back onto my mat, palms up.

"Welcome to yin," the instructor said. "Make sure you have a bolster for tonight's class. We'll be relying on it to make the poses more accessible. We'll be holding some of these poses for up to four minutes, so make sure you are comfortable." The lights were low, and candles lit, music softly warming the room.

"If you haven't been to a yin class before, you're in for a treat. But it won't be easy for those of you who fight being passive. We'll work on slow movements that soften the connective tissue, and all that lies beneath. It takes a lot of energy to keep things suppressed. Tonight we're going to let it go."

Slowly, minute by minute, I started letting go. Being safely locked inside the yoga studio was the first layer of release. Then I tried to let go of the other layers that lived in my muscles: rigidity, distrust, fear. Every time I thought of the upheaval in my life, I tensed up. Forcing relaxation felt like one of those paradoxes Nena talked about.

"It sounds funny, but the issue really is in the tissue," the instructor said. "You've stored whatever is bothering you in your body; you can choose to let it go. You don't have to *do* anything. Let gravity do all the work."

This was harder than any interval training I'd ever done on the track. It was clear I needed more practice. There were more layers to uncover, and an hour wasn't nearly enough, but it was a tiny, peaceful start for now. When class was done, I stayed in corpse pose longer than usual, then hurried out. If I didn't leave soon I'd break Finn's rule, and I did not want to be there alone.

BJ was in the back room when I left the studio, so I didn't say goodbye. The night was clear as I went outside, dodging mosquitos that were so big they were getting cocky. As I drove home, my phone rang; it was BJ.

"Change your mind about Saturday?" I joked.

"No, but I forgot that Nena wanted me to ask you a favor. She wants to offer a class on assisted yoga and was wondering if a few of us would help. She wants to practice the training on real people before she teaches it. Would you be interested in helping her out?"

"Of course. When?"

"Actually, she was hoping tomorrow night would work? The studio doesn't have any late-night classes, and we thought we could grab a beer afterward, too."

"Free yoga and booze? I'm there," I said.

⸙⸙⸙⸙⸙⸙

The next day passed uneventfully. There were no notes, snakes, or damage to cars, but the lack of anything felt ominous. Finn was a messy but reliable roommate, and police cars patrolled my street routinely. My neighbors had to wonder. Celia, busy with her clients and the hair they grew while she was in Vegas, finally returned the calls I'd made to her. She apologized for ghosting me but explained that caring for Bitsy was all-consuming. And it was working. Bitsy was healing faster than expected, which Celia attributed to her new Nurse Crotch-it skills.

Buck had called on my lunch hour and apparently alerted Eli and Levi of my latest upheaval because they called and left messages, too. My phone had never felt so popular. The only person I didn't hear from was Ryan, which was somehow both a comfort and a concern.

"It's so weird being back in Maine. It's like the whole experience in Nebraska was a nightmare," Pen said when I called over my lunch hour. "I'm exhausted. I'm going to lay low and work from home for a couple of days. I'm also going to have my ex keep the kids. I'd feel better."

"I don't like the idea of you being alone," I told her.

"I know. I thought about that. But my neighbors are close by. And my dog Chloe is intimidating. She's a sweetheart, but when she barks, she looks mean as hell." I wasn't sure that would be enough, but Pen sounded resolute.

"I'm so sorry about all of this, Pen. Do you regret letting me back in your life?"

"Not for a second. I feel so much better now that we're back on track, even through all of this. But it isn't over, Sam. You know that, right? I worry that you're not taking this seriously. Like I think you shouldn't leave the house until this is resolved."

I started to disagree, but she cut me off.

"I know you think this is related to Ryan. There are times I can write it off as actions of a stalker, but Sam, I still think it's tied to Ashley."

"How? When I trace everything that has happened, I can put Ryan in every scene," I said.

"What if you're wrong? What if you're looking at all the wrong things?" She sounded defensive and testy. Understandably.

"I'm working on it. And until I can figure this out, I'm being careful." I told her about Finn moving in, the police scouting my place, and how I'd limited my movements. "I only go to work and yoga. The only people I'm seeing are my family, coworkers, and my yoga folks." As I heard myself explain it, I appreciated the simplicity of it all. I was keeping my circle manageable, and I suddenly realized that between my family and yoga, my little circle made me feel loved. Cared-for.

"Are you sure you can trust them?" Pen asked.

"With my life," I said.

HEADSTAND POSE is one of the more difficult and invigorating poses to master. Before attempting, make sure you're conditioned, using proper technique, and not alone.

The consequences could be dangerous.

CHAPTER 25

FINN WASN'T THRILLED ABOUT ME GOING to Nena's assisted training event, but I thought it sounded divine. I couldn't think of a better way to get out of my head and focus on my body. Ever since Nena's hands-on assistance helped deepen my stretch and my awareness, I understood the value of touch. I knew I verged on being a sycophant who idolized Nena, but after her gentle touch had helped me shift between pain and possibility, she signified growth to me. She embodied competency. And consistency. I could never figure out if her teaching style was built on improvisation or if she had a planned agenda, but the combination of her precise cues, wisdom, and subtle humor always made me feel in good hands.

I reassured Finn that, once again, I'd be careful. When I got to the studio, the buzzing of cicadas was atmospheric and loud amidst the almost-empty parking lot. I parked right next to BJ's Malibu and grabbed my mat and workout bag from the car. When I opened the door to the lobby, there was only one little light on in the back office.

"Hello!" I yelled, jangling my keys.

BJ came from the back office, dressed in a plain black sweatshirt with the hood up.

"Hey, Sam. Didn't hear you come in. Look what I found after you left yesterday," she said, handing over my water bottle. It was Yoda doing yoga which always made me smile. "I even filled it up for you. We're all set." She handed me the bottle. I noticed that her hand was shaking.

"Are you okay?" I asked.

"I'm fine. It's been a crazy day." A corner of her dark hair peeked out from the edges of the hoody when she shook her head.

I held up the bottle. "Thanks for finding this. All is right with the world again."

BJ laughed awkwardly and tucked the sprig of hair back into her hood. "We'll be in the small studio tonight." She was talking quickly, her eyes searching the parking lot behind me. "I started the radiant heat already. Nena just called; she's running a few minutes late."

"Only the three of us?"

She nodded. "She wanted to keep it small. I'm going to lock the front door and then get my stuff. Do you want to go on back and get settled? I'll meet you in there."

I made my way down the dim hallway and tentatively pushed open the door. The dark room was eerie. There was a slight intermittent clicking of the heat panels, and without the usual backdrop of music or chanting, the room felt abandoned. Once I was inside, the door closed silently behind me. The only light came from the window to the north, and even that was muted. It was disconcerting. Hopefully Nena would at least light a candle.

After carefully choosing a spot in the middle of the room, I spread out my mat. The room felt cavernous but didn't smell like perspiration for once. I tried child's pose, but it felt awkward all by myself. I pushed myself up and looked around. In one corner of the room was a shelving unit that held cotton straps and foam blocks, and in the other corner was a small electric fan. That was it. Nothing else but the mirrors and me.

I took a long drink of my water. It had been a busy day at the bank, and I hadn't had much to eat or drink. The water BJ used was fresh and cold, and I didn't come up for air until my taste buds complained. The water was a bit tinny, but I assumed that was because it was the purified stuff. I took another drink, and it tasted even worse. Funky. I decided to go back to the lobby and fill it myself. This was nasty.

I got up from my mat and headed to the door. When I pulled on the handle, it was stuck. It was usually an easy open because of all the moisture in the room, but this time it didn't budge. I tried again, but it felt locked. I rattled the door, hoping it would jimmy itself loose. If nothing else, I figured the noise would alert BJ so she could let me out.

Nothing happened. I rattled some more but now could tell the door was locked. I moved to the window facing the lobby and knocked loudly. I yelled BJ's name. She couldn't be that far, and the studio was quiet without people moving around.

"BJ!" I yelled again. Nothing was happening—except that it was getting hot.

Very hot.

Panic started to crawl up the back of my throat as my heart started beating faster. I stopped yelling and stepped away from the window. *Okay. Think. BJ's probably in the back room and can't hear me. Or maybe she's on the phone. I'll give her a few minutes and try again.*

I waited five seconds and pounded again. Nothing. Putting my forehead against the glass of the window, turning from side to side, I tried to see the length of the lobby. BJ was nowhere in sight. I could feel my temperature—and my panic—rising. My throat was getting sore, and I began to feel lightheaded. Lightheaded quickly turned to dizzy.

Besides feeling like my heart rate was getting out of control, my fingers started to tingle. It was hard to catch my breath. I reached for my water bottle but decided against it when I remembered the taste. I had nothing but a locked door.

I moved to the door and yanked on it, then pounded as loudly as I could. I kicked at it, sending a shock of pain through my heel. When I

241

grabbed my foot, my vision started to blur.

"Dammit!" I screamed. "I need help, BJ!"

The intercom clicked on, and I could hear the crackle from the front room of the studio. There was a moment of silence as I stopped yelling. I tried to focus on the sound.

"Sucks, doesn't it?" The voice was low, coming from the speaker in the corner with the fan. I turned toward it, trying to hear.

"Guess we won't be getting that coffee this weekend, Sam. You'll be dead."

In **REVOLVED HALF-MOON POSE,** two opposing movements happen at the same time. While you're rooted to the earth, you're simultaneously lifting yourself up, all while acknowledging a twist. The combination of these two forces generates a powerful, life-affirming force.

CHAPTER 26

"NOT FUNNY, BJ," I YELLED. I plopped down with relief at her familiar voice through the intercom speaker. "The door is locked. Can you hear me?"

"I can hear you, Sam," she said. "And I *can* unlock the door. I'm just not going to."

"What are you talking about?" I felt unsteady and put my hands down on either side of me on the floor, trying to focus on her words. "BJ! Unlock the door!"

"Afraid that's not going to happen, Samantha." The intercom made her voice sound metallic and shrill. My arms were shaking, and none of this made sense. I started to see spots, floating specks that danced around my peripheral vision. Sweat made tracks down my arms and over my legs, pooling onto the floor. All in slow motion.

"This is for Larry, Sam." BJ's voice creaked.

"What?"

"Larry Jacobsen. Your classmate. My brother."

The room started spinning, and I tried to get up on my knees. What was she saying? *Larry had a sister, but she was younger. I didn't even know—wouldn't recognize her if I saw her. Pen had said that Larry's younger sister was named Barbara.*

Barbara Jacobsen.

Oh God. BJ.

Thoughts of the past few weeks flashed through my mind as I tried to make sense of this.

"Please, BJ, come in here and talk to me. I don't understand any of this."

"I know the feeling, Sam. I couldn't understand how somebody like you, somebody who had it all, could be so mean. So uncaring. You act like you're a good person, but I know who you are. My brother was always the target, and you didn't give a shit. You got to live a normal life, while every day, you dug a blade deeper into my brother. You basically killed him. And you didn't care."

Slowly, like opening a door to the cellar that you've been afraid of for years, I started to see the whole picture. I started to whimper. My brain couldn't function well enough to process what she was saying, but somehow my heart knew it was true. My heart sank as I recalled Larry, his bird-like face, his darting eyes. Stringy-haired, small, and wiry.

"BJ, I didn't know. I didn't know." I cried earnestly now, and waves of darkness played with my consciousness. "Please come in here so we can talk about this. Please."

There was no sound from the intercom for a few seconds, and I waited it out while I tried to slow my breathing. I thought maybe I was getting to her.

If anything, she was only getting started. "Everybody knew that Ashley was the worst. She was the hardest on Larry. He hated her so much. After he died, I needed to do something in his honor. She deserved what she got." Her ragged breath over the mic was as terrifying as her words.

"Then, when I saw your parents' obituary, I thought karma had taken care of it for me. I let it go for a couple of weeks, but I needed to see the destruction after losing your perfect parents. I needed to see your demise. It didn't take me long to find you," she said. "And when I got this job, I realized it was all turning out perfectly. I've been watching you for a long time, following you everywhere. You're a terrible driver, by the way. Seeing you every day, seeing your new, improved life, made me *sick*. And when I watched you stand outside with that cop next to my artwork—the word *Bitch*—I *knew* this was what I was meant to do. It's all perfect. Because you *are* a bitch, Samantha. You didn't even know what you had done to Larry or me. I watched you live the life I should have had. I can't ever have a normal family. I can't have a niece that adores me. I can't ever be an aunt because you killed my brother," she yelled.

"I don't understand. How—"

"I'm alone!" she howled. "Understand that? You think you're so damaged because your parents died, but you have no idea. You *had* them. You had the family Thanksgivings and the birthday parties. You have people who care. You have people to help you out—like when I messed with that stupid dog—people were coming and going like it was a party that night." I could hear the anger in her voice, and then the intercom went dead. Her voice reverberated in the silent, hot room, making my head pound.

When she turned the intercom on again, her voice was low and modulated. It was almost scarier than the emotion she'd just unfurled. "You have no idea what it's like when the one person who understands you ends his own life," she breathed. "When my brother died, nobody cared."

I hung my throbbing head, guilt and tears spilling onto my lap. "I'm so sorry," I cried.

"Larry is gone, and you get to move on like it never happened. You even got a boyfriend, although I was thrilled to see you choose such an asshole." She chuckled a deep, empty sound. "That was a stroke of luck. Most guys are so shallow. Sleep with them, and they'll do anything — lend you cars, run your errands, do what you say. But that Ryan guy?

He was a control freak. It was pure karma, too. Once he came into your life, I knew I could use him *and* his past."

"BJ, I know I made mistakes. Huge mistakes. But I've been trying to fix them. I feel terrible about your brother."

"Shut up!" she screamed. The sound was raw and piercing and echoed through the studio. The intercom went silent again.

I was shaking uncontrollably and could tell my heart rate was dangerously high. The little orbs in my periphery were getting larger, blurring my remaining vision. When the intercom clicked on again, I tried a softer tactic.

"BJ, I'm so sorry about Larry. Truly. But look at your life now. You have friends, a great job, a life here." My words started melting together as my lungs were giving out, but I pushed myself harder. "Why mess all that up just to get back at me?"

"Because you deserve it," she said. Her voice sounded edgy now. "I need to see it. I don't remember actually taking out Ashley—it's all a blur. Afterward, I stood there and looked at what I'd done. The blood in the bathroom? It was like a Pollock painting. But this time, I'm going to *be mindful*." She cackled a dry and brittle laugh. "I've been watching you try to reinvent yourself like the past doesn't matter. Like Larry didn't matter. But I KNOW WHO YOU ARE!" she yelled.

My heart pounded so loudly I could barely hear her. The room was starting to get darker, and I cried harder, thinking of the words on Pen's car. *You're next.*

I wouldn't get a chance to warn her.

She seemed to know what I was thinking. "And Pen. She hasn't changed, either." She chuckled. "You're both clueless. I followed you in Omaha, and you two never had any idea. Once again, it wasn't hard to find you. I knew you'd go to Faust's. Then I followed you to the hotel. I thought you saw me once, but then I realized you're both too self-absorbed to even notice anybody else."

She stopped suddenly, and I could hear her deep intake of breath.

"BJ," I pleaded, but her voice railed over the top of mine.

"Shut up," she said again. "You brought this on yourself. I even gave you a couple of warnings, but you're clearly too stupid to catch on." The mic crackled as she warmed up to this.

"I thought for sure you'd figure it out after the snake. Don't you remember your stupid mascot? The ASP, from the first letters of your names? *Ashley, Sam, Pen.*" She sang in a falsetto voice that was chilling. "A snake on your doorstop—I thought that was almost too obvious. I was pissed that it died before you opened it. I wanted it to scare you."

She made a sound, a combination of a growl and a sob. "But it was worse that none of it meant anything to you."

"BJ," I croaked, "I know that's how it seemed. But it all mattered. And your brother was probably struggling with mental issues and didn't get the help he needed. Your mom, too. None of it was their fault. Let's stop all this and see if we can do something about it. I can help."

"You're blaming me now?" Back to yelling. "Mental illness, my ass. My brother was fine. My mother was fine. They were just weak." Her voice shook with rage. "This isn't about mental illness. It's about you, Sam, and how you ruined my family. And left me alone."

She started to cry, gulps of air that were full of agony. Then silence, as she apparently moved away from the mic. I heard a crash in the background, as if she threw something heavy. I knew I needed to do the same, to quickly find some way to break out. I crawled toward the supply shelf, toward the blocks and straps, but sweat was dripping from my body, and the floor was slippery. I fell, landing on my back. The spots in my peripheral vision turned to moving swirls. I wanted to stay there, where breathing was easier, and a sense of peace was beginning to radiate from my core. It would be easier to remain still. So much easier.

BJ's voice filled the room again. "It's time, Sam."

I looked up at the shelf. It looked too far away.

I can do this. I can.

"It's funny, though. It's the ultimate paradox," BJ said slowly. "I can't wait until you're gone. But I'm going to miss you."

I could hear Coach F's voice over the top of hers. He was in my ear as he had been so many times. "Dig deep. You got this." One of my strengths as a runner had been my kick at the end of a challenging race. It was time to kick it.

I pushed myself onto my hands and knees. Blackness started to envelop the room, but I steadied myself.

And then I heard something new over the intercom—another voice.

"What are you doing?" It was a female. Maybe Nena? Relief gave me a second's pause but was quickly replaced by more fear.

Maybe Nena wasn't who I thought she was, either.

The intercom went silent as I realized I didn't have time to find out.

Digging deep, I crawled closer to the shelving unit. I pulled myself up to my knees—hero's pose.

I need somebody to know I'm here. If they both leave, I'm dead. I grabbed the closest shelf and with one final burst of energy, pulled the structure to the floor. As it started to fall toward me, I rolled to the right. It crashed next to me with a deep thud, straps and blocks raining over the room.

Waves of pain and nausea washed over me as I curled on the floor. My lungs were screaming, and I was losing feeling in my arms.

I can do this. I can.

My breath was shallow and fast, so I inhaled and exhaled deeply, pulling from my diaphragm like I was taught. My throat felt like it was on fire, and I clawed at my neck as if scratching open my throat would help. The room was fading. So was I.

I thought of Ella and willed myself to be strong. I got myself to my knees again, this time scooting toward the window. Using my left arm to pull the shelves along with me, I made my way to my feet.

I can do this. I can.

I lifted the wooden unit and, using a force that had been dormant for too long, twisted my obliques and threw it toward the window. It crashed through the glass as I flew backward, landing on my back. A sharp pain shook through me as I gasped for breath. It sounded like somebody was running toward the door, but I wondered if it was the sound of blood coursing through my brain.

The room got dark, and I could feel myself slipping away. Breath was losing its importance, and surrender seemed like a better goal. I thought about my parents. Maybe I didn't need to fight so hard after all. Maybe it was time to let go.

As my vision dimmed, I heard the door open. It slammed into the wall, and I thought I heard screams. Was that real? Darkness surrounded my head and ears, blocking everything I thought I knew.

Then I heard Nena's voice.

"Sam! Thank God! Are you okay?"

I looked at her but couldn't respond. I wanted to move—to use my strength to speak, move, or get myself out of this room, but I couldn't push myself anymore. Darkness was closing in on me again, and suddenly it didn't seem so terrible.

"Sam!" Nena yelled. I could feel her next to me on the floor. She put her face close to mine.

"Help," I whispered.

"I'm here, Sam. Listen to the sound of my voice and stay with me. Nothing else but the sound of my voice. Help is coming. Help is here."

RECLINED BUTTERFLY POSE: Let yourself be as supported as possible. Sink into this restful, compassionate position that calms the mind and the nervous system.

Let it all go.

CHAPTER 27

I WOKE TO SOMEONE BRUSHING THE HAIR from my forehead with cool fingers and a delicate touch. For a few confused moments, I thought the hands were my mom's. The soft strokes felt like love personified. I wanted to wake up and find her there, with Dad standing behind her, eyes clouded with tears and worry until he could get to me, too. But as I meandered through layers of consciousness, I started to comprehend the futility of wishing my parents were there. It wasn't going to happen. I didn't want to address that yet, so I fought to stay in the peaceful, safe place, where I was quiet and still, instead of being awake where coherence only brought pain.

"There you are," Aunt Dorothea whispered. My eyes fluttered open despite myself. I tried to swallow, but my throat screamed in pain. Aunt Dorothea turned toward the tray next to my bed, then lifted a plastic cup with a straw toward my mouth. I moved to it greedily.

"Take it slow, honey." I tried to follow directions but was so parched I wanted to cry. I took too much water at once and coughed, pain slicing down my throat. Dorothea took the cup away and waited. When I was ready, she poured more tepid water from the nearby pitcher, and we tried again.

"Slowly," she said. This time I listened. The water felt like little needles coursing down my throat. I leaned back against the pillows and closed my eyes.

Hospital. Pain. So tired.

Disjointed images of the night before began to insist themselves in my brain, and I fought them. I didn't want to remember.

The yoga studio. Nena.

BJ.

"How long have I been here?" I whispered, eyes still closed.

"Overnight. They brought you in from the studio," Dorothea said. She fussed with my sheet, pulling it closer to my neck. "The police are waiting until you're more coherent to take your statement. They have to come through me; I'll arrange it. But Finn is here, and Buck is on his way. He's waiting for Ella, and then they'll head over together. I've been giving Eli and Levi updates, too. They want to come, but I asked them to wait. I had Finn take Celia downstairs to get some coffee. She's a bit, well, worked up."

I would have smiled but was afraid it would hurt my face. The fire in my throat was dwindling, and I wanted to sink back into the place where pain couldn't find me. I could imagine that Celia was being a colossal pain in the ass. It was good somebody else took charge of her. Aunt Dorothea was perfectly adept at air traffic control, and I couldn't even control my eyelids.

"Can I get you anything?" Aunt Dorothea's voice pulled me back, and I simply shook my head. "I'll let you rest, then. When you're up to it, Nena would like to see you, too."

I felt her soft lips on my forehead. The tenderness of it made me want to cry.

Falling asleep again led to frantic dreams of darkness and heat and voices booming from the sky. I woke up once, and Celia was watching a soap opera. She was engrossed, and I wasn't ready for her, so I closed my eyes again, desperate to return to the cocoon of sleep.

Once in a while, I heard voices, remnants of conversations in a whispered state.

"How is she?"

"Has she been awake?"

I heard the door open and close, and people come and go. When the door opened, I could hear the squeaks from equipment carts and the footsteps of busy staff on a tiled floor. When I finally opened my eyes, the sun had shifted and the room was almost dark. There were green and red lights from digital monitors, rhythmic clicking from machines behind my bed, and a headache so tight that my skull felt close to cracking. Even the light above the sink was too much.

What felt like only a few minutes later, a nurse came into the room for my next round of vitals. I shifted in the bed; my legs were so stiff they didn't feel like mine.

"Oh good," he said. "You're up. I need another blood draw, but I hated to wake you."

As I turned to respond, I saw Finn standing in the corner. He was in jeans and a plaid shirt, untucked and disheveled. His whole face looked untucked and disheveled, crumpled with such worry that it made me uncomfortable. He smiled and came closer.

"Loser," I whispered to him.

"Butthead," he whispered back. Then he leaned down and kissed my forehead. "Way to freak us out."

"Sorry," I said.

"Me too."

The nurse finished filling a vial with my blood. It was so maroon that it looked nearly black. The thick volume made me queasy, and I closed my eyes. When I opened them again, Finn was gone. Night had turned into day—or the other way around—it was impossible to tell. I tried to sit up a little, sneaking into the movement in increments so my head wouldn't crack open.

Celia was in the chair again, hair separated into two braids and a baseball cap on top. She looked like she did when I first met her. Bitsy was in her arms, snuggling on her chest but hidden under a blanket like a nursing baby.

"Hi," she said softly. "I brought somebody who wants to see you." She took a quick look at the closed door and then turned her body so I could see the little furry face. Bitsy's soft brown eyes looked into mine. She had better eye contact than most people I know. It made me want to cry.

"Hi, Bits," I whispered. "How are you, sweet girl?" She seemed to recognize me, blinking slowly like some little wise Buddha.

"How did you get her in here?" I asked Celia.

"Big purse," Celia said, nodding to the suitcase-sized bag at her feet. "They come in handy." She stroked Bitsy, who was completely still except for eyelids that mimicked the up and down movement of Celia's petting. Watching the two of them was mesmerizing.

"How is she doing?"

"She sleeps a lot. Her poisoning—accident—took a lot out of her, but she cuddles better than ever."

I lifted my hand, heavy with an IV tube, toward Bitsy. Celia scooted closer. As I grazed the top of Bitsy's head with my fingers, she tipped her head toward my hand for a deeper touch. Some buried emotion that felt like a mixture of love, guilt, and relief rushed through my body with such force that I unleashed the tears. It was the first I had seen Bitsy since the day of the poisoning. I'd been so buried by guilt that her response felt like forgiveness. I smoothed the top of Bitsy's head, and she leaned harder into my hand, and for just that moment, I felt better.

Celia took herself out of the equation longer than I imagined possible. Then she reached down to her bag and pulled out a box, the same dark chocolate candy that Tommy had given us at dinner long ago.

"It's from Tommy," she said as she placed it on the bed tray. "He feels awful about what you've been through." She looked at me with such hope that I set aside my sarcasm and doubt. It felt like a tiny truce wrapped with a gold bow. I'd take it.

"Tell him thank you," I said.

"There's more," she finally said. "I'm so excited. Bitsy is going to be a big sister. Dr. Brisbain told me about a puppy that was surrendered, a Pomeranian that's diabetic, and the clinic is having trouble finding him a home. I met him and he's amazing. I can't imagine not taking him," she said as she dug her face into Bitsy's fur. "I already named him Versace."

I looked at Bitsy as if to read her thoughts. It felt like a betrayal to her after all she'd been through.

"Bitsy is my forever love," Celia explained. Her voice got thick, and she put her cheek on Bitsy's head. "I'd give my right butt cheek to have Bitsy live forever, but we all know that can't happen. Versace isn't a replacement; he's a surprise. A good surprise for me and for Bitsy. Sometimes you love whoever is in front of you, despite what has happened in the past. All we really have is this moment, these souls, this love. It's not ours to control; it's ours to enjoy."

She and Bitsy both closed their eyes. "It's simple. We all just want to belong," she said.

I stared at my golden-haired friend and took in her t-shirt, denim shorts, and pink flip-flops. She had makeup on, of course, but this was a new, wiser, softer side to Celia that I was just getting to know. And love.

We heard my door open, and Celia quickly covered Bitsy with her nursing blanket. In one swift move, she opened the suitcase/bag and gently placed Bitsy inside. A quick kiss on my cheek and she was gone, leaving a perfume trail in her wake.

⁂

Out my window, new construction filled the sky. Cranes moved slowly on the horizon, and reverse signals from trucks permeated the thick pane of glass. Life was in motion around me—regardless of me—and I didn't even know what day it was. I reached for the TV remote to check in on the outside world as Nena walked into the room.

"Hi," she said softly. "Okay if I come in?"

"Hi," I croaked back. "I'm glad you're here."

Her hair was loose, giving her a bohemian look. She looked lovely and lithe in jeans, a long taupe sweater, and silver earrings so long they touched her shoulders. It was the uniform of people with normal lives, someone who wasn't prone in a hospital bed and got to make decisions about hair and earrings.

"How are you feeling?" she asked gently.

My throat was fiery again, and I pointed at the water before I could speak. Nena poured fresh water into the cup and handed it to me. I drank, slowly this time, and handed her the glass.

"Thank you," I sighed. "For the water and for—for the other night."

"You're welcome." She tipped her head with pity, eyes boring into mine. "I'm so grateful I came to the studio when I did." She looked like she wanted to say more but didn't.

I nodded. It was all I could do. Memories of the night were becoming more vivid, and my recent dreams had been chilling versions of being strangled and unable to breathe. I'd been avoiding it as long as I could; it was all too raw.

"I can't believe it, Sam. What BJ did to you." She reached for my hand on the bed. So much hand-patting in a hospital. Touch is the doorway to comfort, and hands seem to be the welcome mat. Nena's hand was warm, and when I squeezed it back, it somehow felt intimate and bold. Even though she had already put her hands on me during assisted yoga, escorting me through a layer of grief, and had held me until the ambulance came, this was the first time *I* had reached out to *her*.

"I owe you," I said, but the words felt like cotton candy. Inadequate. Flimsy. Disappearing without the appropriate weight.

"You'll make it up to me," she said. "Mind if I sit?" she asked, reaching behind her for a wooden chair. As she scooted it closer to my bed, she winced. The gravity of what may have happened in the yoga studio's office suddenly occurred to me. I wasn't the only one who had been caught off-guard.

"Are you okay? What happened to you?" I asked her.

"I'm fine. Really. Let's just say BJ and I 'tussled' before I even knew you were locked in the heat."

I shook my head, ready to tell her not to downplay things on my account, but she elaborated. "When I first came in the studio, I could tell something was off. BJ was in a frenzy—almost incoherent. I was trying to reason with her, to get a sense for what was happening, and she came after me." She looked down at her lap and shook her head. "Now that I know what she's capable of—"

A moment passed—a white ghost of a frightening possibility. Nena started again.

"Anyway, I was able to defend myself and took advantage of every kickboxing move I've ever learned. She's tough; I'll give her that. I was trying to get her under control when you threw the shelving unit through the glass. I didn't even know you were in there, Sam. It was so loud that it startled us and gave me the chance to race to the door and unlock it."

She took a long breath that lowered her shoulders and relaxed her face. It was like watching water settle. I involuntarily copied her, as I had so many times in class, and tried to avoid a meltdown. She'd already done so much for me that it was hard to sit this close to it all. I took another breath and looked around the room. There was a showy bouquet of Stargazer lilies and white daisies on the ledge behind Nena that I hadn't noticed before.

"They're beautiful," I said, nodding toward the arrangement.

"Aren't they? I was here earlier when they were delivered. They're from your friend Pen."

That did it. Hearing Pen's name come from Nena's lips brought the last few months full circle. It made me feel worthy and worthless at the same time. I cried, big gulping sobs that hurt my head. I couldn't stop.

"I am so grateful, Nena. If you hadn't been there—"

She put her hand on my arm. She handed me the box of tissues and let me unroll. As the tears abated, sounds of the hospital corridor floated into my room, and my breath stutter-stepped to a normal pace.

I wiped my nose and my face and nodded a thank you to Nena.

She nodded back. Something passed between us again, but this time it felt like strength.

"Okay," I said, resolve building as an antithesis to my vulnerability, "I'm confused about a few things. I still have questions."

She smiled and scooted closer to the bed. "Shoot."

"What made you come to the studio when you did?" I asked.

"It was a fluke. I was meeting a friend at the brew pub and drove by the studio. I saw BJ's car, so I thought I'd stop in and invite her along. I didn't recognize yours. The minute I walked into the studio I could tell something was wrong. The air felt tense. She came out of the office and freaked out. I couldn't understand anything she was saying. Like I said, I tried to get her under control. When you broke the glass, she lost it. I've never seen anything like it.

"When I ran to open the door to you, she screamed and tried to grab me but only got a fist full of my clothes. She followed me into the studio until I found you. And then she sort of deflated. She was catatonic. She watched us from the floor, and when the police came in, she was limp, like she was ready to get caught. Ready to get it over with."

I didn't remember any of that. I had missed so much, even from the very beginning. Piecing it together would be an embarrassing walk backward. As I thought more, pieces clicked into place.

"All those times I left my phone in an open locker during class? She probably used a tracker app. It must have been easy after that."

Nena watched as I started to put it together.

"And later, when I thought I lost my keys, she called me to say they were found. That's when she probably made a copy of my keys. That's how she got into my place." My throat started to hurt again as I went on. "That means she poisoned Bitsy to get back at me." I pictured Bitsy's face, her eyes, her trust in me. The guilt still blanketed my thoughts of her. I wanted to cover my eyes, but my arm was tethered to the IV.

Nena handed me another tissue. "Do you want me to leave? This is probably all too much."

"No. I want to figure this out. I want to be done with it. Things have been out of my control for so long. I just want to understand it all." I readjusted myself as pain shot up my spine. And then a new, stark pain came to the surface.

"She had a right to hate me," I said.

"Sam." Nena's voice was soft, but the admonishment was clear.

"It's true. Her brother—"

"I know. I know about that. And that will be something you'll have to deal with, eventually. But BJ needed help, Sam." She smoothed my sheets while she gathered her thoughts. "She should have had help. Losing her brother was traumatic, and something like that changes a person. She should have had support, therapy, and people to help. Any loss is hard, but surviving after losing someone to suicide is one of the hardest. And she did it alone."

I nodded but didn't feel any better. "She wanted somebody to feel the pain she felt," I said. "I can see that now."

Nena's phone rang. She didn't answer it. It was another reminder that life was going on outside this hospital, regardless of the mess I was in. People kept moving whether their hearts had little fissures of pain or were gutted, open wide.

I continued. "The doctor was in here a little bit ago and told me I had a toxic amount of potassium in my system. They suspect that she laced my water bottle. That's why I couldn't handle the heat in the studio."

"Or maybe it was the fact that she turned the radiant heat panels to their maximum. Sitting in a room that was 122 degrees might get anybody."

"Well, normally I'd be able to handle that," I said, trying to smile.

She leaned in closer. "Are you still trying to convince me you're invincible? Yes, she played you. She knew about your disease and your past to get to you. You are strong, Sam. I've seen your determination. But sometimes, being strong means asking for help. Letting people in."

The truth of that sat heavily on my chest. I drew back a bit, trying to get comfortable.

"I've been thinking about something," she said. "You know how I'm always trying to get students to use blocks or straps to get deeper into a pose?"

I nodded.

"You never do. Why?"

I felt like I was in second grade, Mrs. Peterson's unabashed teacher's pet, trying to answer perfectly.

"Blocks are for pussies," I said weakly. And grinned.

Nena shook her head, but kindly, like Mrs. Peterson once did, too. "I know you think you're kidding, but I've seen it, Sam. Have you ever considered why you resist help?"

The room went silent except for the hospital din.

"It's called support," she said. "Tools to help you go deeper. It's true of the padded bolsters, too. I was watching the students in my yin class the other day, and it occurred to me: the people in our lives are like bolsters. They're meant to support us when we're uncomfortable and are a soft option when things are challenging. But it's our responsibility to admit that we need them. You have to pull it off the rack, put it by your mat, and not tie it to any judgment."

"I'm too short to reach them," I tried to joke.

"That's what you tell yourself. But let this sink in, Sam. Admitting you need help is showing yourself compassion. The same compassion you'd show anybody else."

I nodded. She was right.

"So here's your mantra for the day: it's okay to take advantage of support. It's okay to need people. That's why they're here." She put her hand on my forearm, and it felt warm. "In fact, there are a lot of people here. I'm going to give you some time with them." She motioned toward the door, where a heavy white curtain blocked the opening, but people I loved waited beyond. Nena leaned in to give me a careful hug.

"Thank you," I whispered. "For everything."

"Thank you," she whispered back. "I'm honored to be here for you. To walk through this with you."

After a few seconds, she righted herself. "I'm going now so you can rest. It looks like you're in good hands." She nodded to Aunt Dorothea, who was hovering, eavesdropping, at the door.

Nena left, Dorothea came in, and I had to shut my eyes from it all, just for a second. When I opened them again, my sweet aunt stood beside the bed, hands clasped in front of her, watching me. Tears pooled in her eyes, ready to fall, and I could see the pain of all those who stand by bedsides, wearing prayers for their loved ones to be whole again. Aunt Dorothea's eyes were so full of emotion that my own heart lurched, returning her love in a way words couldn't hold but fracturing at the same time. BJ never had anybody stand by her bedside like that.

Aunt Dorothea pressed her palm against my cheek. "When you're ready, we'll talk about the secrets you keep. In the meantime, there's a whole swarm of people who want to see you," she said.

"Family," she clarified and, once again, patted my hand.

The intent of **CORPSE POSE** is to provide a deep rest with full awareness.
It's the most important yoga pose, simply requiring that you remain.
Be. After a few minutes of stillness, notice how you feel. Ironically,
corpse pose helps you feel more alive.

CHAPTER 28

SOMETIMES THE HARDEST PART OF YOGA is the last three minutes, in savasana. Corpse pose. Nena often tells the class to "find your savasana" because this pose isn't passive; it takes some chasing after. Although it requires simply laying flat on the mat, legs relaxed and open to the corners, palms facing up, the challenge is to acknowledge the change that just took place.

This is when the good stuff happens. The body's cells acclimate to the work that was done, and deep restoration is the reward. By the end of the practice, the body has experienced an unfolding, and hopefully, the mind can follow. The first time I tried it I was afraid I'd fall asleep, but strangely, it has the opposite effect: I feel alive. Awake. Whole.

Like in savasana, I'm still absorbing what happened to me. I'm slowly acknowledging what transpired and the consequences that remain. BJ left me notes that said, "I know who you are," but she didn't; she knew me at a point in time. I've realized that we're all works in progress and can't change the future or the past. I'm taking responsibility for my part in the chain of events, but that's all I can control. All we really have is the versions of ourselves that exist this very minute.

BJ awaits trial, and Nena visits her. I don't ask Nena too many questions about BJ. I'm not sure I want to know the answers. She and I each have a lot to reconcile about ourselves, but I'm not ready yet. BJ confessed to Ashley's murder and will be extradited soon. Once she's transferred to Nebraska, Pen's mom has organized a schedule for our old neighbors, the ladies in the grapevine, to visit BJ. Nobody should be alone.

Ryan is gone. He tried to deliver flowers to the hospital and Finn promptly shut him down. After I got home and finally made sense of my feelings for Ryan, I mailed him a letter to set things right. Because I don't love quickly, retracting it takes me a long time. I needed him to understand what had happened to us, and I wanted to acknowledge that what we had mattered, but I couldn't see him again. Our conflicts had been starting to build anyway, but the restraining order was a deal-breaker. Lying about it made it even worse. Writing the letter helped me make sense of our relationship. It helped me see that my need for affection and attention clouded my common sense. I ended up trusting him instead of trusting myself.

I decided to keep my job at the bank, for now. I signed up for a class at the university in the exercise and fitness department. Even though I'm intimidated by the freshmen that look like they're twelve, I'm going to take it slow and figure out my next step. I have structure during the day and uncertainty at night, which seems like a good balance for now. I need to focus on what's right here in front of me—not the next finish line.

Ella still fights with her dad but on a smaller scale. She and I shop when we can, and although I still mostly listen, I'm trying to be more transparent with her. She understands much more than she gets credit for. I've realized I won't find redemption for my past through Ella, but I'll be by her side.

Aunt Dorothea fits me into her schedule, but she's more popular than ever at church and started taking Zumba classes, too. Finn, Buck, and I have Sunday evening meals most weekends, and we're planning a visit to see Levi and Eli over Thanksgiving. I'm noticing more of Dad in Finn's gestures lately, and I can hear the start of Mom's laugh when Ella giggles. It's both lovely and painful. I'm finding that accepting the loss of my parents didn't constrict me like I feared; rather, it opened me up. They're with me more often now, like seeing flowers my mom would have loved or the clouds that would have made my dad smile. Their essence is everywhere.

I'm trying to get Celia back to the gym, but she's still pissed at the hospital for kicking her out when she snuck Versace into my room. She says anger is all the cardio she needs.

Pen and I talk regularly, and I'm planning a trip to Bar Harbor this fall. I can't wait to meet her twins. I'm hoping Finn will come, too.

I keep tabs on my electrolytes, and I'm trying to run again, slowly. I took a long, measured run in the arboretum recently, and the sound of my feet on the earth was almost reverential. It's a way to hold tight to those around me, remember the past, and keep its vigil. I'm working on forgiving myself, which is hard. Forgiving others seems easier.

When I look back at all that happened, I can't help but compare it to the before and after of a yoga experience. Before class, I'm distracted, closed-off, achy, and stiff, looking for reasons to leave. Then class begins, and somebody leads me to me. I start to open slowly, gently unfurling until my body and mind are stretched, still, and warm. As much as I have tried to force myself toward this feeling, I know now that I can't do it by myself.

It's August now, a time for transition, when parents buy school supplies, robins' nests that are empty and dry spill from trees, and thistle leaves turn maroon on their way to a deep brown. I'm trying to transition into my own new life. I'm trying to be more grounded and present and to let people in. It's a way to honor my parents—living a vulnerable, courageous, balanced life now while I can, despite losing them too early. I think they'd be proud. Sometimes this seems daunting, but I'm practicing daily until it's *no sweat*.

ABOUT THE AUTHOR

LESA KNOLLENBERG is a freelance writer who
enjoys country living just outside of Madison,
Wisconsin. When she's not writing, you can
find her in the hot yoga studio, in nature with
her family, or giving presentations on the
writing life to students. *Corpse Pose* is the first
in her series of suspense novels set in the world
of fitness. To learn more and sign up for her
newsletter, visit www.lesaknollenberg.com.

ACKNOWLEDGMENTS

AT LEAST ONCE A DAY, MY DOG WENT OUTSIDE and rolled around. Paws up in the air, scratching his back against the earth, picking up everything near him and bringing little pieces of it inside. I can relate, because I eavesdrop a bit. Okay, a lot. If you tell me a story, I roll around in it, revel in it, and eventually can't remember if the story is yours or mine. So if you see a piece of your personal history in this book, I thank you. It means that you and your stories are embedded in my fur.

There are many things I could never do, like design urban traffic routes or live in a submarine. Teaching algebra is out, too. But I feel most at home when I write, and I want to thank the many people who helped me along the way, whether they knew it or not. I've always wondered about those authors who have pages of acknowledgments for their books. Can it really take so many people to put out a book? Turns out it does.

To Madison Writers' Group: Thanks to Michelle Wildgen and Susanna Daniel for creating a safe and sage learning environment. Your encouragement has been everything. SD, sometimes I hear your voice when writing, and it's a comforting sound. Thanks to co-member Julie Loeffler for your empathy and friendship.

It's rare to meet your heroes and find out they're just as personable and kind as you'd hoped. Julia Dahl, I so appreciate your enthusiasm and all you've done for me. And Barbara Rogan, remember when our class joked that you were Barbara the Horrible? Talk about a misnomer. You're anything but horrible. What joy to find that the writers behind some of my favorite books are wise, generous, and astute.

Thank you to Kristin Mitchell at Little Creek Press for helping me unearth my dream and to Shannon Booth for buffing it.

I don't even know how to adequately thank Camille Pagán and the rest of my mastermind crew. Camille, your influence has been the catalyst for a prodigious season of growth in my life, and I'm forever grateful. Combined with the warm support of our phenomenal group, I'm walkin' on sunshine.

Thanks to authors and critique partners Julie Holmes and Susan Richards for your wisdom, laughter, and kindness.

I'm so grateful for these people and their expertise: Sue Hodges, Chandru Solraj, Carol Ellis, Tiffany Kvalheim, Sergeant Papa JoeJoe Maurer, and Rachelle Fenster (friend to animals and mermaids all). Kristen Weber, thank you for being both wise and compassionate. Dr. Tom Murwin, thank you for patiently and thoroughly answering every weird question I ask. Even the naughty ones. Thanks to my authenticity and accountability partner, Katy Meuer, for helping me uppercut self-doubt.

Abigail Arttus, thank you for teaching me about resilience and hope. You've been a crucial part of this journey, inside and out. You're wise beyond your years, and I'm so proud of you.

Sky Showers, thank you for all the ways you've enriched our lives. Your heartwarming support and encouragement have added layers of meaning and joy at home and on the page.

Jenny Gordon Parker, every friend I've ever made has been measured against the yardstick of you.

To all the wonderful yoga teachers along my path, I'm grateful for every one of you. Madison is rich with talented instructors, and I've learned from each of you. Angele Walcott, you had me at Maslow and have been foundational ever since. Karen Rigsby, thank you for all the bright days of transformation. Deep thanks to Hally Marlino for so many things, especially your good heart. Your hands-on assistance years ago was the genesis for Sam's healing, and you continue to remind me who I am every week.

Unlike Sam, I'm blessed with a lovely crew of compassionate women who regularly lift me up. My gratitude to Darcy Edl, Marcia Ellestad, Shari Engel, Michelle Eversoll, Doreen Gudlin, Jordonna Hall, Judy Hawkins, Karen Kilroy, Kim Knollenberg, Laura Knollenberg, Lisa Mazzara, Louise Luessman, Karin Mandli, Joan Murwin, Tracy Preston, and Bev Semmann.

I'm so lucky to be born into the Knollenberg family and gifted with the Turecek family (starting with my favorite in-laws, Don and Shirley Turecek). You've all been so supportive on this journey, and I'm grateful for each of you.

Thank you to my brothers, Bill and Dan Knollenberg, for deep roots, strong and twisted. Neither of you is Buck, and neither of you is Finn. You're a combination of the best of both. You and your families are priceless to me.

Thanks to my boys, Noah and Caleb, for a glorious family life. When I dreamed of having a family, I couldn't have ever conjured up such a thoughtful, funny, encouraging, talented team. Noah, your imagination, love of words, and curiosity helped start me on this path. And Caleb, all those long nights when you didn't sleep and I talked to you about this book lit the way, and now your humor and observations continue the conversation. I appreciate the way you both inspire and support me.

To my parents: Thank you for teaching me how to live a creative, joyful life. You have been the gardeners of my soil and my soul. It's been a privilege to watch you navigate life, and being one of the recipients of your love is a gift I don't take lightly. Aside from the murdery parts, this book is a love letter to you and the family life you've built.

Infinite gratitude to my friend and husband, Doug. Your support has been vast and unwavering, and my love for you is the same. Every time I lost faith in myself, you helped me find it. I'll never be able to thank you enough for the life we live and the creativity you cultivate. You've been supportive in thousands of ways, from your Neil Young dreams, to calm IT savior when I accidentally deleted entire chapters of my manuscript, to writer of expunged sex scenes. For somebody who loves words, I can't find any that are adequate for how much I appreciate you, your insight, and your integrity. I'm so grateful we get to walk through this life side by side.

And thank you, dear reader, for your part in making my dream come true. If you'd like to continue along the journey, sign up for my newsletter at **www.lesaknollenberg.com**.

9 781955 656641